FLICK

by Lola LePaon

I would like to dedicate this book to my Aunt Margie whose words of encouragement propelled me, and enthusiastic support is responsible for a great deal of my first book's sales. It hurts that I never got to tell you face to face how appreciative I am for your love and endorsement. We always think we have more time, the last and hardest lesson you've taught me. I miss you dearly. R.I.P. MM

Table of Contents

FLICK

Hoelistic Healing 6

- Boxing 12
- Yoniverse 16
- Boxing Cont'd 19
- Herd it all 26
- Icy Ivy 29
- Naughty Nina 31
- You're So Fly 34

Mustache... 38

- Royally Fucked 42
- A Mes of a Mess 46

Company... 50

- Tandem 59
- Joy-ner 62

Sex Rolodex ™................................ 70

- Luxury Suite 77
- Mascara 83

Trixxx are for Adults 90

- Blowing O's 95
- Dutty Wine 97

Family Affair 99

- Held in High Ahh-steam 105
- Mom's Maple 110

Hostel Situation 115

- Secret Swap 121
- Double Trouble 124

Fonder 127

- Clamp Countdown 136
- Lit 139

The.rapist 145

- CUNT 156
- Risk 163
- Remove the Period 169

- Splash 171

124 174
- Cat and Mouse 181
- Hard On 183

Bridal Blues 185
- Something New 189
- Something Borrowed 193
- Something Old 196

The-eat-er 202
- Tribulation 204
- Brush Up on Me 208

Kinky Crank 210
- Show and Tell 220
- 'Lest you Forget 223

Drilled 228
- Cheat Code 234
- Instrumental 236

Babydoll 239
- Get Dolled up Marion 245
- Get Dolled up Heiran 247

Hell of a Dilemma 250
- Hail Mary Pass 257
- Lent a Hand 260

It's Written All Over You 262
- Suds Away Sins 268
- Menial Matrimony 272

Cumming to 277
- On the Roof 285
- On the Rohypn 287

Tea With A Twist 293
- Boba Tea 299
- Cooch Hooch 301

Fucking Falconry 303
- Wi-Fired Up 308
- Meet Moana 311

TEASE

Titillating, Erotic, Anecdotes, Symbolism, Etymology

There are spoilers, so I wouldn't advise reading this until you've read all possible outcomes

Hoelistic Healing 316

Mustache.. 317

Company... 318

Trixxx are for Adults 319

Family Affair 320

Hostel Situation 321

Fonder 322

The.rapist 323

124 325

Bridal Blues 326

The-eat-er 327

Kinky Crank 328

Drilled 329

Babydoll 330

Hell of a Dilemma 332

It's Written All Over You 333

Cumming to 335

Tea With A Twist 337

Fucking Falconry ....

Bonus Stories

Edict 340

Nip Quick 350

Acknowledgments 351

Hoelistic Healing

I missed the last two monthly outings with my girls Nina, Arden, Haven, and Ivy because I was wallowing in sadness over my stupid ex-boyfriend. This time Nina told me I had to come, or she was coming to drag me out herself.

They were all chattering, but I sat stirring and staring into my caramel macchiato.

"Listen, I know what you need to do, P." Nina's voice lowered to a whisper. I could feel her joke building.

"And what is that?"

Her tone still hushed, she said, "You need to go to the 'Cum Clinic' downtown."

I nearly spat my gum clear across the room! "I'm sure I'll regret asking, but what is that your version of a euphemism for?"

"Nothing! I mean go downtown to the building that has two large C's on the front. Though it's a huge building, it's fairly unassuming. You probably walked right past it thousands of times. I didn't notice it myself before I got put on."

"So wait, this is a real, actual... thing?"

"Yes! Some Doctor, what was his name again, Arden?" Arden bared her teeth and tilted her head. She'd forgotten. "Anyway," Nina waved at her dismissively, "this doctor had this concept about the actual health benefits of sexual healing. He studied why Happy Ending massages were so popular and it was more than just the obvious people enjoy cumming. Long story short, he got clearance by pitching some shit about increased endorphins, relaxation, healthy outlet for fantasies, safer space for sex workers, etcetera, etcetera and he got the green light."

"To… make prostitution legal?"

"To heal yourself, sexually."

I scanned their eyes for signs of humor, but everyone seemed serious. "So you're telling me there is an actual place that I can go, and like, fuck a random person?"

"It's bigger than that, P. Think of the ability to have your biggest fantasy played out, your dirty little secret kink fulfilled, and know they won't chop you up and put you in a freezer afterwards, or blab about it in the streets to anyone."

It did sound promising. "So why didn't you tell me about this before? All of you have been there and no one told me?

"Not Haven's scary ass. I offered to get her an appointment but she wasn't with it. Plus, you were with Rick the prick. Just me, Arden, and Ivy."

My mouth dropped. "Ivy!"

Ivy cast her eyes down and shrugged. "I was curious, P."

There were so many questions in my mind all at once. "Did you guys go together?"

Everyone leaned back in their seats looking disgusted. "No, P! We went on our own. I just have the connect to override all the official referrals and shit. Are you with it or not?" Nina stared at me waiting for my response.

"Set it up."

"Yes! You won't regret it, P. And I want all the details after. I know your freaky ass is gonna choose something wild."

"Thanks for the pressure, Nina, but I'll see what my options are before deciding, thank you very much. Maybe I just want to be kissed passionately in the rain."

All motion at the table stopped as their skeptic side eyes were on me.

"Okay, so maybe not something that simplistic, but damn, y'all act like a girl couldn't want some romantic shit." We laughed.

Conversations jumped to at least twenty different topics before we finished up and parted ways.

The next morning I awoke to a text from 646-470-7739 that told me I had a Thursday afternoon appointment at the CC. Something about having an appointment made it real. The solidification created knots in my belly. It was only Monday, so I wouldn't let my nerves interfere with the day's productivity. I turned on the hot water for my shower and closed the door to let the room steam as I made my coffee and selected the day's outfit. In the shower, I ran through potential scenarios I could request at this freaky ass clinic. I'd never been the type to hold back with a loving, trusted partner. This was different though. This was going to be with a stranger. This was permission to do anything because you weren't going to have to look into those eyes the next morning. But what is it they always say about fantasies? They should remain that way because they never live up to your expectations? Or was that in reference to meeting your idols? Whatever, I had time to think of something good.

Wednesday night I got a text from Nina.
You nervous about 2moro?
Yes, actually!
You want me to come hold your hand?

Lol. No thanx. According to you, you might not be ready for what I'm about to do.

Oh I can handle anything your kinky ass is into... or whatever gets into your kinky ass. Lol

I think I'll be fine.

You know what you're going to do yet?

Nah. I've been mulling over some scenarios but haven't chosen anything definitively yet. What did you do?

That answer doesn't come without a bottle of wine sweetie.

Fair enough.

We can exchange stories this weekend. Deal?

Deal.

   Nina always had a penchant for the forbidden. My guess was she was going to be underwhelmed by whatever I chose. My selection would be rooted solely in my desire, not with the intention to impress a friend. I drifted to sleep with kink on the brain.

   Thursday morning rolled around in an instant. It felt as though I'd blinked, and it was Thursday. The week had never moved so expeditiously in all my life. The day was here and my mind was no more certain of what I wanted than it was on Sunday when I first learned about it. I showered and dressed in what felt like slow motion. I chose a colorfully printed pencil skirt and semi-sheer black scoop tank with my six-inch heels and priciest perfume. I wanted to be somewhat provocative but not slutty. I had no idea what you were supposed to wear for a dick appointment with a stranger.

Nina was right, I had passed this building several times without so much as a second glance. That day it towered over me.

It was your standard medical office. Clinical, but an air of mystery that alluded to the deviance that loomed behind the doors. There were faint sounds permeating the room but nothing that would make you feel uneasy. On the frosted coffee table were porn mags; different fetishes and body types were featured on their glossy covers. I was greeted by this woman who had sparkly, inviting eyes. Everyone was wearing scrubs like a regular doctor's office. I'd begun to believe that this was a prank for a moment. If I hadn't spotted those magazines, I may have bolted. I think the receptionist could sense my trepidation. "First timer? Don't worry. You're safe and can leave at any moment without questions. Though, I hope you do opt to stay and indulge. We haven't had one complaint to date." That was certainly reassuring. "I have some paperwork for you to fill out. If you have any questions about anything on there or anything else, you let me know."

I was given a stack of paperwork that asked questions about my medical history, but also my exploration history as well. If I was allergic to or had an aversion to anything. If there was something I'd like to try but hadn't, my sexual fluidity, if I was open to group sex, any fears like claustrophobia, etcetera. After a few of those questions were answered, there was a section that asked if I knew exactly what I wanted to have executed or if I wanted to check the fetish files. The last line on the page just said "I'll do anything, Surprise Me" with a box you could check next to it.

Choose from the file? Page 12
Surprise Me? Page 34

Boxing

Shit, I wasn't quite into "anything" so I thought it best to check the "fetish files," whatever the fuck that meant. As my eyes wandered the room wondering what it could mean, there right in front of me, my eyes stopped on a big, gray file cabinet that had a sign above it that read "Fetish Files" in bold black letters. It seemed silly that I hadn't noticed it before. I leapt from my seat, stepping curiously over to the file cabinet.

I'm not sure what I expected would lie within but I partly envisioned a bunch of dildos, lube, and whips would fly out as soon as I slid the door open like some clown trick, but it was anticlimactically just a bunch of papers. As I peered in closer I saw, very organized,quite possibly every fetish known to man. The drawers were separated by categories in: submissive, dominant, versatile, and fetish. Then each drawer had alphabetical folders for every kink with its definition and potential pros and cons of each. I was astounded and overwhelmed. I knew I wanted to choose something submissive, but the whole point of my being here was that I didn't want to see it coming. So I began thumbing through the sensory deprivation section.

There were so many options it was beginning to feel stressful and I'd only made it to the letter B in the file. All things with blindfolding felt so... trite. I wanted something that felt riskier than that. So I quickly flipped through that section, and just before the letter C, I saw a file that said "boxing." Images of someone sitting in a ring, being tied up against the ropes getting abused sprang into my mind before I even read the file. It piqued my interest so I began to skim it and it was nothing like

I'd imagined. In fact it had nothing to do with the sport at all.

As the patient, you go into a room that has nothing more than a box in it. You strip naked, bend over, and are strapped inside the box. What happens after that is a surprise—within the realm of what you have signed off on in your file. This was it. I could feel it in the way the idea aroused me. It was perfect. I wouldn't see it coming and I would just have to be subjected to whatever happened in whatever order. The file also mentioned a "safe button" inside the box if at any moment you wanted to bail. I wasn't going to drive myself crazy with more options. I liked the sound of this one and I was going to do it.

I walked proudly back to my seat, confident with my selection. I excitedly finished filling out my paperwork, eager to fulfill this recently discovered fantasy. The minutes ticked by slowly as I waited for them to go through my paperwork and set up my fantasy or whatever the hell they do back there. A bundle of nerves, I sat doing every stereotypical thing that denotes anxiety: tapping my foot, biting my lip, twiddling my thumbs. I decided to lose myself in social media until they called for me. About forty double taps down my timeline later, a woman in a lab coat emerged and called my name.

"Pentz?"

"Yes?"

"Come with me."

I followed her through the doors to what felt like a holding area. I was impressed with the cleanliness. She stepped away momentarily to a closet and returned with a handful of things.

There was a folded robe, a towel, some toiletries and flip flops like they give you at a spa. In fact this entire step felt like a spa experience.

"We require all patients to shower before their appointment. If you find you need something else, give us a ring from the phone in the bathroom and we'll do our best to accommodate you. Otherwise, when you're finished you can just step out and we'll know to take you back for your session."

Momentarily caught up in the doctor and spa sensations, I'd nearly forgotten why I was there. I showered quickly and slipped into my fluffy white robe. Somewhere in that steamy water I'd found my courage. I was ready to do this.

When I emerged, I noticed another woman sitting in the post-shower holding area. She was beautiful with thick wavy jet-black hair against her glowing brick-colored skin. She looked Indian, or maybe just mixed with Indian. I didn't want to outwardly speculate. I sat down across from her.

She instantly struck up a conversation. "First timer huh? I see that virginal panicked excitement in your eyes. I'm a regular. You will be too. I can feel it!" She cackled at her proclamation. "I'm Amrita." She outstretched her hand.

I hesitated.

"You don't have to tell me your real name. Heck, I'd never know. Just making small talk to ease your nerves."

"I'm P."

"Nice to meet ya. I'll be doing a version of a gangbang, but only having my pussy sucked. It's called 'Yoniverse.' Add it to your to-do list. I'm all about variety, but even I had to do this one more

14

than once. It's the most empowering thing you can do. Trust me."

Another attendant in a lab coat appeared. "Amrita. We're ready for you."

Check out Amrita's Yoniverse experience? Page 16
Continue Boxing? Page 19

Yoniverse

Before my official fantasy, I was brought to the crowning room.

Everything was plush from floor to ceiling. I sunk into a velvety rose throne with gold accents. I read over their drink menu displayed on a pedestal beside me. The first one immediately caught my eye. A "Golden Haute Chocolate." It seemed fitting given what was to come. It was described on the menu as *"Guaranteed to be the most delectable hot chocolate to ever grace your lips. Brewed with rich, decadent, gourmet Tuscan chocolate, spiked with vodka distilled quintuple times and filtered through diamonds to remove any impurities not fit for a queen. Garnished with edible 24K gold flakes."* Sold!

Next, I was laid on a massage table as they began to cover me in 24K edible gold paint. Seeing my thick body covered in gold instantly made me feel regal. When I sat up, they crowned me.

After being crowned, you begin the Yoniverse experience. Though I knew what to expect, it was always a pleasure to see a room full of strong, powerful-looking men genuflect as you enter. In the center of the room was a black hanging bubble chair painted with shimmering glitter in purple and deep blue tones so it looked like a painting of the galaxy.

"You may rise." I told my awaiting lovers.

Each man asked permission to touch me and when I gave it, they worked together to remove my silk robe. With each body part that was unveiled, they complimented it. They were in awe and

16

fawned over me. Parts of me that don't normally receive recognition, let alone praise were flattered with such specificity that it allows it to resonate. Admiration for my clavicle became a request for permission to kiss it. Each petition of allowance to touch ends with Queen. It was "May I touch you, Queen?" or "May I kiss this, Queen?"

Eventually, all hands were permitted and they rubbed my back and shoulders, kissed my fingers and toes, allowed me to bathe in sensations and adoration.

At that point, I was sitting with one man on either side of me sucking each of my nipples. Two men holding my legs up were allowing another two men to suck my toes.

They each asked if they may taste me. I spread my legs and granted them access. One after another they sucked, fondled, tongue fucked, licked, and lapped at my pussy.

One man crawled from the back of the pack closer to me on a leash. "May I have the pleasure of tasting that sweet nectar?"

Everyone else stopped what they were doing and gasped as though they were mortified. He forgot to call me Queen.

"I'm sorry, Queen. I was just so excited by the sight of you, but I will spell Goddess with my tongue until you demand I cease to make up for it if you'll allow me."

I leaned forward and grabbed his leash from the floor. "Take your time. I want to feel you spelling every letter." I pulled his leash, instantly ensconcing him in my yoni. He made good on his promise until I creamed all over his tongue. I pushed his head away while I caught my breath.

He slinked away and returned with a package he opened to reveal a chin strap dildo. My legs were so weak I didn't know if I had the energy to sit on his face. I momentarily relished in having such a fantastic dilemma before me. He fastened it to his face and asked if I would sit on it. I never used one before and I was curious what it would be like to have someone suck on my hot button while feeling penetrated.

I walked as gracefully as one does when they're orgasmically exhausted and squatted down on the dildo strapped to his chin. I leaned forward so he could have direct contact on my clit and the dildo would push against my G-spot. The remaining men in my yoniverse came from everywhere to rub my ass, lick my nipples, kiss my neck, suck my toes and I felt an orgasm gurgling inside me that seemed like it would tear me apart. Between their whispers of worship of how beautiful, sexy, and amazing I was, their moans were music to my ears. A full body orgasm ripped through me that caused me to convulse until I collapsed. They rolled me over, massaged me and stroked my hair. I soaked up every moment. If only the universe beyond those doors felt the same.

Boxing Continued

"Welp, that's me. Enjoy your session" Amrita followed the attendant giddily, chattering with her like an old friend. Before she disappeared, she mouthed "Yoniverse" with a thumbs up.

That smile was better than any review website endorsement. If this session went well, I would be adding the Yoniverse experience to my list.

The same attendant that came for Amrita returned to get me.

"Your session is ready."

Some of my newfound courage dissipated but I wasn't going to back out. I stood up and followed her down a hall and into a room that was mostly bare. At first sight of the box, my heart raced.

"Okay, you'll strip completely bare and bend over into the box. We've already adjusted it for your height but if you feel uncomfortable, let me know and we'll adjust it before beginning. There are two metal pegs inside that you can hold on to. The red safe button is just above the right peg. It glows dimly in the dark. You said on your form you do not have any sense of claustrophobia correct?"

"Yes."

"And you are okay with multiple partners in one session correct?"

"Yes."

"You have no issues with same sex partners correct?"

"Correct."

"There will be leather straps tied around your thighs, knees, and ankles to restrict your movement. Are you okay with this or would you prefer to make an amendment?"

"Wow. Umm, nope. You know what, that's okay."

"Perfect. There's the safe for your belongings. Do you have any questions for me?"

"Not at this time, thank you."

"Okay, I'll be back to strap you in in less than five minutes."

"Great. Thank you."

I disrobed and walked over to the box. It opened like the ones magicians use to saw a woman in half. It would close over me, and I'd be latched inside. Just as she described, there were two pegs and a safe button. I bent over and held on to the pegs. The height was good. I didn't have to be on tiptoe or bend my knees.

She returned with a respectful knock before strapping my legs as she said she would. She confirmed none of the straps were too tight before shutting the top of the box so I was completely enclosed in darkness. The only sound I could hear was my own heavy breathing as I anxiously waited for what was going to happen next. I know I ordered sensory deprivation, but this eliminated four of my five senses. I couldn't see, hear, smell, or taste anything. I hadn't a clue who or what would be touching me either. Anticipation built like it does when they pull the lever down on you for a roller coaster ride at amusement parks. I was in for a wild ride indeed.

Suddenly there was a nose nuzzling my exposed lady bits. I flinched, but quickly relaxed. Whoever this was made sure to be very gentle. I suspected it was a woman, but I couldn't be sure. Nails raked across my ass before they spread the cheeks open and tongued my asshole. Definitely a woman. Her tongue was warm and slick. She

20

probed gently as saliva ran down my crack onto my lips. She slid a finger in my pussy, then two, curving them down to reach my G-spot. If I had a question in my mind before which gender was pleasing me, I'd know it was a woman from that alone. A man wouldn't have thought to make that adjustment. They would stick to the "come hither" motion even though in this position it was upside down. Generally, women think of shit like that.

She was skilled in the amount of suction and licking. Her rhythm was perfect like she knew me and my body before; like she knew what I liked. I couldn't see this stranger's face and she knew how to suck me better than Rick's dumb ass in over three years. She slurped on my pearl, making it pulse. When she slid her fingers back in my soaked pussy, it tightened on them reflexively. My body was communicating what I couldn't. She was especially intuitive and responded with an insider's knowledge.

I wanted to spread my thighs more and let her really bury her face in there. In an awesome moment of symbiosis, this stranger lifted and spread my ass, granting her the permission I silently craved. My legs trembled in their straps. My moans echoed inside the box like surround sound. The sincerity of genuine pleasure reverberating back at me turned me on. These were not sounds to stroke someone's ego. This was basking in the uninhibited pleasure of a skilled oral pleaser.

She latched on to my thighs with her hands, and onto my clit with her mouth and practically pumped that orgasm out of me. With nowhere to run or hide, I thrashed in the minimal space I had until her mouth was left covered and dripping. I caught my breath reveling in this amazing experience. I knew for certain I'd be back again because nothing had ever... Oh!

There were hands on my ass. Not hers. Not a woman's. Was something else about to happen? Where did she go? How many people were in the room now? Were they watching what just happened? Will they watch what happens next?

The unmistakable stiffness of a hard cock was rubbing up and down my lips. He jerked off right against my pussy, his fist pounding against my lips. He pushed the head in just enough for me to feel pressure, then moved away. It was driving me crazy. I squirmed tortuously in my box.

"Please." I murmured from inside, but my pleas could or would not be heard. His thick head toyed with opening my slit. My pussy made smacking sounds, relaying from below. My body begged at least one set of lips to be heard. If he would just push in the full head, I could grip him and suck him in. I pushed my thighs against the box hard and inched away from him as much as I could. When he tried that shit again, I had just enough room to push back and suck him in. He clasped my ass hard as he got his bearings. Then, as if to punish me, he pulled out completely. I ached with frustration, but it hurt so good. It built my desire up in a way I'd never known.

Smack!

I couldn't be sure but it felt like a leather paddle or riding crop of some sort smacked my ass.

Smack!

Then that fat head rubbing across my ass again.

I was trembling with suspense.

Fuck me. Just fuck me.

Smack!

Gentle hands were rubbing my ass. The woman's hands from before! She was still here. She slowly rubbed her finger over my opening, but didn't slide it in. It's like they knew the only thing I wanted more than penetration, was wanting penetration.

Teasing was my favorite as long as the payoff was worth it.

His head pressed against me again, and her hand was beneath me making circles on my clitoris. He pushed the head against my opening, then he crept his way in inch-by-painstakingly-slow-inch until he filled me up.

Finally!

All the while her fingers never stopped making their circles.

He probed in and out of me slowly, almost cautiously, like he wanted to build up my orgasm in the slowest way imaginable. I throbbed graciously after getting what I'd been craving.

Just as my orgasm was building, all sensations stopped.

No pumping. No circles. Nothing.

Breathless in the darkness, I wondered what fucking happened. I wanted, no I needed, to cum.

His dick pushed in me full force.It was bigger and longer somehow and he was more forceful almost like... it was a different guy!

It had to be a different guy.

A familiar mouth came from below and covered both of our parts in the warm wetness of her tongue. He stroked harder, deeper, faster and her sucking kept right up with him.

I'd had an intense clitoral orgasm, I'd had an intense G-spot orgasm, I'd even had them together but I'd never had a dual orgasm as intense as this was building up to be. I held on to those pegs for dear life. I was almost there.

Don't stop.

He fucked me like he knew I was a first-timer and he would get a bonus for ensuring my return. And I came back... to back to back to back all over his dick and her tongue.

I shook, screamed and cried. It was overwhelmingly fantastic.

She slowed to a stop and he withdrew. Panting with the biggest grin on my face, I knew I owed Nina the biggest bouquet of flowers that...He was back!

How? He just... it wasn't him. It was the first guy. I think. I was almost sure.

I didn't know how much more I could take, but he took his time, just as before. Slowly but surely, I felt another orgasm rise up within me and cum crashing down all over him. When he withdrew, I knew if I felt so much as a finger on me I was going to whack the safe button before I fucked around and had a heart attack in this damn box. Thankfully, the next thing I felt was the unlatching of the box opening above me.

As light poured in, I screeched like a vampire. I went from sensory deprivation to sensory overstimulation. It was going to take me a minute to adjust.

The same attendant who brought me in was here again, her voice soothing and calm. "I know you'll need a moment to pull yourself together. Take your time. I've untied all bindings and set aside a fresh towel and more toiletries should you wish to shower again before you leave. If you don't need anything else from me, I'll leave you to it."

All I could muster up was a grunt and a head shake.

"Great. Call me if you need me. I'll be in earshot."

However many minutes later when my legs felt strong enough for standing, I hobbled over to grab my stuff and head for the shower. The cleansing was amazing but nothing could be as rejuvenating as the experience I'd just had in that room. I was a new woman.

The receptionist handed me a goodie bag and information on how to book my next appointment if I was interested.There was no question as to whether I'd be back, but how soon.

Amrita was right. That Yoniverse experience did sound good. Maybe next time. Maybe not.

Me and the girls got together for a late brunch at my place and let the wine flow. Haven couldn't make it, but she didn't have a story to share anyhow. After polishing off the second bottle, we were ready to swap clinic tales.

Arden's Adventure? Page 26
Ivy's Intimacy? Page 29

Herd It All

Arden began in her no nonsense tone, "Well y'all know I'm not into any of that submissive shit. I need to be in control. I also love wearing latex. It feels so tight and intensifies every touch like you're on X. I took my shower and put on my favorite latex catsuit. It's red, has nipple holes, and is crotchless. I lubed it up you know and..."

"Wait, lubed it up? Your pussy?" Nina asked.

"No silly! The suit. You need to lube it up so it's slick and smooth."

"Oh! I didn't know that." Nina admitted.

"Yes, hunny! So after I lubed it all up and put on my heels, they took me to my session. I ordered nipple to clit tweezers and fortunately they arrived the day before."

"Tweezers? Girl what?"

"Yeah they clamp on. They're similar to the ones you use for your brows, but they're tipped in a soft silicone so it's just pressure, not necessarily pain you feel."

"So you got two sets of tweezers to clip to your... business?" Nina piped up again.

"No, they're on a chain. They're three clamps. When I'm fucked hard, my titties bounce and they pull the clamp on my clit."

"Shit! And you... like this Arden?"

"Nope. I love it! Don't knock it till you try it," Arden answered without the least bit of shame.

"Okay, so what was the room setup like, were there several men, women, both? Spill it girl!" Nina wanted no detail spared.

"Well the space was traditionally clinical because that's what I asked for. I wanted to act out my doctor fantasies."

"In a latex catsuit?"

"Yes, exactly! My doctor, my rules."

"Okay, so then what?"

"Well I had the man they selected for me dress like a doctor. I requested for him to lie down on the table and I told him to use a stethoscope to listen to my heart while I rode his face so he would know if he was doing it right. If he didn't, I would use my electro stimulation wand."

It was my turn to chime in. "Your what the what?"

"It's a wand that has a nice little electric current that gives a zap. Not too much. It's similar to a cattle prod. It helps me herd him to my orgasm."

We all had a good cackle at that.

I had to know, "Where are you shocking him, girl?"

"I reach back and shock him on the side of his ass like I'm riding a horse."

"Damn, and does it help?"

"It does. I feel like the stethoscope helps more. His hearing is muted a bit and I'm not feeding him no fake ass moans for a fantasy. If you aren't getting my heart racing, you know you're not doing it right. I want him to know in a way that cannot be faked what is working to get me off. And if that alone isn't motivation enough, I herd that ass!"

"Damn. You're making me want to take notes, Arden. I never thought of a stethoscope as a teaching tool."

"Yup. I like to use it too. Y'all remember when I was dating that doctor Gary?"We nodded."Well I used to love sucking him off and listening to his heartbeat gradually rise until it was pounding in my ears. *The* best motivational soundtrack. Trust me."

Mental notes were being made in the minds of all women in attendance.

"After I rode his face, I made him beg to fuck me. I told him he better make it good or he'd be getting shocked. After that, he made damn well sure to do his job. Those tweezers did their part too."

"All this time I thought P was the freakiest and then here you go!" Nina laughed.

Arden shrugged before reminding everyone, "We haven't heard everyone's yet. Let's reserve judgment until we have, thank you!" She giggled. "Okay, someone else share."

Icy Ivy? Page 29
Naughty Nina? Page 31

Icy Ivy

"I had them set the temperature to about forty degrees. I'm wearing a fur. One chick is wearing a leather trench, the other is wearing fur as well. The one in leather is wearing rubber-textured gloves, the other one has those gloves you know... for arthritic patients? They vibrate."

"Nope. Never even knew they existed, but continue." I laughed.

"The room had an emperor-sized bed with pure Mongolian cashmere bedding."

If it were anyone but Ivy's bourgeois ass telling this story, I'd question how she knew those details.

"Beneath the furs they're both wearing the dopest lingerie I've ever seen. They pulled out all the stops. Garters, thigh highs, all that. The temperature has everyone's nipples at full attention just begging to be sucked. So we did. A mouth feels exceptionally warm in the cold climate and every exhale of ecstasy became a visible confirmation cloud of pleasure. The cold creates a craving for body heat so there's this added layer of hunger that isn't generally present among strangers. We desired each other's closeness like our survival depended on it... and we devoured each other that way too."

"Well shit!" I unintentionally muttered. I was surprised at how thoughtful all the elements were. I never would have thought of that. I tuned back in to Ivy describing the way the girl with the textured rubber gloves rubbed and pinched her nipples while the one with the vibrating gloves used two fingers like a bullet on her down low. Afterwards, they managed to form a circle so no one was left out and she was getting sucked and finger fucked in the ass while doing some licking of her own on the girl

29

who was pleasuring the woman who tended to Ivy. It sounded like synchronized sex. It also sounded unusually intimate and attentive. I wouldn't be opposed to trying it out.

According to Ivy, even post-snuggle time was included in her session. She claimed she would try something a bit more hardcore next time, but this seemed like the best way to get her feet wet.

"Alright, that's enough about mine. Who's next?"

Naughty Nina? Page 31

Naughty Nina

"My first time, I went in for a nuru massage. All of us got butt ass naked and oiled up..."

Arden cut her off, "Umm, we've heard this one, Nina. Tell us what happened when you went on Thursday."

"Thursday?" I asked. "You never mentioned you would be there the same day as me."

"I didn't think I had to run it by you," Nina answered defensively.

"I'm just saying. I was nervous and shit. We could have gone together. That's all."

I excused myself to go to the bathroom. "But don't start the story without me!" I shouted back towards the living room as I exited.

As I was washing my hands, I heard a tap on the door. I guess I'm not the only one whose bladder called.

I opened the door hurriedly to offer relief to whomever was on the other side.

"Hey."

"Hey, Nina. Let me get out of your way." She wouldn't budge from the doorway. "I'm sorry, you need something?"

She wriggled in the door and closed it behind her. Then she just stood there, looking at the floor.

"What the hell are you doing Nina?"

"I told the girls a different story of what happened on Thursday..."

"You were supposed to..."

She held a finger up. "I lied to them. I want to tell you the truth."

"Oh. Okay. Well this must be pretty juicy."

"Have a seat."

31

"You want me to sit on the toilet for this story? This must be wild." I put the lid down and had a seat. "Should I have brought my wine in here too?"

"P, you know how growing up you'd go to sleepovers and whatnot?"

"Of course."

"Well, I always had this fantasy about hooking up with one of my friends."

"Oh. Which one?"

"None specifically. I mean, there were some I preferred over others but I really liked the idea of fucking a friend. It feels almost forbidden. You're all supposed to be asleep and then the two of you brush against one another. You start exploring and discovering each other in new ways, you know..." She chewed her bottom lip nervously.

"Okay, so you recreated that? You had a sleepover?"

"Yes, and no. I didn't have a sleepover. But I... I indulged in the forbidden."

"I'm not following."

"My friend. She didn't stay at my house. She wasn't home either. She was at the clinic... in a box." She finally raised her eyes to me.

I was frozen. My mouth was opened, but words refused to form, my voice silenced in awe.

She began filling the silence by babbling on. "I'm sorry. In my mind I tried to justify it because you signed up to fuck people without knowing their identity and the Cum Clinic is a place where fantasies are fulfilled and selfishly I saw an opportunity to fulfill mine and... well no matter how I tried to justify it, in my gut it felt wrong. You signed up to be with a stranger and you had a right

32

to know it was me and I feel awful like I betrayed your trust and I'm really sorry. I am."

I took a deep breath and tried to digest all that had been said to me. Was she wrong? Yes. Did she have to tell me? Nope. Did I feel betrayed? Mildly I suppose, but the fact that it was bothering her says something too.

"Pentz, say something please. Tell me to get out or give you a few days or whatever, just say something. My nerves are shot over here."

She never called me by my full name. This could put up a serious barrier between us if I let it. This infraction was not worth that kind of shift in my opinion. It didn't hurt that she was damned good at it! I wanted to make her sweat a bit first.

"Nina..."

She stared intently with bated breath.

"I think that you should...."

Her eyes began to fill. Okay, I didn't realize how scared she was. That's enough torture.

"...know that if you wanted to fuck me, all you had to do was ask."

She heaved a huge sigh of relief, she blinked and her pending tears fell.

"And if you still feel bad, you can make it up to me right now."

She grinned so hard I may have seen all 32 of her teeth. Then she locked the door. "Lights on, or lights off?"

"Oh I want to see this time."

Arden and Ivy could occupy themselves for a few minutes. Nina and I had some making up to do.

You're So Fly

Hmm, I have always liked surprises. That file cabinet is overwhelming. This will take out the guesswork. I already stated what kind of shit I'm into on my paperwork. Fuck it.

Immediately upon deciding on this raunchy roulette, I anxiously launched into the possibilities. Thankfully the wait wasn't too long and I could only get so worked up. The attendant handed me toiletries and a towel for the prerequisite shower. I thoroughly, and quickly, cleaned myself. I was eager to find out what I was going to do! I wrapped myself in the robe behind the door and sat in the holding area until the attendant returned. My legs bounced restlessly as they do when I'm nervous. She arrived from behind a door where I heard screaming and then it closed to being nearly silent. She could read the fear in my face. "That's Ronnie. He's a veteran & our self-proclaimed resident pain slut. He's got a slew of women in there strapped up and pegging him. He loves being watched if you want to take a peek. They are having a very enjoyable experience in there. Trust me."

"I'll pass."

Some of my fear absolved, but I still hadn't a clue what I was walking into. Four doors down she stopped and we entered a room with what appeared to be a life-size spider web.

"Is that for me?"

"It is. You'll be the fly, and I'll release some spiders to weave you into that web with silk ropes. They'll blindfold you and eat you and well... I don't want to spoil all the fun. They won't do anything you haven't signed off on. If at any moment you feel uncomfortable for any reason, say your safe word and you will be unbound, everyone will leave, and I

34

will come in and check on you. You don't have to give an explanation, but if you want to discuss it, I'll be here. We also have on-site therapists. You are in a safe space. Okay?"

I felt relieved. I felt safe, and this seemed like something I could handle.

"Okay." I smiled.

"I'm going to exit, and then you may disrobe. After that, your handsome 'spiders' will be in," she said, her voice sing-song.

I looked around the room. It was mostly bare. Considering the quick turnarounds they have to do after such elaborate planning, it makes sense that they don't invest too much in everyday decor. They're focused on fantasy details. As long as that paid off, it didn't matter. The space was clean and safe. I felt odd thinking of just standing there nude and decided to wait until my spiders arrived. The lights dimmed and faux candles began flickering red lights. Eight men entered in two lines of four, dressed in all black.

They removed my robe for me and silently went to task hoisting me up onto the web and tying me securely, and comfortably. Once both arms and legs were bound, one of my spiders walked toward me with a silk blindfold outstretched. He nodded. I nodded affirmatively and tilted my head forward so he could tie it around my brown locks.

I felt what I suspected to be a pounce wheel across my nipples. Someone was sucking on my ear on one side. On the other side, someone was biting my neck. Below, someone was kissing up and down my thighs. I loved feeling sensations all over. It was titillating. I knew I was being prepped for more. Two fingers found their way inside me but none of the other spiders stopped their kisses, licks, caresses, or nibbles. He worked with the winding of my hips to have the perfect cadence and pressure for G-spot pleasure. He turned his hand counter-clockwise and pushed his pinky in my ass. I rocked with my limited range of motion to help him penetrate further.

Suddenly I heard buzzing and before my ears could even be sure, I felt the familiar vibration of a bullet on me. The sensations were immense in the most extraordinary way. Simultaneously vibrating nipple clamps were clasped on as anal beads were being pushed in. I was writhing with overstimulation. I wanted to push myself; I didn't want it to stop. I wanted to crack open and release.

Next, I felt a man's hand on my ribs as he guided himself into me. He wasn't uncomfortably long, but he had incredible girth. That was my preference anyhow. That bullet on my clit was going to bring this orgasm sooner than later. He held my ass with both hands as he discovered a way to get deeper penetration. My moaning became screams I'd never heard myself make before. With all the twitching and twisting, I'm surprised my straps held. Screams grew to grunts and growls. I felt sweat trickling down my face, I was so worked up. I cursed those men like they stole something from my mama.

Turns out, those anal beads could vibrate too. I suspected my partner could feel those vibrations through me because he started fucking me with wild abandon. I bucked and shuddered as I climaxed. They pulled the beads out slowly and it prolonged my orgasm until I squirted for the very first time! It surprised the hell out of me. My partner didn't seem to mind. In fact, three pumps later he followed suit. They removed the bullet and nipple clamps and he withdrew. It got really quiet like I was alone. I felt a hand on my ankle and if it wasn't strapped, they would have gotten a swift quick to the head.

"Sorry. I'm going to untie you now."

He released my legs first, then my arms. He told me I could remove my blindfold whenever I was ready. I left it on a minute, reveling in the experience I'd just had. Once it was off, the fantasy was over and I was back to real life. I wanted to extend my pleasure for a few more moments. Two minutes of basking later, I removed the blindfold and grabbed my robe. I looked around the room, drinking the last bit of my experience in. My first experience would not be my last.

Mustache

I run a very popular anonymous erotic blog. You've probably heard of it. The Make Me Moan site started as an option for me to record sex in a way that I was comfortable with. Sex tapes leaked too often for my taste. No shade to those who didn't mind exhibition that way, but it wasn't for me. Instead of recording visuals, I only recorded the audio. There was something so thrilling about hearing the sounds you make with a lover. I found it interesting to see how different people could bring out different sounds in me. I also loved hearing their varied sounds, reliving their commands and ass slaps. Slurping and heavy breathing came to be more of a turn on for me than seeing it.

With as many followers as Make Me Moan had, it became clear I wasn't alone in being turned on by audio sex. I felt like the Banksy of the amateur porn world, so I uploaded all posts under the pseudonym "Bangsky." Originally, it was just my audio. Then I began accepting submissions to hear how others were getting down. User admissions became pouring in so quickly, I renamed it MakeBangskyMoan.

I got an account on the app Just For Tonight, better known as JFT, to feed my addiction—we'll get into that in just a minute. The app is self-explanatory. People in search of a one night stand can find others looking for the same in their area. On my profile I revealed that I was married. They knew upfront there was no room for growth. My marital status didn't seem to affect their willingness to participate. Though they didn't mind the marriage, some of them weren't interested in how I wanted to fuck.

I had this addiction to fucking in places my husband might catch me. I can't explain it and I won't even try. I loved him and he satisfied me sexually, but this was a hunger he couldn't satiate. I tried. Make Me Moan was originally just a space of our audio sex sessions. The first time I cheated on him, I recorded it out of habit, and blogged about it out of guilt. My readers' response was amazing. I had a few judgmental folks, but for the most part people loved the idea of knowing and hearing my sexual tryst firsthand. It egged me on. I would blog about a prospective "date" and then post audio of our session. The first time, my subscribers tripled in two days.

Like many areas of my life, I had a hard time following rules. My JFT app interaction was no different. It started with a bunch of different guys who wanted to have a one night stand, but eventually it became a place to arrange regular meet-ups with Justin. Justin must have had some version of my same fetish because whatever I suggested, he was always down—or suggesting ways to kick it up a notch.

Justin was supposed to be a one off like the others. Though when I told him I wanted to do it downstairs in the parking lot near my husband's car around his lunch break, Justin offered to fuck me in my husband's work elevator and try to make me cum before my husband possibly got on. I knew then this was the start of something more. I'd found my kink soulmate.

My husband worked on the fifth floor. We took the elevator to the top, on the thirty-fifth floor. We were able to fool around a surprising ten minutes before the elevator was called down. It was someone on the seventh floor. It may not have been my husband, but we couldn't be caught by anyone. We needed to finish fast. Justin must have had the same thought because he started jackhammering the fuck out of me so hard both my titties flew out of my button up. The elevator was in the teens when he seized and filled me with his cum.

He pulled out quickly as I tucked in my twins and yanked my skirt back down. He zipped and fixed his trousers. I smoothed over my hair and clothes, doing my best to look presentable. There we were, flushed, but mostly decent as a gentleman walked on from the seventh floor. He pushed G and looked at us as though he wondered why no other buttons were lit up before his arrival.

We made another stop on five. I hoped my husband Tahir was there. The doors opened and there he was, among a bunch of other folks waiting for the elevator. When I shifted to the side to allow more passengers in, I felt Justin's warm cum trickling down my inner thigh.

"Baby! What are you doing here?"

Excited by the rush of my recent indiscretion and nearly being caught, my walls pulsed. It squeezed the cum out faster. Oddly, that excited me more. I squeezed my thighs together before it oozed out to a visible space beneath the hem of my gray pencil skirt.

"I was thinking maybe I could surprise you for lunch."

"You're too good to me. Where do you want to go?"

"Wherever my baby has in mind."

I smiled at Justin who was grinning to himself in the corner.

I said goodbye to Justin as we separated in the garage. I fully expected Tahir not to say anything.

"I'm sorry, I didn't realize you knew each other. I'm Tahir Trotter." He extended a hand.

Justin accepted. "Justin Cider. We just came down together."

I had to bite the inside of my lip to keep from grinning at his word choice.

Tahir and I went on to enjoy a great lunch. First I dipped into the restaurant's bathroom for me to rub out a quick one and then to clean myself up. I was too aroused to wait till a more respectable time or place.

The next morning I had an inbox message from Mr. Cider. Two words: Again. Soon.

He wasn't a man of many words, but he didn't need to be. I preferred he used his tongue for other things anyway.

We repeated our wild trysts, each time increasingly riskier.

One Night? Page 42
On Repeat? Page 46

Royally Fucked

I decided the next time it would be in my bedroom. He agreed.

My suggestion? Tahir took long showers. We could do it in our bed. Try and finish before the water turned off.

Justin's even better suggestion? Do it on the floor next to the bed while Tahir slept.

I gave Justin my alarm code so he could disarm it on the way out if he had to escape alone in the event we had to split up so I could distract Tahir or something.

I met him at the door in my silk robe. Without turning on any lights, I helped him find his way to our bedroom. Tahir was snoring peacefully loud. I hoped it wouldn't drown out any sounds from my recording session with Justin. Though we couldn't make much sound without risking Tahir waking up, there was no way I wasn't going to record reaching the peak of my fantasy.

I pulled Justin onto the floor on top of me. He was grinding his hips, kissing me passionately. It was hardly ever like this with him. It was usually hard and fast considering time restrictions. He put a hand over my mouth to mute my orgasm and buried his face in my massive breasts to mute his own. Tahir didn't stir once though I secretly wished he had. The scent of our sex calling his nose to suspicious attention would have made me cum harder. We crept down the stairs and I bid him farewell. I returned to my bedroom and climbed into bed next to my husband with Justin's sweat fresh on my skin.

The next morning I was cooking breakfast on a high. I packed Tahir's lunch and ironed his clothes. I'm not sure if it was a replacement for my guilt, but I always wanted to dote on and spoil Tahir after a session with Justin. I leaned over our island to shower him in kisses and compliments before he headed off to work.

I was tempted to call Justin over to fuck in our bed as a cherry on top but I didn't have the time. I had an important meeting at work that could not be missed. This fantasy would have to be put off for another day.

Justin must have had the same thought because shortly after getting ready for work, I had a text from him asking if we could do it in the house again this afternoon. I told him I had the same thought but couldn't shift my schedule around today but I definitely wanted a raincheck. I lingered in the doorway before leaving, lovingly looking at the home I created with my husband. The frames of our family lined along the wall, trinkets from our travels placed about. I hoped one day this would be enough.

I killed my meeting at work and kicked ass in the productivity department for the rest of the day. My boss even pulled me aside to commend me on a job well done, before asking me to stay late. The only reward for doing your job expeditiously and efficiently was receiving more work. At my next review I was going to make sure it was reflected in my pay as well. But for the time being, I'd just be the accommodating team player I was known for. I received a call from Tahir around 6:30.

"Hey baby. I know I'm late but I had to put in an extra hour. I'll pick something up on the way home if..."

"Tymber, I'm not sure how to say this but, we've been robbed."

"What? What do you mean robbed."

"Our house was broken into. Well, I'm here with the police and they're confused because there are no broken windows or locks. The house isn't even ransacked.

"Are you sure you locked the door this morning and that all of our windows have been locked? I don't understand how someone got in here without setting off the alarm. Did you have someone come in for repairs that may have seen our passcode that I was unaware of?"

As soon as he mentioned the alarm passcode, I felt a mix of fear and anger in the pit of my stomach. It couldn't have been Justin. It... it couldn't.

"Tymber?"

"Sorry. I'm still in shock. No. No repairs."

"I'm sorry. I should have waited until you got home. We'll figure this out together when you get here. We have insurance and these things can be replaced. They didn't take anything of sentimental value. Try not to get worked up. I need you home safe and sound."

"Okay. I'll be there soon."

I called Justin just to eliminate him as a suspect and ease my conscious.

The person you have dialed cannot be reached.

Shit!

I logged into the JFT app and checked my inbox. In place of his photo was a black silhouette above our conversation thread. In place of Justin, it read 'unknown user'.

This wasn't coincidence, but I couldn't wrap my mind around it.

I couldn't tell Tahir about Justin and how he knew our alarm code. I couldn't tell the police. I couldn't find Justin. I wasn't sure if that was even his real name. I didn't know where he worked or lived. I was so focused on granting him access to invade Tahir's spaces, I never thought to inquire about his. I was fuming with the kind of anger only self-inflicted pain can bring. I cried a fountain of guilty tears, ashamed of my foolishness. I made sure my tears were gone before I showed up at home. The least I could do was not force Tahir to comfort me in this mess I created.

I stepped into my home, devoid of all expensive electronics.

Guilt cascaded across Tahir's face. "I'm sorry. It's my job to protect us and I've failed. I'm going to upgrade our system to include video surveillance and get a dog. I'll work from home more. I'll do whatever I need to to make sure you feel safe again."

"They're just things, my love. We're okay."

He embraced me tenderly. "What have I done to deserve you?"

I promised myself I wouldn't cry but salty guilt burned down my cheek, knowing Justin fucked me in a way I never imagined.

A Mes of a Mess

I'm not sure when, but at some point I became hooked on my trysts with Justin. I couldn't get enough. The recklessness of our adventures fueled my sex life at home as well. Tahir had no reason to suspect anything as I was as attentive as I ever was, and applying how electrified I felt from fucking Justin into our sex life. Things hadn't been better.

I confessed to Justin that I wished he could sneak in each night. He suggested that he move in instead. When I balked at the audacity of him thinking I could hide him in my house, he laughed. "Nah, tell your man I need a place to crash for a while." I felt my lips curling into a sly smirk. He continued his pitch,

"I'm sure you can think of something to sell it. Come on. Think of all the fun we'd have all over the house." He enveloped me in his arms, kissing my neck.

I caved. "Okay. I'll see what I can do."

The following week, I told Tahir a sob story about learning of someone who had fallen on hard times and needed a place to crash. He asked who it was. I told him a friend of a friend. I explained that I wanted to help but I didn't know how.

Tahir asked why he didn't just rent a room until he could get his own place. I told him he was trying, but it was difficult when you don't have a support system. I quietly added, "I wish I could help him out." I tacked on a sniffle for good measure.

Tahir turned to me. "We have the room, babe, if it means that much to you. We can give him a month to save and get himself together."

"Really, baby? Are you sure?"

"I'm not signing up for a lifetime roommate, but we can help him for a little while if he needs it."

"That's so sweet of you, babe. I'll send word today and start making arrangements."

I raced out of there eager to message Justin. He bought it. You're in. We've got a month. Justin replied shortly that he knew I could pull it off.

By week's end, he had moved into our guest room. Justin and I hadn't had sex in the house yet, but every time we passed each other, he'd intentionally brush against my body or grab my ass or squeeze my titty. The next thirty days was going to be incredible.

Monday came, and Tahir and I completed our pre-work ritual. I left the house first per my usual. He departed roughly ten minutes after me. What he didn't know was I just made a run to the coffee shop and would be home bound after. I waited an extra ten minutes for good measure after getting our coffees and returned home. Tahir's car was gone. It appeared the coast was clear.

I entered, singing out to Justin, "Got you some coffee." He exited the guest room and nearly knocked me and the beverages over pawing at me. He banged me right on my kitchen island. I suggested we shower in my bedroom's en suite. We got steamy in the bathroom for round number two.

I handed him Tahir's robe and slippers and we lounged in our bed. Just being there started to arouse me again. We watched some television and as I turned my head to look at him, I could smell Tahir's scent on the pillow. I shared that with Justin who chuckled, "And that probably makes your crazy ass want to do it again, doesn't it?" He knew me so well.

He turned me over, ensuring my face was buried into the pillow to soak up Tahir's scent as he fucked me. The smell of my secret lover's sweat while pounding me combined with my husband's scent on the pillow was the perfect elixir to help me get off.

"Just think, we've got an entire month of this," I reminded him happily.

The more we incorporated Tahir's belongings, the harder I came. He tied me up with his ties, spanked me with his belt. He once lubed up my wedding band and fingered my clit with it.

By the third week, Tahir and Justin were remarkably close. They played video games and drank beers together. Justin told me he started to feel guilty because "T's a nice dude."

I sneered at Justin. As if he was telling me something I didn't know. I knew he was a nice guy. I married him! I loved him! But my defensiveness was guilt in armor. "So what? You want to stop now?" I asked coarsely. He paused long enough for it to be uncomfortable.

"Nah. I just felt bad. I can fuck you in your man's car in the garage while he's upstairs, and in your bed when he's at work, and all over this fucking house, but I can't share with you that I felt bad for the guy for a second?"

"I'm sorry. I feel bad too."

Palpable guilt dripped from my tongue as it took my lover to yank my conscience from her hiding place."You're supposed to be out of here in a week anyway so..."

He stared at the floor. "Yeah. We knew it couldn't go on like this forever."

"I know."

We didn't touch each other for three days. Try as we might, we couldn't maintain a strong enough front for Tahir not to be suspicious. When we're not fucking, he finally suspects something. Go figure.

"What's going on with you two? Y'all have a fight or something?" Tahir asked.

"Nah. Just thinking about leaving and looking forward to the next chapter," Justin answered.

I shrugged. "No issues here. Got a lot on my plate at work, but no issues with either of you two weirdos."

As this month-long indulgence came to a close, Justin and I had our last night together. I crept to his room while Tahir was asleep as I'd done many times before. Our encounter wasn't like any other time. It was gentler, tender, more sensual and loving. It was a goodbye fit for two lovers who'd grown to love each other and justly, the man between them.

Once he moved out, we never spoke again. I deleted the JFT app. I was finally cured of my addiction. Anybody know the cure for guilt?

Company

Jaxon and I had been talking about the swinger lifestyle and even though it seemed to fit us on a logical level, if we were honest with ourselves and each other, we were scared about the potential jealousy issues and emotional ramifications associated with the behavior. After much deliberation, we decided to go for it.

We made a decision to go to a swinger club, then decided to make some ground rules. I suggested that we have code words that were seemingly benign to a third party, but would be a prompt eject button if either of us felt uncomfortable. "I'm a bit thirsty" seemed like a safe bet.

The venue said there would be refreshments and either of us would just excuse ourselves, say "I'm a bit thirsty," and we could head out of there, no questions asked.

A rub in the palm of the hand was granting permission, a squeeze of the hand was a no. We hadn't decided if we'd be participating, or if we'd just be voyeurs that night, so on the cuff indicators were necessary in addition to set limits. No kissing other people, no missionary sex, and always use protection if we did decide to engage.

The date was a week away and I was beside myself like it was my first date. I wasn't sure what to wear, or how to do my hair. I wanted to be invitingly sexy, but not look like a hooker. We giggled all week long about what we thought it would be like, swaying between whether we were leaning towards having a threesome or just watching others get busy.

As the date neared, I found myself getting nervous about the potential consequences in my relationship. What if Jaxon really wanted to engage, and I didn't and he became resentful? What if I wanted to engage and he became jealous? What if no one found us attractive and we didn't even have the option to try? What if we loved it and regular sex seemed too vanilla and we ruin a good thing?

I started working myself up so much, I nearly backed out. I came to Jaxon the night before with all my concerns. He was more than understanding. He reassured me that nothing we could do would outweigh the intimate, loyal, and loving relationship that we had. He said we didn't *have* to do it because the point was to try something fun for both of us and if it's upsetting, then we're missing the point. His understanding was just the reassurance I needed. No matter what happened, or didn't happen, we'd be okay. If anything about it upset either of us, we could communicate and fix it.

The day of the party, I had massive butterflies and apparently an inner glow that radiated to my exterior. All day at the office, everyone asked what my weekend plans were because I looked like I was going away for my honeymoon. I just smiled and told everyone my husband and I were going to binge stream a series and eat ice cream.

Finally, the day had arrived. Forget about first-time-sex-with-a-boyfriend preparation, I did pre-gyno visit prep. No, new, hot *male* gynecologist visit prep. Everything was waxed, exfoliated, slathered in moisturizing cream, and a few dabs of my finest scent in a few deliberate places. I'd decided on a nude hued, semi-sheer lace dress with strategically placed overlays to barely cover naughty parts. It hugged my curves tighter than my husband, and panties were nowhere to be found.

My especially dapper-looking husband gave me a visual reminder as to why I was lucky to be with him as he stepped into the bedroom to ask if I was ready. In a crisp button up with a fresh cut and the perfect five o'clock shadow, I drank my man in and considered keeping him all to myself for no other reason than I wanted to jump his bones immediately.

"Damn, baby, you look good!"

"Thank you. Joyce, you look…" I turned so he could get the 360 view. "You look like I don't want to leave this house!"

"I thought the same thing!" I shouted excitedly.

He extended his hand, "Let's get out here and show off before we devour each other in here."

I grabbed his hand and we walked out the door.

When the fresh, warm night air hit me— especially as it swept past my thighs to tickle my bald pussy—my sense of what was about to happen was heightened.

I squeezed my lover's hand as we walked to our Mercedes. I realized this was better than a first date; it was a first date with your best friend in tow.

For most of the duration of the ride we listened to music instead of talking, just holding each other's hand excitedly. When the GPS announced that we had arrived at our destination, my stomach did a somersault.

I looked over at Jaxon. If he was nervous, he was wearing a brave face.

My nerves died down as it took us forever to find parking. It gave me time to collect myself. I checked the address in my phone several times because it was a large unassuming door in the middle of the block. By the address of the adjoining buildings we guessed this had to be the entrance, but there was no sign of us being in the correct place.

We stepped in and it was far more elegant than you would expect from the outside appearance. I was pleasantly surprised. The outside's ambiance gave no indication that this was a place one would want to remove their clothing. The open lobby space was plush, pristine, and inviting. There was a beautiful chandelier and large mirrors that served as my final check before introducing myself to potential partners. As I spun and looked at myself over my shoulder to check out my backside, a woman stepped in and cleared her throat startling me.

"Oh. Hey! Sorry. We were looking for 'Compagnia.'"

Her face warmed instantly, "Ahhh, yes. Do you two have a reservation?"

"Yes, we are Napier & Quinn." Jaxon and I decided to go with the surnames of our favorite villain duo Harley and the Joker as our aliases for the night.

She scanned the list with her finger before finding our names. "Ah, I see you right here! V.I.P. guests for the night. Well, I hope that we make you feel important enough to return." She handed us each a pamphlet with some communal guidelines that we'd already reviewed on their website, along with key cards like you receive at a hotel. We stepped into the elevator and as the glass doors closed in front of us, she asked if we had questions before traveling up. We shook our heads no.

"Okay then. As VIP cardholders, you have unlimited refreshments and alcoholic beverages. You have access to all three levels as well as the pool and Jacuzzi areas. On the first level is the "Mixer Room" where you can mingle as clothed or unclothed as you'd like, while getting to know other guests. We ask that sexual activity not take place on this floor. On the second floor, there are private beds separated by curtains if you two, or whomever you'd like to bring, desire a private undisturbed session in the front. In the back, there are private rooms for VIPs only. There's also a sex toy vending machine so people can be sure products are new, clean, and safe. On the third floor it's an open space, with open beds, and you can be as involved or uninvolved in the activity taking place as you'd like. There are various forms of contraceptives near the showers in the back. On the roof there is a bar, swimming pool and Jacuzzi. Sexual activity is welcomed in this area as well. Any questions?" Jaxon and I looked at each other then decided we could take it from there.

"Have you decided which floor you'd like to begin on?"

"You said there's a bar on the roof and on the first floor?"

"Yes ma'am!"

"Roof," my lover and I said in unison.

"My pleasure."

When we reached the top and the doors opened, I was relieved to find the roof looked as luxurious as the lobby. The pool was lit up from below, the bar was bigger than I'd imagined, and the scene was bustling with happy, energetic, normal looking people. It had a typical nightclub vibe, but there were a few clusters of people who were nude

54

or semi-nude that were making out. We stepped out and both made a beeline for the bar.

"What can I get you?" The bartender leaned over and asked, cupping her ear to be sure she could hear our requests over the thumping music.

"I'll have a Scotch, neat. She'll have a 'Pink Pussy Martini.' She looked like that was a new request. "It's vodka, cranberry juice, lemonade and peach Schnapps."

"Specific vodka?"

"Something top shelf."

While she whipped up our drinks, we surveyed the scene: lots of attractive people who looked happy to be exploring their sexual freedom. There was a nice variety in age, race and body type. Women outnumbered men roughly three to one, but I expected that as the venue did not allow single men to attend on certain nights—just women and couples.

Our bartender returned surprisingly fast with our drinks. She scanned Jaxon's card and we left her a tip before walking arm in arm around the rooftop. All eyes were on us like cows before the slaughter. They could smell the fresh meat. There wasn't uncomfortable staring, just noticeable. We chatted a little as though there weren't naked people all around and like we didn't hear the moans of pleasure surrounding us until something made us stop in our tracks.

A petite woman with perky natural breasts in the Jacuzzi was squatting on a man in reverse cowgirl, with a mouth full of dick, and holding on to a cock in each hand. Her curly wet hair clung to her face as she splashed up and down in the bubbling waters. They were pounding her holes as fast as she was jerking the others. Not only did she appear to be so happy in all her sexual glory, but she seemed even more thrilled to have gained a captive audience. She stopped briefly from her multitasking to wink at us, but then it was right back to the tasks at hand... and mouth and... well, you get the point.

We wandered back over to the less intense area of the bar to refill our glasses.

"That is too much for me!" Jaxon whispered in my ear.

"You? That is too much for *me*!"

We laughed, deciding right then and there that our night wasn't going to get quite that wild.

"Same?" the bartender asked.

"Yes."

We observed through two more rounds and even danced a little. The alcohol had definitely loosened us up. We decided to take the fourth drink to go investigate other floors. We took the stairs and for a brief moment we were in the staircase alone. Jaxon pinned me up against the wall saying, "You are by far the most beautiful woman here tonight. I knew that'd be the case before we left the house." We kissed like high schoolers between classes. Drunk on him and a bit of my martini, I stumbled a bit down the steps, holding his arm for balance. I pulled my key out of my soft leather purse.

"This floor or second floor?"

"Let's check them all."

"Right. Good idea."

We opened the door to the third floor and it was the same as on the roof, all eyes on fresh meat. It was a huge room with wall-to-wall beds except for one small corner with someone to monitor the space near a doorway that led to an adjacent room that I assumed were the showers the hostess mentioned, and a small table of contraceptives. The lighting in here was dim, forgiving even. All the beds made it very obvious what this space was used for.

Jaxon and I chose a bed to sit on and watched a couple make very passionate love. For some reason I expected all rough and kinky sex. But this couple, they were intense and nearly oblivious to their surroundings. It was… endearing. Amidst all those people, they could not get enough of each other. I had no way of knowing if they were actually a couple or just met that night, but their closeness suggested that they were pre-existing lovers.

There was an eight-person orgy that was so fluid it was if they'd all known each other too. So many limbs and yet none in the way. It was intuitive and graceful, like a dance. I realized that no two experiences were alike. From the Jacuzzi gangbang to the octo-orgy to the one-on-one couple, their experiences were all sexual and all very different. There were silent boundaries and openness co-existing. It was art, and it was beautiful.

The sensual sights and liquor combination had heat coursing through me. I reached for Jaxon and kissed him passionately. We lost ourselves in sexual sensory for a time I could not give a number to. Eventually we were interrupted by a gentle tap. A woman who appeared to be alone was staring at us.

"Umm…" she looked as though she hadn't quite thought through what she was going to say. "… I noticed…Uh, you guys looked so passionate and it was turning me on so much I have been touching myself watching you and I was wondering if you wanted some company or if I should just resume watching. No pressure. Either is fine. You guys look new and I thought you might be more inclined to accept an invite than to ask for one."

I looked at Jaxon, he looked at me. We sized her up. She was beautiful. Warm honey colored skin, thick in every place that counts. Her smile was friendly and she had dimples so deep you could see them when she pronounced certain words. She had long, straight chestnut hair that appeared to be all hers. But you never know these days. We sat up and I thought at the very least we could introduce ourselves,

"I'm Quinn. This is my husband Napier. You are?"

"Sioux."

"I expected a more exotic name than Sue from such an exotic looking person."

"Well, it's Sioux, like S-I-O-U-X, not S-U-E. Does that help?" She laughed, her brilliant dimpled smile on display.

"Sioux, you're correct. We are virgins here." I reached for Jaxon's hand and…

Hand Squeeze? Page 59
Palm Stroke? Page 62

Tandem

I clasped Jaxon's hand and squeezed. I was enjoying the thrill of watching and being watched. It was fulfilling and exciting enough. This girl was beautiful and it wasn't even jealousy that prevented me from accepting the invite, it just didn't feel like the next step. I was on a high and I didn't want to push it. I turned to Jaxon ready to search his face for disappointment, but he was staring lovingly at me.

"You can continue to watch. Right?" I said, making sure to check with my love.

"Of course."

We resumed our make out session but this time we weren't completely lost in ourselves. We were aware that at least one other set of eyes was on us and in fact, our lovemaking would serve as the catalyst to her pleasure too. I'd never felt so connected and aroused. I was porn! Me! Little ole Joyce. Being a live show and seeing how someone reacts to your pleasure is an experience I found surprisingly enjoyable.

She fed off an invisible thread in tandem with our passion. When Jaxon raised my breast to my mouth, she did the same with her breast. When I rode him slowly as he gripped my full ass, she inserted two fingers inside herself, rocking slowly onto them. When he turned me and pulled my legs toward him for missionary, she laid on her back and pushed her fingers deeper inside. When he sped up and started doing hard, deep thrusts, she reached deep within fondling her G-spot. I found myself swallowed in the sounds. The grunts, moans, and sighs of all the other patrons engaging in their own pleasure, the sound of Sioux in tandem with my sounds, making me so much more aware of my breath, my body, my pleasure. Seeing her masturbate on one side of me and several bodies touching, sucking, and fondling one another on the other was a sensory overload.

When he began giving me long, deep strokes I circled my hips in rhythm with his as I felt my orgasm build. Sioux was feverishly rubbing her clit moaning. In perfect time, her confession mirrored mine. "I'm about to..." moans replaced words and my body succumbed to the ecstasy. Instead of one giant climax, a continuous full body orgasm rolled in like thunder over and over. Jaxon would slow down just enough for me to start to come down, then he'd aim for my spot and thrust so deeply I cried for him never to stop as another orgasm took over. Sioux had stamina, she hung right there with us even though I was on the edge of insanity.

When Jaxon wrapped his hand around my neck and started fucking me in search of his own gratification, Sioux switched from clitoral stimulation to deep internal pleasure. The harder he pumped, the faster she fucked herself. When Jaxon said, "Shhhhhhhhhhhhhhhiiiiiit," as he released, Sioux clenched, snatched her fingers out and squirted so far it shot past us and hit the wall as she convulsed for a few seconds. It may have been the most erotic thing I had ever witnessed up close.

When body twitching stopped and breathing became normal for all parties, we sat up and looked at one another. I wasn't sure what to say to break the ice with someone who you've never been more aware is actually a stranger, but with whom you have just shared such an intimate encounter.

"That was amazing!" seemed like a safe and true admission.

"Yeah," Sioux agreed

Jaxon just nodded, exhausted.

I rested my head on Jaxon's shoulder. "Shower?"

He nodded again.

"Can she?"

"Hell yeah!"

"Just shower, Mr. Excited," I teased.

"I know, babe." He kissed my forehead "Sioux, we're gonna shower. You want to join us?"

"Yeah, Yeah, I'd like that very much."

We walked quietly to the shower and grabbed towels & flip-flops.

Washing each other proved to be erotic as well. She and I washed each other, which Jaxon liked very much. Then the two of us washed him, which he loved. She supportively rubbed our backs as we kissed and held each other. She was never out of line, and I never felt threatened. Everything was respectful and nothing felt forced or unclear. It was the perfect experience for a first timer.

Once we dried off and dressed, we walked to the elevator together. She didn't come in. She said she had a wonderful night and would be honored to share another experience with such a loving couple. Who knows what she went back to do or how she had the energy for it. Maybe she had a wild gangbang with a raunchier couple, maybe she went home shortly after. Whatever her decision, she deserved to live it to the max. As for me and my lover, well, we would never forget this night. Would I do it again? Maybe. Would I engage next time? Possibly. Would I do it regularly? Don't push it.

I excitedly stroked his inner palm. I'd never done something this wild in my life! My heart was thumping out of my chest. What were we about to do? How well would I perform? Would I be jealous if he touches her? Would I be aroused if she touches him? There were so many things I had no answers to. I figured just being honest was the best way to go.

"Okay so, we're new at this. I'm not sure what happens next or how."

"Well, that depends entirely on what you two are willing to do and what I'd like to do. Also, what you don't want to happen. Like, if you guys have rules, it's best I know them in advance. Do you?"

"Yeah, a few."

She ran down a checklist so fast, it was evident she was a veteran here.

"Oral?"

"Yes."

"Give or receive or both?"

"Receive."

Jaxon chimed in, "She can give... to a woman."

"Right. And he can receive from a woman."

Jaxon looked at me, surprised. We hadn't discussed that, but I had been thinking about it and it didn't bother me.

"Yeah?" he asked smiling.

"Why not?" I giggled back to him.

She continued, "Vaginal penetration?"

"No males penetrating me."

"And may he penetrate?"

I hesitated. "I don't... I don't think I'm ready for that yet."

"Okay, that's totally fine. Anal?"

"I'm not receiving that from anyone but him, and he's not doing it to anyone."

"And I'm not receiving it from anyone!" Jaxon clarified.

"I assumed that was a given, baby."

"Don't say 'given' when talking about my ass," he laughed.

"So Quinn, have you ever been with a woman?"

"In college a friend went down on me once when we were drunk, but I didn't reciprocate. I guess that doesn't count. But... I'm a fast learner!"

"Hmm, okay. So you've never penetrated a woman?"

"With fingers or a toy?"

"Toy."

"No."

"Would you like to?"

I looked at Jaxon, puzzled. "I... I... don't know. Can you explain more?"

"Sure! There's a vending machine that sells all sorts of stuff: vibes, crops, strap-ons, lubes, etcetera."

"There is a vending machine downstairs that will dispense a whole strap-on?"

"Yep."

"And you want me to fuck you?"

"I want you both to fuck me."

"But..."

"Before you say what you're about to say, allow me to clarify."

"Okay."

"If he fucks you anally while you're wearing the strap-on to fuck me, every stroke of his will also be yours, as though the two of you are fucking me together. Some couples like that shared experience.

It's cool if you're not into it, it's just an idea. I have others."

Jaxon and I stared at one another. Secretly I pleaded he wouldn't suddenly get "thirsty" because I was really intrigued by this idea. Being penetrated while penetrating a gorgeous girl never even occurred to me.

"What do you think, babe?" I asked.

"Sounds interesting to me." Jaxon stared at me intensely, no doubt checking if I was really okay with this.

"Me too." I returned my stare to Sioux. "Okay, so we're headed to the vending machine."

We walked hand-in-hand all three of us downstairs to the vending machine. Again, eyes fell on the trio that was two-thirds fresh meat.

I'd never seen a vending machine quite like this in my life. Everything Sioux said would be there, was there, and more! We selected between three options and she swiped her card once we decided.

"Consider it a virgin gift," she said, nudging me.

Once it dropped down with a thud, it started to become very real what we were about to engage in.

"You want to put on a show or you want some privacy?"

"I think..." I looked at Jaxon; he frowned and nodded in support of whatever I chose. "I think I'd like to be private this time."

"Great. Private areas are this way."

The private rooms weren't actually rooms. It was one large room with curtains between for privacy.Sioux began taking the toy out of the box.

64

"We don't have to use it right away but it's better to have it out and ready to use so we're not fumbling around with it when things heat up."

I really appreciated how open she was. It helped me feel at ease.

Jaxon and I kissed and Sioux helped us undress. She removed her own clothes as well.

She had a tattoo of a purple dragon on her ribs that wrapped around her hip and ended just below her ass. She had another tattoo that was writing in another language on her shoulder. Sioux had both nipples, her belly button, and the hood above her clit pierced. It surprised me because none of them were visible before she was nude. She sat on the bed and patted next to her.

I sat beside her and she asked if I wanted her to suck my pussy.

I looked at Jaxon and he looked back at me, shrugging his shoulders.

"Okay."

Sioux turned to Jaxon, "I don't want you to feel left out. Head up there and give her some kisses, suck her nipples, you know..." She smiled that deep dimpled smile.

Jaxon kissed my lips just as she did. Soon, I realized her tongue must have been pierced too. Sioux did some shit with her tongue I never felt before. It felt like she could make it move in waves and it felt incredible.

I felt like I would cum hard and fast. I kissed Jaxon deeply, moaning into his mouth.I held tightly to him, surprised by the force and the quickness she was able to bring me to orgasm. She was going to have to teach Jaxon that shit before we left!

I sat up and grabbed Jaxon's hand, pulling him around the bed in front of us.We leaned forward together and tongue kissed each other with Jax's dick between us.He watched with widened eyes like he couldn't believe it was happening. It was like a synchronized dance going over and under the shaft. Then as she deepthroated him, I took both of his balls into my mouth.

His legs trembled.

Sioux came up for air and we switched places. I knew he liked it rough but I wouldn't expect that from her, so I grabbed his ass to make him throat fuck me.

Surprisingly, she seemed really into that. She grabbed my hair and forced me down on his cock while she fondled his balls. He looked down but only for a moment. It seemed looking at us overwhelmed him. I could tell he wanted to draw out this experience a bit.

Sioux and I stopped for a second and pressed our breasts together before resuming our original double dose of tongue on the shaft routine.

Jaxon moaned for me."Joyce."

I knew he wanted to cum. I pulled him on top of me so he could hump my throat. Sioux got behind him and sucked his balls from the back as he pumped my mouth.

He came so hard he pulled the sheets off the bed and grunted loud enough for the people on the other side of the curtain next to us to stop and say, "Well, damn,"to which we all had a good laugh.

I'd never experienced the afterglow with a third party but it was cool.

We talked about what brought us here, how long she'd been coming, more of our likes and dislikes. As we started talking about our likes, Jaxon started stiffening up, signaling round two could begin.

Sioux had me lie down on top of Jax. She spread my cheeks and started tongue fucking my asshole. She was an expert at tongue play. The same way I climaxed quickly when she sucked my pussy, I did when she licked my ass.

She stopped for a moment. "Put this on."

It was the strap-on. She was ready to get fucked. Jax and I got up, and she sat down while we secured the strap-on. She sucked the strap-on the way she did Jaxon. It didn't do anything for me physically, but somehow it made me feel powerful. I later realized she was lubing it up the way she lubed up my ass. Sioux was a fucking pro! Literally.

I entered her slowly until I felt I was all the way in. She kissed me soft and deep. I was grinding my hips the way Jaxon does when he's inside me. I hoped it felt as good to her. Her facial expression read that it did.

She grabbed my ass, opened her long legs wide and moaned as I got deeper.

I peeked over my shoulder to find Jaxon watching and stroking himself.

"Fuck us, baby," I moaned.

He looked excited with a slight tinge of panic. He pulled both of us down to the edge of the bed. Sioux shoved two of her fingers in her mouth, repeatedly gagging herself collecting thick spit, before pushing them between my cheeks, and lubing my asshole. Next, she pulled my ass cheeks apart with both hands.

"Fuck us baby" She echoed my statement.

Jaxon just exhaled loudly. I know my man. He was elated. He pushed inside my ass slowly the way I did with Sioux. Once he was able to make it all the way in, he gave my ass a moment just to get acclimated to him before he started any grinding.

Once he did, I felt a bit overwhelmed. He felt extraordinary and her reaction to being fucked by me, and Jaxon by proxy, was really fucking amazing. He grabbed my breasts and I put my hands over his so I could remove one of his hands from my breast and put one of them on Sioux's.

She looked at me before sucking one of his fingers. I smiled at her and sucked one of his fingers grabbing my breast.

Two mouths, two breasts, stuffed deeply in my ass, with moans surrounding us, I'm surprised he didn't cum immediately. If it were his first orgasm of the night, I'm sure he would have. I was grateful for his stamina because he was able to fuck my little asshole hard, and that meant he had both Sioux's and my eyes rolling back with orgasms.

When I could tell he was close I begged, "Cum for me, baby."

Sioux repeated me. "Yes! Fuck! Cum, baby. Harder. Make me cum." This was the most vocal she had been.

I came before either of them. Sioux followed soon after, and Jaxon came hard and loud again.

In our secondary afterglow, Sioux asked, "Are you always that loud when you cum?"

We laughed. "Not usually. There was an awful lot of stimulation going on."

Sioux played with my hair and it felt like a sleepover with an old friend. All the anxiety I had leading up to this week was so unnecessary. We hadn't even left yet and I couldn't wait to come back.

"Want to hit the showers?"

"Yeah."

Instead of putting on our clothes, we wrapped ourselves in towels and scurried to the shower area.

Staring at Sioux's sexy tatted body in the shower got me thinking. Maybe I wouldn't have to wait till our next visit for round three after all.

Sex Rolodex™

I'm a slut.

I was never innocent. I never wanted or claimed to be. No one made me this way. No one harmed, molested, de-valued me.

But by society's standards, and my own, I am a slut.

Thankfully, what people thought of me was the only fuck I couldn't give.

Monogamy made absolutely no sense to me. No matter what I told the partners I dealt with, none of them seemed to believe me. They all wanted to be the one to change my mind and heart and get me to settle down.

I was a challenge.

I couldn't understand it. All my friends were looking to settle down and I couldn't keep guys from begging me to commit! I was starting to question where the hell my friends were looking for spouses.

They'd ask if I wanted to have a family one day. Nope.

I don't want children. Never have.

If I changed my mind, which I was 99% sure wasn't going to happen, our orphanages aren't empty.

I didn't feel a compulsion to have someone to come home to or share everything with. I didn't crave to be part of a team. Choosing one person's point of view to listen to, face to stare at, and body to fuck sounded like the most boring shit I could think of. I wasn't sure why everyone else found it so normal.

"You'll change your mind." was said to me so often, I didn't hear anything after "You'll change" anymore.

No man, no age, no sight of babies, nothing was going to change that.

It's weird how society accepts that you know what's best for yourself, until you deviate from it.

Most nights I would settle in at home, pull out my Rolodex™ and spin it like a magic wheel; whoever it landed on was who I called to fuck.

I liked my old rolodex™ because I kept anecdotes on the card about each contact. Notes on their appearance, their kinks, what they taste like, and a GS that represented "gold star" to remind me what their proficiency was.

I stuck my fiery red stiletto nail between two cards and then spun for fun.

"Stori."

Hmm. Stori?

Short. Thick. Huge Tits. Pierced nipples, tongue, and twat. Pretty dominant. Into some light bondage. Tastes sweet and juicy. GS: strap-on stroke is A1 and she sucks pussy like a champ.

Sounded like a fun time to me. Time to make the call.

She picked up on the first ring.

"Stori?"

"This is NOT who I think it is!"

"Well, that depends. Who do you think it is?"

"Hampton."

"Then you'd be correct."

"I can't believe you're finally calling me back."

"I'm not calling to chat. I'm calling to get fucked. You with it or what?"

"Shit, I'm out of town. But look, I can be there in a couple hou-"

End call.

Next!

Spun it again.

Luxe.

It must be ladies' night.

I chuckled to myself. I remembered Luxe. I always thought it was interesting that her named alluded to being so posh and lavish and to an extent, she was... for the world. But behind closed doors? Completely different story. Her card said it all.

Skinny, but has a phat booty. Has a tattoo on her ass that says "slave." Total masochist. Loves being degraded. GS: Sucking pussy and toes.

Okay, let's see what's up with her.

It rang a few times, and just before I assumed voicemail would pick up, she answered in a hushed tone.

"Hey, Hampton, I'm working late but I didn't want to miss your call. I can swing by in a few."

"What's a few?"

"Umm..." she sighed, "I think..."

"Hurry up, bitch. I don't have all fucking day."

I could hear her smile through the phone. "Hour and a half, two tops."

"I'll think about if you deserve me. Call when you're getting off. If I don't answer, I'M already getting off. Don't call again. Capisci?"

"Understood. I'll try as fast as I..."

"Luxe," I barked

"Yes?" she answered, her voice breathless with sensuous fear.

"When have I ever given a shit about trying?"

"Never, Mastress."

"And I didn't start today."

End call.

Another spin.

Hendrix.

Well, looks like dick may be on the menu after all!

Hendrix: Slender, but very fit. Average height. 9" and thick. No specific kinks, but mostly down for anything. Strong and silent type. GS: Amazing stamina with no refractory period.

Ahhh, yes. I remember that part. No refractory period. He could cum and keep going no problem. No reboot necessary. He was a deliciously fascinating anomaly. Let's hope I have better luck with him.

Three rings. "Hey, Hampton."

"And you know who I am. Points for not pretending I'm a stranger."

"I'm never deleting your number. Ever."

"Are you as full of cum as you are compliments?"

"More so."

"Perfect. How soon can you be here?"

"25 minutes."

"See you then."

Now that I knew what kind of night I was in for, I mentally prepared for Hendrix's arrival. After the potential night with Luxe, I began to acquire a taste for domination tonight. I had to shift gears. No problem.

Hendrix arrived in just under 25 minutes dressed comfortably with a bottle of cognac in hand.

I led him to my bedroom by the hand. "Lie down."

I stood above his face, touching myself in my crotchless red teddy.

He began stroking himself.

"Did I say you could touch yourself?"

He was shocked. I'd never been this way with him before."Uhh, no."

"Then don't."

He smirked and continued watching me.He began writhing beneath me, unable to touch or taste anything, so I squatted just over his face.

He was breathing so hard I could feel the warmth against my pussy even though I stayed just out of reach where his lips could meet mine.

"Hampt…" he whined.

"Mmm. You want this pussy don't you?"

"Fuck yeah! Why you playing?"

Knowing that not being deep in my tight little cunt was the source of his frustration turned me on.

"Open your mouth."

I rubbed my clit feverishly, bringing my orgasm to the brink. Then I dug my fingers deep inside, fucking myself until I knew I was about to gush and then I let my cum spray all over his face. He stuck his tongue out, and pulled me down onto it so he could suck what remained out of me. I came so hard my thighs quivered around his head, twitching with orgasmic aftershocks as he tongued my hole and slurped my entire pussy.

When he finally got air to breathe, he said, "Turn over."

He gripped my thighs, flipped me, pressed down between my shoulders and pushed inside my pussy without warning.

I cried out but it didn't throw him off one bit. Pounding my pussy, he released a stream of curses while smacking my ass. I threw that ass back but made sure to sustain my arch for him. He started asking a bunch of rhetorical questions like, "Why is your pussy so damn good? What the fuck do you have inside there?" Telling me it's too good and shit. He turned me slightly to the side so he could grab a fistful of titty while maintaining a powerful grip on my ass. I sucked my free tit moaning, "Fuck me Daddy" and it was sensory overload.

He pulled out and came all over my thighs, some managing to shoot up on my stomach. Before I could suggest a clean-up, he was right back in it.

Damn it! How could I forget?

He was back with a vengeance, like he knew I'd let that fact slip my mind and he wasn't going to let me forget again. He pushed me back onto my stomach, grabbed my throat and served me deep thrusts with his chest pressed against my back, sinking his teeth into my neck.

Growled adjectives between each stroke, he asked, "Who you calling Daddy while gripping my dick with this tight... fat... wet... pussy?"

I squeezed my pussy so tight on him he couldn't pull out if he tried. I had a Chinese finger trap grip on that dick and was about to unleash a tsunami wave.

"Hendrix!" I shuddered, releasing all over his fat dick.

"Damn!" He stopped moving, trying to hold his nut back. I don't know what for. It's not like the party was over if he came. So I wouldn't let the friction be stopped.

I reached beneath and stroked his sack while I threw that ass back at him. "Give me that nut, Daddy." I could feel him throbbing inside me, but he was determined to hold on. He gripped my neck harder and pushed me close to the bed, limiting my range of motion.

My phone began blaring my ringtone, jolting us both. I'm such a "don't call me, I'll call you" type of person I hadn't a clue who it could be. Then I remembered Luxe. It had been nearly two hours. I grabbed the phone and silenced it.

I turned to Hendrix and asked, "You want to have a threesome tonight?"

"What? With who?"

"I made tentative plans with someone else before you and..."

"Are you serious right now?" he began to withdraw from me.

I stayed in sync with him and tightened my grip.

"She's cute. She'll do whatever I tell her to do to you."

Yes? Page 77
Not her? Page 83

Luxury Suite

"Whatever?"

"Whatever. What do you want?"

His eyes lit up with options. "Both of y'all to suck me off."

"Of course. But I mean, something you wouldn't normally have someone do."

He began rocking back and forth inside me at the expectation. It was then we both realized we'd never disconnected.

"She take it in the ass?"

"Yup!"

"Okay."

I called Luxe back.

"Listen, I was getting fucked too hard to answer the phone right away but you can still come over and be my little slut. You're going to have to share me now that you made me wait and you're going to be his slut too. So I hope that ass is ready, and I mean that literally. Move fast too, bitch, you hear me?"

When I hung up, Hendrix was staring at me bewildered.

"She loves it. It probably made her pussy wet. Now, back to my pussy. Since I had to wait for that nut, you better hold it until our slut gets here."

Then I tried my best to make that impossible for him. But he would not be defeated. Whenever he got close, he would just force me into a position where I couldn't move and pull away just enough to have a respite.

When Luxe arrived, Hendrix and I went to meet her at the door. I snatched it open, grabbed a fistful of her hair and pulled her down to the floor in front of Hendrix. With the door still ajar, I told him he could finally let that nut out by spraying her face.

He looked afraid.

"Beat that dick and spray her face for making us wait."

"And you," I gripped Luxe by the chin, "open your fucking mouth like you have some damn sense."She opened her mouth and stuck out her tongue, kneeling before this stranger.

"Slap your dick on her tongue or fuck her mouth if it helps, but when you cum, I want to see it."

He beat his dick, occasionally shoving it in her mouth for wetness. Her eyes watered as he skullfucked her. Luxe's breasts bounced as she worked hard rocking back and forth, jerking him off with her mouth.

It was turning me on so much watching them together I had to touch myself. I came hard and fast. Self-achieved orgasms never took long for me. My hand was soaking wet and I thought all those juices shouldn't be wasted. I walked up behind Hendrix, wrapped my pussy juice-soaked fingers around his dick and took over stroking his shaft. I took my other hand and grabbed Luxe by the hair again.

"Deeper, bitch."

I wrapped his arms behind me and planted them on my ass. I took over and jerked his dick like it was an extension of me. Grinding my hips, forcing his forward, while pulling her closer. I had to peek around his torso to see anything, but I partly enjoyed not being able to see. It aroused me just imagining what I'd want her to do to me, focusing on receiving and stroking him as I would.

"Oh fuck."

"Yesssssss," I encouraged. I was eager to see this happen.

"Fuck."

Something primal washed over me and I bit him."Paint your fucking slut's face Daddy"

"Shiiiiiiiiitt." He shot nut all over her face. I felt the remaining warm gooeyness dripping over my fingers like a melting ice cream cone.

"Hendrix, meet Luxe. Luxe, this is Hendrix."I walked into my guest bathroom and returned with a washcloth I tossed to Luxe. She was instructed to get herself together, strip down to her panties and lie down on the couch. I brought Hendrix into my en suite so we could clean up together.

"You ever bust all over a stranger's face before?" I inquired, electrified.

"Hell no!"

"How was it?"

"That shit was amazing."

"Right?"

When we finished, we returned to find Luxe laid out on the couch, just as she'd been ordered. She stared expectantly, wearing only purple boy cut panties with lace trim. Her ass was perfection.

Hendrix just stared at her. Suddenly, an idea popped into my head.

"You know what? You're so filthy. I think I need to use my vacuum on you."

Both of them looked perplexed, but I was going to change that.

"Hendrix, please retrieve my vacuum from the closet near the front door and roll it over to this piece of filth."

His eyes widened as he was still getting used to such harsh language being used to describe her, but she squirmed excitedly each time I did it. Once he had it in front of her, I plugged it in and pulled out the hose attachment. I told her she could touch herself while she watched me sit on his face.

She stuck her hand in her panties.

"No. On the outside. Clit only."

Hendrix had pulled my thick, black throw blanket I kept on the love seat onto the floor to lay on top of. Once he was comfy, I made myself just as comfortable on his face.

"You can beat off this time. But you," I returned my attention to Luxe, "no more touching. Move your hand."

I turned the vacuum on and put the suction right on her clitoris. Oh how she squirmed!

I was smothering Hendrix's face. I glanced over my shoulder to see him jerking slow and steady.

"Put your hand in your panties and separate those lips. Gimme that clit."

Luxe followed directions perfectly. She squealed as the suction took hold through her panties. Even though he couldn't see, Hendrix started jerking faster just hearing what was going on.

"Ooh, you filthy, filthy cunt."

I noticed a slit of wetness darkening her panties.

"Damn, look how wet that pussy is getting when I call you filthy. You love being a nasty little slut for me. I can't wait to let Hendrix pound your asshole, you nasty bitch. I might consider letting you suck my pussy while he does it. I haven't decided if you're worthy of such an honor yet. But maybe, just maybe you can suck my toes, while I finger myself and make you watch."

I would only suction her clit in small bursts. Sometimes, I'd pull it away and use it to suck on her full nipples. The wet stain in her panties got larger.

I hovered it over her clit again. She raised her pelvis to the hose. She started bucking beneath it, the sound of the suction changing as it varied in pressure. She grabbed hold of the nozzle to direct where she wanted it to go.

Normally her taking so much control without permission would get her in trouble, but watching her soak through her panties, while riding a face, and knowing that he's jerking off was more than enough for me to handle.

Her moans grew louder as she allowed more and more time to be spent on her hot button. I was grinding my clit on Hendrix's nose, fucking his face with no respect for his ability to breathe or potential lack thereof. The firm grip he kept on my thigh with his left arm let me know I had no reason to be concerned.

"I want to see these panties so wet, they cling and I see every detail of that fat print throbbing when you cum for me."

That sent her over. "Oooh!" she convulsed, snatching the hose away.

I couldn't hold mine back either. I flooded Hendrix, who shot a load in tandem with the both of us.

"I've got at least one more in me," Hendrix proclaimed, shocking the hell out of Luxe. She'd just watched him cum twice, this time with no break. I'd briefly forgotten they were strangers and she was unaware of his secret talent.

"Take those panties off. You owe the mister that tight asshole."

She scooched her ass to the end of the couch and cocked her legs open. It took some patience to get him in there but after a few minutes he made it.

I just watched for a while. Luxe was taking a pounding. I don't think she was used to that kind of girth in that hole. She was enjoying herself though. I decided to let her suck my nipple and stroked her face lovingly as she did so to reward her for her endurance.

Hendrix loved the visual. He reached around and pushed two fingers in me. I guess he wanted to make sure all three of us were connected before he got ready to let off.

"Tell Daddy where you want him to cum," I told Luxe. By the look in his eye, she'd better answer fast.

"My tits!"

He pulled out and made a glorious glaze on her. I came for the last time of the night on his fingers. Hendrix lay on the floor as Luxe and I cleaned him with a warm cloth. That almost turned into another round, but everyone was just too tired for it.

We laid down on either side of him and fell fast asleep. We needed our rest, dual head was for breakfast.

What? You thought I forgot?

"Whatever I tell her to do?"

"Yeah. She likes being degraded and told what to do. Like a dog."

"Nah, that shit sounds a little too crazy for me."

"So is it that you don't want to share, or you don't want to share me with *her*?"

"How many options you got?"

"Enough to know I've got someone who will fit the bill for whatever you're into."

"Okay."

"So, what you into?"

He started to pull out and sit down so we could discuss.

"Uhn-uh. You're still hard and I'm still wet. We've got unfinished business here. If you can't think and pump at the same time, then I suggest you stop thinking."

He answered with strokes. After he emptied his ejaculation, he was free to spill what he had in his mind.

The way my Rolodex™ was organized was by their proficiency, which was far more useful information than their name on the off chance I preferred a particular kind of play, versus the luck of the draw. Turns out Hendrix wanted someone who was a bit bossy. He said he's always in control, but he would like to experience relinquishing it for once. The first person who came to mind was Lash. She was dominant, and fine as hell.

"Lash is 5'10", busty, thick hips, booty is okay. Very pretty face. Domme that likes bondage and paddle play. She's good at aftercare. That's great for a beginner like you."

"Did you just pull a card with all that info? Is that your list of partners? Are all those cards full? What does my card say?"

"Oh honey, this is none of your business and if you try to see any cards, yours is removed… permanently."

"Well, okay. So what does aftercare mean?"

"It means that sometimes the play can get a bit rough. She has some oils that she'll use to rub down and massage all your areas she made sting or burn."

"Burn!"

"From spanking, not fire, baby. Relax. You think you can handle it?"

"Yeah, yeah!" he said, I believe convincing himself more than me.

"Well let's see if she's available."

Lucky for us, she answered.

"Lash! Are you busy tonight? Please say no. I need to be punished. I've been real bad."

"You are hard to pass up, Hampton, but I…"

"Oh, no! No buts, just say yes. I need you. And I have a treat for you. A virgin; a man."

Lash took a deep breath like she was considering it.

"He doesn't need breaks after cumming. He's ready again in like ten seconds. You really should. He's never had someone take control before, and you're the best."

Stroking her ego won her over.

"I'll be over in a half."

"Mmmm. Thank you, Madam," I purred.

I poured Hendrix a glass of my twenty-year-old scotch and spent the time waiting on Lash's arrival to prep him. I told him about safe words and how they could be used at any moment. I asked if he wanted to have a non-verbal signal for me to pull him out of anything without letting her know. I gave a brief lesson on which items resulted in particular sensations so he knew if he wanted a flogger, or a paddle, or a riding crop. I explained she would begin softly and allow the blood to form in that area and create a cushion for more impact so it wouldn't hurt. Generally, Lash didn't even have to use anything, unless I desired her to. So chances were Hendrix wouldn't need to be reprimanded tonight. We were just going to have fun with him.

Just as I was finishing my crash course in sex slavedom, Lash arrived. I'd sent her a text with all of Hendrix's preferences. On a scale of 1-10, he was willing to go to about a 6 for pain. He wanted to be tied down, and was open to being blindfolded. He wasn't that into being degraded but he didn't mind vulgarities. He was willing to try a leather paddle for the night.

Lash walked in as the force that she was, wearing thigh high patent leather boots, a black corset, and her hair in a single braid ponytail that was at the very top of her head resembling a whip. She didn't typically look the stereotypical part, but I presume she wanted our newbie to have the full experience.

"So thissssss is my virgin," she hissed, eyeing him predatorily.

I could hear Hendrix's heart thumping.

"Why are you still wearing clothes?"

"Oh! I, umm..."

"Shh!" she snapped. She gestured for him to silence himself and just do it.

He stripped clumsily and stood stark naked, afraid to make a move and be scolded again.

She grabbed his dick. "Nice."

His shoulders relaxed a bit after the compliment.

"I've seen better though."

His shoulders tensed again.

Lash would build you up to tear you down, to build you up again. You never knew which direction she was going to take you in, and it left you wanting to please her desperately.

She dug in her bag of tricks and pulled out a ball gag."No more talking for you."

He looked at me like I was supposed to save him. He knew he had both safe words and gestures if he wanted to tap out, but he used neither. Soon the panic faded from his eyes and only curiosity lingered.

"You. Stop standing there like a fucking imbecile and help me strap this pig up."

In all my excitement about his first Domme situation, I forget about my own responsibility to serve our mastress of the night.

"Yes, Mastress."

I pulled my silk scarves from my drawer and we tied Hendrix to my bedposts. Lash obstructed his vision with a blindfold.

"I might have to change my plans for you. See, I was going to torture you. But you look weak. Your chest is heaving and if I didn't know better, I'd think you were seconds away from crying. So I have to do to you, what I do to little bitches. I smother them."

She pulled the ball gag from his mouth, ensuring not too much spit had collected and our little piggie wouldn't choke.

"I don't think you deserve my pussy, but this filthy slut will do whatever I demand she do, isn't that right?"

I nodded.

"Then why the fuck are you just looking at me instead of climbing on top of him?" She spanked me with her riding crop before I could mount Hendrix. Stood over him, facing me.

"I'm going to smother you with my fat pussy and you're going to love it. The ass is going to cover your entire nose and I don't know how the fuck you'll breathe but that's not my problem. You should feel honored to die between these thighs."

Virgin or no virgin, she was not taking it easy on him.

"And you, make sure you can ride dick and suck titties. I don't care how good it feels, getting me off is the priority for both of you. Don't fucking forget it."

Then she squatted right onto his face, like what she said was law and neither of us better find the gall to protest. I felt Hendrix tense beneath me the moment Lash planted herself on top of him. His dick throbbed inside me. I was momentarily distracted.

Lash cut her eyes at me, and pulled my head down to her plump E cups. She pushed them together so I could suckle both nipples at once. She swirled her hips on his face and clutched my head closely to her bosom. She used us as her pleasure saw fit. She pushed my head down further so I could lap at her clit while she reached behind, and grabbed a handful of his locks, demanding he tongue fuck her. She growled as she bucked on both of our faces.

"Harder, bitch. Yes. Don't stop." She had a fistful of my hair as well and was pulling me so far forward, my clit was pressed against Hendrix's pubic mound. If I came before she did, there'd be hell to pay. For everyone's sake I hoped she was close because the way he pulsed inside me said he and I were on the same page even if she wasn't. She bounced on his tongue and held my head still while she shivered and finally released on his face.

I gripped his dick so hard, he had no choice but to cum. I held my breath as I shuddered, trying to minimize my orgasm. She hadn't given permission for either of us yet and yet, we'd both defied orders. Though she did cum first, I suspected Lash wouldn't care about a technicality.

Her head and eyes rolled forward.

"You came."

I lowered my head.

"Did he?!"

I shook my head quickly. There was no reason to rat him out. She didn't believe me.

"Get up."

I clenched my walls tight, attempting to suck up any remnants of his cum. She grabbed his dick. It was still hard and throbbing. She attributed its stickiness to me.

"Well, at least one of you can follow directions. You'll be rewarded for that." She turned to me with cold eyes. "Suck yourself off of him."

I knelt, sucking, trying not to let any of his cum leak out of me. She knelt beside me and began sucking his balls. He writhed with excitement.

She stopped momentarily to scold me.

"What the fuck are you doing?" She pushed my head down and force-fed me his dick. She wasn't happy until my eyes produced tears and thick spit from choking poured down the shaft.

She grabbed something from beside her but I couldn't see what it was. She pulled a glove onto her hand, yanked my mouth off of him, and shoved her two gloved fingers in my mouth the way she had with his dick. Then she motioned for me to resume. I did with no questions asked. She sucked his balls and then pushed her fingers inside him.

The restraints tightened and he made a sound I'd never heard from him, or any other man before, and immediately erupted like a volcano down my throat. That new sound and the projection of his nut turned me on so much my walls seized and out poured his cum from earlier. When Lash finally sat up from sucking on his balls, making sure they were fully drained, she looked back and saw my exposing puddle.

"You're both going to pay for that. Especially him."

Fuck.

Trixxx are for Adults

Some people practice their Dom/sub lifestyle when they have the time. For them it's role-play. Even if it's frequent play, it's just play. For others, it's as much a part of their life as their career. Being Kelvin's slave was not just a job, but a job I took quite seriously. We met like many other couples, on social media. Likes became private messaging which graduated to text, which turned into phone calls that lasted hours.

Fortunately we were only thirty-five minutes away from each other so we picked a restaurant in the middle and had a casual meet-up. There was chemistry there but I didn't want to put too much pressure on it. I wore jeans and a tank with some accessories to dress it up. I just wanted to feel out his energy.

People can be whoever they wish behind a screen and over the phone. They create alternative lifestyles that they begin to believe so much that sometimes they forget to convey the behind-the-scenes version of themselves that they actually are the majority of the time. He only had a handful of photos on his page in all, and most of those he was tagged in. Of the few he uploaded, they were mostly memes showcasing his humor, or scenic portraits from his travels. There were five of him, but in each he was wearing sunglasses or a hat, sometimes both. Never one to care all that much about physical attraction, I didn't bother to ask for more photos. As long as when he showed up there was some resemblance to the person on his page, that'd be fine with me.

When I arrived, I was more nervous than I anticipated. I sat on the bar stool tapping my foot on the rungs below, trying not to look like I was waiting for someone in case he stood me up. Every time the door opened I perked up, putting that plan to shit. I was early so I couldn't exactly fault him for my building anxiety.

I heard the familiar jingling of the door opening and I looked up to find him panning the room searching for me. He removed his hat and sunglasses to get a better view. Finally, I got a better view too. Photos did not do him justice.

"Kelvin." I raised my hand to help him out.

"Taylor!"

He sounded sincerely happy to see me. His walk was confident, his smile approachable, his eyes had a twinkle in them that lit up his entire face.

He sat his sunglasses, hat, and phone on the bar, and approached me with his arms outstretched. I hopped down to embrace him.

"Glad we're finally doing this."

I agreed.

The conversation was light-hearted, fluid, and intriguing. His vibe was everything I'd hoped and more. I knew with certainty I'd be seeing him again.

After we wrapped up and paid the bill, we walked out together hand in hand. We lingered in front of Leila's Restaurant, not wanting to end the conversation. He reached in his pocket and pulled out a Black to smoke.

"Mind?"

Normally, being a smoker was a deal-breaker, but the fragrance wasn't as bad as a cigarette and we were in a public space. "Enjoy." I shrugged.

The moment he lit it and exhaled, I knew I was hooked. I nearly toppled over leaning in so closely. Envying his exhalation cloud of smoke, I longingly followed it as a child watches bubbles. For a woman not into smokers, he proved that every rule had an exception. Watching his full pink lips come together around it and suck, then push out to blow made me want to get on tiptoe and suck his bottom lip. Aside from our greeting hug, I hadn't been close enough until now to notice all his features. He was around 5'11 or 6'0 I'd guess. It appeared he kept in shape but he wasn't obsessed with the gym. His arms were really nice. I could envision myself wrapped in them. I did a quick scan to see if I could get a penis print in his dark wash jeans, but I couldn't tell. I noticed as he focused on our surroundings his sea foam green eyes would transform from sparkly, to piercing and intense. I couldn't tear myself away from them even when he was looking elsewhere.

Two years later, those eyes trained me with a glance.

When he entered a room, I stood with my head and eyes down with my arms behind my back until I was given instructions. I had an area of our living room that was for me to be "in park" when I was not actively being used by Kelvin. He used to have me kneel there, just to be on display for him. To be living art to the objection of your affection is beautiful. It also provided an opportunity to show my devotion and submission—both of which give me great pleasure. However, he said if I'm kneeling, he'd prefer I be used or at the very least, petted somehow. So he'd say "here," and I'd crawl beside him on the couch and kneel. The first time I did it, his eyes lit up. He assumed I'd stand up and walk over to him when he said "here" but when I crawled, his chest swelled with pride, and he became noticeably aroused. He stroked my hair as I knelt beside him like you would a pet. I found it soothing.

If I wasn't in park with my eyes cast down, he made eye contact and snapped, and I knew he meant to come to him. His command of me with just a finger motion gave me chills. Sometimes he told me to "worship" and I had to place both palms on the floor, stretch like a cat with my ass way up and chest touching the floor. He kept me in this position for up to an hour. Even if my body got tired, I wouldn't move. The ache reminded me I was his and I was honored to serve him.

Sometimes my position was functional. He had me in "table" and used me as just that. I strutted to him and brought him his dinner, then got on my hands and knees with my torso facing him and let him eat dinner off my back. After clearing his plate, he sometimes propped his feet up on me in that position, but then we found a more comfortable position for me to be his ottoman. I faced away from him with my ass in his face on my elbows and knees. I loved this position because often times he couldn't resist sliding his fingers inside me or stroking my pussy through my panties. He loved seeing me stripped down to just panties. He had a fetish for seeing them dampen. He wouldn't stop stroking me until my pussy soaked through the panties, and when it did, he snatched them off and ravaged me.

This was general play time. On the weekdays after a long day of work, Sir needed special pampering.

As was our ritual, I removed his coat so he could be seated. Once he sat, I knelt and removed his shoes. I rubbed his feet silently, giving him about a half hour to decompress. After this relaxation period, he patted his lap and it was my cue to curl up in it like a kitten, an action I relished. He told me about his day, listened to mine, we'd vent, share dreams, kiss, or be silent. It was our special time to connect. His cue to know I was satisfied with bonding was for me to ask if I could get him anything.

He smiled his single dimpled smile and thought up something for me to do. That day it was:

Trick 1? Page 95
Trick 2? Page 97

Blowing O's

He smiled a crooked smile, showing his solitary dimple in his left cheek. "A black."

Not often, but sometimes he smoked a Black & Mild™. He may have preferred one of his cigars, but just didn't feel like heading down to his man cave to smoke them.I didn't mind the scent of Black & Smooths nearly as much and he smoked them so infrequently that it wasn't a big deal for him to light one up in his favorite chair in our living room.

I went to grab one from the drawer within our antique mahogany pub bar.I walked over with lighter in tow and asked if he'd like me to light it for him.

"Yes, please, baby."

"Between my lips or yours?"

"Yours," he responded, smiling devilishly.

I placed the black between my lips.

"Uhn-uh."

"Kelvin." I blushed, catching on.

With raised eyebrows, he tilted his chin up at me, silently edging me on.

I shimmied out of my panties. When I turned to place them on the nearby couch, he grunted approvingly at my round bottom. I smiled over my shoulder, still blushing.

He swiveled his chair to face the couch for a front row seat. I sat on the edge of our fittingly smoky gray sectional and opened my legs. I pushed the plastic tip in and searched for the lighter beside me.

"Actually, I think I'll light it for you, babe."

He ignited the lighter and the end of the cigar. I sucked in my walls like I did with him inside. One hard drag and it was lit as brightly as his eyes. When Kelvin removed it, he cupped his hands around my sex, leaned forward, and inhaled as I blew like a shotgun.

Then he sat back a bit, putting the tip to his lips and taking a pull. "Mmm, these taste so much sweeter laced with you."

He pushed the tip back inside me, I pulled again. This time I spread my legs wide so I could blow O's and watch them dance invitingly to him.

We repeated this process until the cigar was too close to comfort for my precious lips. He tongue fucked me until I was wriggling and creaming on his lips.

After an orgasm like that, even a non-smoker deserves a smoke.

How should it be lit?

DuttyWine

"I'd like you to feed me."

"A meal or a snack, Sir?"

"A snack. Something… refreshing."

"Yes, Sir."

I stood up and went to the kitchen to hunt for something that fit the bill. I remembered I wanted to make a white grape martini for myself later, so I'd popped a bunch of grapes in the freezer. He may be initially disappointed by something as stereotypical as feeding him grapes, so I'd make it interesting. I grabbed a sheet from our linen closet and draped it over the table. I climbed on the table stark naked and lay down. I arched my back so my hips would spread and my tummy looked flat and my breasts were perky.Then I called Kelvin in.

"Sir, I have a refreshing snack for you."

It was unusual for me to be calling out to him, so I knew his wheels were turning as to why he wasn't being served.

When he saw me on the table, he smiled. I was relieved. I held the bunch of grapes up over my chest, dragging them back and forth across my breasts. They were still very cool to the touch and my nipples stiffened instantly. I sat the bunch on my stomach and removed two so I could rub them around my nipples. He leaned in, enjoying the show, and I popped one in his mouth. Continuing to rest the full bunch on my belly, I popped a few off their stems.

"Why don't you pull up a seat near my feet, Sir?"

He did, and I scooched my booty down to the edge of the table. I spread my lips and popped a grape inside me. I repeated this until there were about five inside. Kelvin's eyes were wide with anticipation.

"You ready for your refreshing treat, Sir?"

He nodded.

"Open up."

And I squeezed the grapes out. I tried to do it one at a time, but two plopped out. By the time we reached the end of the bunch, I'd figured out the right equation to control just delivering one at a time.

At that point, he was nearly sucking them out of me in anticipation. He must have wanted to make sure they were all out before he pushed himself inside me, So he did a quick finger sweep, then proceeded to do precisely that right on top of our table. He gripped my hips and wound his in deep slow strokes. I closed my eyes from the glaring light fixture in the ceiling and focused on the weight of my lover on top of me. I loved how rhythmically his hips moved. Our pelvises swirled an invisible hula hoop together. He lifted my right leg and tilted me on my side, grabbed a handful of my locs and pumped, winding those hips to repeatedly massage my G-spot until I gushed all over him, more times than anyone can count at a time like that. Once he was sure I was good, he went about chasing his own satisfaction. I arched my back to secure my grip on his dick, and sucked it with my pussy until I milked generations of nut out.

Refreshing, indeed!

Family Affair

"Viri! August! Neme. Dinner is ready!"

I was thankful our prepared meal might serve as a distraction from the silent tension that filled the living room where my sister and brother-in-law sat exchanging heated glares.

The feud between my sister and I was longstanding. Since birth we were oil and water. People always said we'd grow out of it as if it was guaranteed. Nothing was further from the truth. We'd chased each other with knives and spoke in shouts exclusively. I once caught her exchanging my contact solution for bleach.

My mother Leña would separate us, beg us to stop, and try to force us to apologize. She finally gave up by the time we were around fifteen. My father, a man of few words, would simply say "enough" whenever we were arguing or things would get out of hand. Since he didn't intervene often, I tried to honor his requests.

Viri was Mom's favorite. That was clear from the beginning. She didn't use those exact words, but there are many ways to express it. "Viri reminds me so much of me! Viri will be the one who keeps this family's traditions. Viri has a handsome husband and will be giving me grandbabies soon. Viri's is so successful. Why can't you be more like Viri, Neme?"

Whenever she began comparing us, my father would say, "Enough, Leña" and she'd temporarily switch the subject. After dinner, he'd watch football and when I'd walk in he'd say, "Sit my little free spirit," and we'd root for the Ravens and have a few cold ones. That was the only part worth coming over for.

I actually got along fairly well with August, my sister's husband, but he'd begun to clam up because they were constantly fighting. They had a huge blowout at dinner a few weeks ago while my father and I watched the game. I heard her screaming in the kitchen and he walked out the front door. They stood in front of the house shouting at each other. She said she was going home and he'd better find another place to sleep for the night and slammed the car door. I jumped back into my seat to pretend I hadn't been listening at the door. When he sulked back into the house for his coat, I walked over to him and offered him a beer.

"If anyone knows what it's like to fight with that one, it's me. This'll help."

He watched the rest of the game with us and downed a few more beers. At the start of the fourth quarter, he was already laughing with us. When the game ended, I grabbed some linens to make up the spare room for August. I placed a wash rag and a towel on the chair and a small bag of toiletries on the dresser. My father got up and headed to bed with my mother. I sat with August, laughing at an old movie that came on after the game. Afterwards, I showed him to his room for the night.

"Those are fresh linens I just put on the bed, you can use those towels on the chair and there's soap, toothbrush, toothpaste, and deodorant there on the dresser. You know where the bathroom and everything is. Umm, Mom usually cooks in the morning so... that's nice."

We stood in the archway pretending this wasn't awkward. I wasn't really sure what to say next. It wasn't until then that I realized I'd never really been alone with August. I decided to break the uncomfortable silence.

"Welp, I think that's everything. I guess I should go."

He looked mournful the moment I announced my departure. I felt bad. Perhaps the gravity of their fight was hitting him. Nightfall's silence, and solitude can do that to you.

"You tired?"

He shook his head solemnly.

"Me either. Want another beer?"

"Yeah." He perked up.

He stayed there in the room, sitting on the bed waiting for me. When I returned, I handed him a bottle, moved the towels to the dresser and sat my ass in the wooden Windsor chair near the foot of the bed.

"We should toast," he announced staring at his beer.

"To?"

"Not slapping the shit out of Viri."

That statement caused us both to laugh so hard I had a coughing fit, and he had tears in his eyes. When we finally collected ourselves I said, "I've wanted to more times than you know. If I had it my way, you never would have had the chance to meet her. I tried to take her out a few times. She's lucky Papa stepped in."

"Oh I know! I've wanted to step in a few times on your behalf too. Your mother doesn't help. She adds fuel to the fire. Comparing you two, praising her because she's like her, never taking a moment to appreciate your individuality and the bravery it takes to be different. Not everyone wants to shack up, get knocked up, and share recipes. If you're happy flying around the world, and can fund that habit, I say go for it."

I was speechless. I'd always felt no one at that table understood me, not even Papa. He may have wanted Mom to stop before things got bad, but he never said he was proud of me. He never said I was brave.

He continued. "Viri and I have talked about how rude she is to you and I wonder why you even show up to be berated by them."

"I come for Papa. And, they are my family. Albeit a dysfunctional family, but they're mine. I just avoid perfect little Viri at all costs, and ignore my mother's backhanded compliments. But hey, I inherited them. You chose us! What the hell is wrong with you?" I joked.

"Perfect little Viri?" he mocked, "Ha! She wishes. It kills her that she's not more like you. She's always going on about how she feels trapped. Like she's stuck in a cycle of bullshit, living a life chosen for her. She thinks the only reason your mother favors her is because she groomed her to be just like her. Like loving her is simply loving herself: an act of vanity. She desperately wants your father's approval. She wants to be the 'free spirit.' She thinks it's too late now. She resents me like I forced her into this life. I remind her that we can move away, get new jobs, travel, all the things she really wants to do... but she doesn't think I'm being realistic. She doesn't want to be the responsible one, and she doesn't want to do anything to change it. She won't even fuck me since she doesn't want to get pregnant. She'd have a nervous breakdown."

August had dropped the bomb of all bombs on me. Viri envied me? She was unhappy? Her perfect life, a facade? I chased those thoughts with the remainder of my beer. I wasn't sure what to say. "She would kill me if she knew you'd told me that. You know that?"

"I don't give a shit," he drawled drunkenly. "What's she going to do? Make me miserable?" He raised his beer as he answered his rhetorical question, "Too late!" He polished his bottle off as well. "You know, I admire your drive and your fuck conformity attitude. I wish Viri was more like that. You can see the beauty of your self-fulfillment just radiating out of you like a light. You're beautiful."

I refused to make eye contact when I responded meekly, "Thank you."

I needed to get out of there before any lines were crossed. Those beers were clouding my judgment. I'd had too many to drive though so I figured I'd stay the night too. "I'm going to go to bed." I'd had way too much to drink. I can drink liquor by the bottle, but beer always goes straight to my head.

"You can't drive! Lay down."

"I'm not. I'm going to my old room."

"Okay, good."

I stood up and bid him good night.

I sat on my bed, undressing in disbelief. Viri's whole life, her holier-than-thou complex was a complete lie. For the first time in, possibly ever, I had genuine sympathy for her. Then I thought of all the bash sessions she and my mother had about me. How many times I had to sit there quietly and take it so I wouldn't stand up and stab her with a carving knife. How many times she paraded August in front of me like some prize that I could never attain. I would be an old-maid holding photo albums of the pretty pictures I took around the world to keep me warm at night, they laughed.

"Hey!"

August startled me out of my thoughts. I quickly pulled the shirt I'd just removed to my chest to cover my purple satin bra. "Hey."

He didn't turn his face away, but instead leaned against the door frame comfortably. "Sorry, I got up to use the bathroom. You know you only rent alcohol. I didn't mean to scare you. I thought you may have heard the toilet flush."

"Nah, I didn't. I was in deep thought I guess."

August was of average height and build. He had kind eyes and a warm smile. He had a drunken grin plastered on his face at the moment, but he looked innocent. He stood with his belt unfastened on his black bootcut jeans. He was a handsome man. More attractive tonight after revealing dirt on Viri and admitting he was a silent ally at the dinner table. I'd never really taken the time to notice him physically before. He was attached to *her*, that made him a sorry ass appendage not worth a second glance. Until tonight.

Now? Page 105
Later? Page 110

Held in High Ahh-steam

"What were you thinking about, Neme?"

"What you said in the room. About me being brave."

"Hmm." He stepped forward, "I should take a page out of that book."

I was too afraid to ask what he wanted to feel brave enough to do. I knew. I could feel it.

"Neme..."

"Au..."

His lips covered mine. Quickly. Urgently. Passionately.

He left no room for me to contest. My shirt slipped from my fingers and I caressed his head as he sunk into me.

Few things are more forbidden than lying on your old bed in your parents' house making out with your sister's husband. We began tearing at each other's clothes as we continued. He was an excellent kisser, not sloppy or too much tongue. I stopped abruptly, realizing the door was open and though my folks had an en suite, the risk of being caught was too great. For that same reason, I tossed the pillows on the floor and pulled him down on top of me where no mattress springs could give us away.

When I dug inside his pants, I was surprised to find August was well hung. I don't know how Viri maintained such a bad attitude with a horse dick like this to ride all the time. I was sure that I was going to put it to good use tonight. He pawed at my bra, unleashing my breasts. Clothes were being thrown about like women ravaging a sale bin. I briefly thought about protection but he proved it wasn't a thought in his mind as he pushed into me.

"Ooh!"

He cupped his hand over my mouth as he dove inside me.

"Damn, Neme. Fuck, your pussy is... mmmph damn." He grabbed my ass for leverage to get impossibly deeper.

Thank goodness he knew he still couldn't remove that hand from my mouth or everyone on the block would know what was happening.

He nuzzled his head in my neck, growling my name. Confessing how many times he'd had to fight staring too long or fantasizing about what my pussy felt like. How it's better than he imagined. "Mmmmm, shit. Oh no." He pulled out abruptly, and flipped me over aggressively. He smacked his thick dick on my ass and then shook both cheeks with his hands. "Mmmph!" He slid back in, burying my face into the pillow. I held tight to the pillow, letting my moans get muffled in the down feathers. When I threw that ass back, he held on to my shoulders with both hands, giving it right back to me. Cursing through gritted teeth, he began holding me so tight I knew he was going to cum soon. I reached under and massaged his balls and felt them empty from the outside and on the inside. He rocked steadily inside me, quaking every so often before pulling out completely.

"I'm mad at myself for cumming. That pussy was too good. Shit!"

I was waiting for guilt to kick in, but it never surfaced. August had fucked any conscience I had right on out of me. I was able to freely bask in the afterglow. Though I still didn't think it best to make it a habit.

"We can't do this again."

"Why not?"

I glared at him.

106

"Well not all the time, but don't say never. Please, don't say never."

"I didn't... I..." He placed a finger over my lips.

"Not saying never is enough for now."

"We should clean up and go to bed."

"Right."

He stood up, and we climbed in our respective beds.

I was up early in a chipper mood, and decided to wash my sins away in the shower before everyone was up so I had time to process my thoughts. Losing track of time in a daydream, I lathered my breasts repeatedly. I couldn't stop thinking about August and his hands being all over my body.

I felt the rush of cool air and the suction of the curtain when someone opened the door. I pulled the curtain back to find August standing there.

"What are you doing?"

"No one else is up. Even when your parents wake up, they'll be in their bathroom first. That buys us some time. I've been thinking about you all night."

"Lock the door."

"Already done."

He propped my leg up on the edge of the tub, sat on the nearby toilet lid, and enshrined his face in my kitty. This time I had to be responsible for covering my own mouth. He was masterful with his full, warm tongue. When I held the back of his head and fucked his face, he grabbed my ass and helped me grind it deeper. Only he and our creator knows how he was able to breathe but he wasn't stopping until I was dripping with cum.

Instead of climbing in the tub with me, he lifted me out like I was weightless and bent me over the sink. He put my hands up above the fogged up mirror and told me that when I was close to climaxing, to wipe it so he could see me cum for him. Then he spread my cheeks and started fucking my ass. It wouldn't be long before I came. Anal always sent me over the edge quickly. He held me in a headlock as he plunged into me from behind. It felt so good tears formed in my eyes.

Though blurry from the steam, I could see him in the mirror, veins bulging in his neck. He too was straining not to make a sound. I could feel my orgasm looming near. I slid my hands down across the mirror, creating a dewy, clear streak that allowed him to see my eyes roll back as I gave in to my pleasure. He followed quickly after, grabbing handfuls of my breasts as he descended into me. Breathing heavily, we smiled at ourselves in the mirror.

"So much for washing myself clean, August."

"The shower's still on. Hop back in."

"You better get out of here before you get us caught."

"Fine." He kissed me like it might be the last time, though we both knew it wasn't. Then he slipped out of the door.

I resumed my shower, toweled off, and got dressed.

When I stepped into the living room, all eyes were on me. Or at least it felt that way.

Viri was smiling smugly like she was the one who knew something I didn't.

I gave her my usual eye roll and frown.

"You even got a stick up your ass early in the morning."

It took all of my good sense not to reply, "Yeah, your man's stick was deep in my ass this morning."

Instead I just said, "Watch your mouth in front of Papa."

I noticed what I could now see as a tinge of jealousy at the mention of me protecting our Papa. She stood up in a huff and walked to the kitchen with our mom. "Ugh, you look awful."

"The mirror told me something different this morning," I answered cheerily, reminiscing on her husband's admiring gaze in our reflection.

August smiled slyly before we both turned our attention to the TV before Papa noticed.

"So, who's playing today?"

Mom's Maple

He stared with lust-filled eyes, drinking in my body. "Neme, I want..."

I had to stop this before he went any further. "August, I am really exhausted. It's been a long day. I'm sure things will get better with you and my sister. You guys do this, but you always bounce back. Try not to worry. Get some rest. It'll help. Good night."

He looked dejected, and mumbled, "Night," before sulking away.

Lying in the dark without distractions can be dangerous. I was plagued with what ifs and wondering if Viri would have this same level of respect for me. August was fucking sexy too. I'm ashamed to admit regret was the most prominent thing I was feeling. With a sober mind, he would reflect upon tonight and I'd never have the opportunity again. Additionally, I had one fucking ally at the table and now I had to add him to the list of people with whom I had uncomfortable tension. Great job Neme!

Well, since the only place I could have August was in my dreams, it seemed to make the most sense to drift off to sleep.

The sun came screaming into my bedroom way too fast and I pulled a pillow over my face to block its unsolicited rays from harassing me. I turned away from the window and closed my eyes tightly, wishing for just another hour to sleep soundly. Masturbation usually does the trick and my body was craving August's heat. The door was already closed so I turned flat on my back, and slid my hands down between my thighs.

I must have taken that idea of dreaming about August to heart because I was met with a level of wetness designed for accommodation. I hooked my fingers inside, slowly gyrating my hips to grant my digits deeper access. I slid my soaked fingers up to my clitoris so it would get nice and wet, encircling it with two fingers, focusing all my pleasure in that one spot. It was entrancing. Once I began to throb inside, I knew it was time to penetrate myself again. I thought of how I wished it was August filling me up. I imagined his girth widening my pussy before his inches stretched me lengthwise. I felt like gravity could work in my favor to help me get deeper. I turned over, snatching a pillow to place beneath my crotch and then slid down onto my fingers so I could grind and maybe get as deep as August. The thought riled me up so much, soft moans of "ah, ah" seamlessly stretched into "Au-Au-August." My hips undulating created a slow building friction of my clit against my palm as my fingers dove deeper. "August... August... August... AUGUST!"

When my eyes fluttered briefly as I ascended my peak, I saw the object of my fantasy standing in the doorway staring at me with the same stunned expression I must have been wearing myself.

"What are you...? Oh my God!" I covered up every part of my body, pulling the comforter to my chin. "What the hell were you doing?"

"I'm... I'm sorry. I was sent to let you know breakfast was ready and I decided to be quiet about it in case you were still asleep and I saw you... Well, I noticed you were... I was mesmerized. I didn't mean to... but I heard you say Aug..."

"Oh no. Ooooooh No! Umm, we can't. I can't. This can't. You have to go."

"But you..."

"Go!"

111

He closed the door with the level of audio I wish he'd used to open it. I was mortified. Shit. Shit. Shit. Shit. Shit! Now how the fuck was I supposed to sit at breakfast with him in front of my parents?

I hopped in the bathroom, handled the hygiene routine on autopilot and grabbed a cami and PJ shorts to wear to breakfast. I didn't want to give off any sexy vibes.

I walked into the dining room to find Viri had arrived for breakfast. Fuck!

Of course she was there to make up with him and maintain their happy family front.

"Glad you could join us, princess. Some of us are hungry you know. But it was totally worth it waiting for you to get so... dolled up." She rolled her eyes, mocking my choice of attire. If she only knew.

"She had a long night, Viri. Leave her alone," August chimed in.

No! Don't start openly defending me now. It'll look suspicious! I screamed internally. If my own sister knew me at all, she would read the guilt all over my face, but instead she just shrugged and made some remark about how we all have rough nights.

My mother was seated next to Viri, and my father was at the head of our table. August sat across from Viri and the only seats available for me were either at the far end from everyone or right next to August. As I stood debating which seat to take, Viri piped up again, "What is going on with you? Sit down so we can eat!"

I quickly sat down next to August and put my head down as Papa blessed the food.

Mom made my very favorites: scrambled eggs with three cheeses, bacon, sausage, pancakes, and homemade syrup from scratch.

"Mom, I love your syrup. It's better than any I've had anywhere in the world."

"You make this? From scratch?" August asked. Being over for breakfast was a rarity for him.

"Yes. Not every time, but sometimes."

He nodded, obviously impressed.

He dropped his knife on the floor between us and grabbed my calf and bit my thigh while pretending to be fishing for his missing utensil.

My eyes were wider than the saucers we were using for our tea. I quickly regained my composure and tried to mask my face as best as I could. I couldn't believe he'd been so bold in front of everyone!

"I can make this syrup if you find that you like it, August. *I* paid attention to Mom's recipes," Viri said, shooting me a smug look.

That was it!

I nudged August's elbow and he put his hand on my thigh. I moved my shorts to the side and pushed his finger inside me the way I had with mine just a few minutes before.

Viri and Mom were too up each other's asses to notice a thing, and Papa was focused on finishing the contents of his plate.

I rocked back and forth until I felt myself about to cum and then I started to rethink my plan. I didn't know if I could finish quietly enough without drawing attention to us. But as I tried to resist, it encouraged him to continue. He nodded his head as if to say the coast was clear. I put my head down, rocking and swirling my hips until my pleasure swelled and I squeezed my juices all over his fingers. I exhaled slowly, letting out all the air I'd been holding inside trying not to make a peep.

When I looked up, it was the same as it ever was at this "family" table. Nothing I did was noticed.

August slid the two fingers he'd had inside of me into his mouth and sucked my juices off them slowly before saying to my mother, "I can't believe you made this! Sweetest I've ever tasted."

Hostel Situation

This wasn't my first time traveling to Morocco. In fact, I'd been a bit of a jet setter since my early teens. My nomad parents pretty much assured I could stay in any climate for a month on what most people would pack for a week. I knew every travel site's fare patterns, and signed up for the best one's notifications. I'd racked up enough miles so I didn't really need funds to fly for the foreseeable future.

Lodging was a different issue. I could have used my points for those accommodations but it seemed like such a waste. I'd stayed at the best, and a few of the worst I'm sure. Always seeking an adventure, where I crashed didn't really matter much to me. As long as it was clean, had space where I could clean myself and a bed, it was fine by me. Skimping on that helped me squeeze in more trips. It wasn't as if I used the room for much beyond sleep anyhow. Occasionally I treated myself, but I was not above staying at a hostel. Plenty of them were quite good.

It was on such trip that I met this interesting girl who reminded me of myself. She wasn't as well traveled, but the fire in her eyes and her desire for adventure were like me, as were the lush curly locks resembling my untamed mane. Her frame was also similar to mine. She had strong thighs like a volleyball player and a nice tight ass. She was more fit than I was. My ass was a bit jigglier, but it was nothing to complain about. My tits were definitely bigger, and surprisingly perkier too.

She noticed me sizing her up in the bathroom and I could tell she was guarded, and wasn't sure what to make of my inspection. I extended my hand and made sure to use a friendly tone. "Hey! I'm Iris, sorry for staring. I was actually admiring your body. You look super fit."

Her guard immediately lifted and she returned my friendly gaze. "Thanks, you look great yourself. My name is Siri." We chatted on about how guys likely never greet each other this way after checking each other out. Siri insisted they did, but you had to say "Bro" or "dude" or some super masculine shit about lifting to "butch it up." We laughed about how the male ego can be softer than baby shit at times. Fortunately, us girls were allowed some liberal freedoms as long as we were discreet about them.

"The societal scrutiny could put a dampening on your pussy party if you let it."

"Which is why I don't!"

"Hey!" We high fived our mutual interests.

"Is this your first time here?" I asked.

"Yes. It was number two on my bucket list so I'm very excited to be here."

"I've been before, so if you're looking for tips, I've got you covered. With it being number two on your bucket list, I imagine you have a full itinerary of things you've been wanting to do."

"That's so nice of you. I have some things in mind but I left room just for suggestions. I'm open to whatever."

"I'm scheduled to do a tour tomorrow. You're more than welcome to join."

"Count me in!"

"Cool. You have the Black Broad Abroad app?"

"Of course."

"I'll message you details and we'll link tomorrow."

"Perfect."

We went our separate ways and I went forward with my plans for the day.

What I hadn't planned on was meeting this dark German chocolate fellow while on my quad bike tour. He was so busy watching my ass bounce around he nearly flipped himself head first into a sand pit.

Once our excursion was over and our group stopped for some tea, he made his move. He shared he was in Morocco for a friend's wedding and was making the most of his trip until then. He asked if I had plans to do anything later.

He was taken aback when I said him.

I knew immediately I was going to fuck him. No need to pretend I wasn't. Hell, I'd fuck him right there with an audience if I thought he'd go for it. I told him he was coming back with me and we were going to have lots of fun. I swiped my hand ever so gently over his cock. I wanted my intentions crystal clear. He smiled broadly and I knew my message had been received.

I tongue kissed Otto all the way back to the hostel, jerking his dick in my hand the whole time. I bent over to suck it, but he shook his head no upon noticing the glaring eye of the taxi driver.

"I don't want this pervert to crash 'cause he's not minding his business."

It was a fair request.

I eagerly pulled Otto into the bedroom where I heard moans echoing throughout the thin walls. I couldn't be sure, but it sounded like Siri had brought someone back to the room too! *Okay, girl. I see you.* My silent accolades were diverted by the dick I had waiting in the wings to ride.

I drew him close to me, yanking him up to my top bunk. Thankfully the ceilings were high because I was in the mood to ride. I was shredding his clothes off like he was hiding a prize from me. I had us both undressed and a condom in place in under twenty seconds easily. I straddled him and bucked on his erection like he owed me more than the orgasm I was chasing. Riding to a song playing in my head, I got lost in the stride and watched his head slide up and down. His eyes rolled around and he bit his lip. I moved his hands from my undulating hips, planting them on my full C cups. He was moaning louder than me, Siri, and her guest combined!

It was time to squeeze this nut out of him. I arched my hips forward so he became fully immersed in me, then picked the pace up, making my walls pulse like a techno beat around his shaft. I started talking shit to him. "You trying to hold on to that nut like I can't squeeze it out of you? Huh?" He made a sound that wasn't quite a squeal, but it wasn't exactly a moan either. Siri's moaning was kind of egging me on. An unspoken friendly competition. "Fuck yeah, put up a fight. I like it." I placed my hands on his chest for leverage. "But" Squeeze "That" Squeeze "Nut" Squeeze "Is" Squeeze "Mine." Squeeze

"Ooooooohhhh!"

He was so loud I quickly planted my hands over his mouth. Just below, some finishing sounds were being echoed back to us.

I think we were fueling one another. I'd like to think I was the winner, but not only am I biased, I was focused on being a good lover. That doesn't always allow me to keep score, but Siri's dude wasn't exactly....

Wait, is this fool snoring? I didn't even pull him out yet!

I held his dick at the base, keeping the condom in place and lifted myself off him. He started to roll over, and I grabbed the condom as he turned, and I slowly crept down the steps to scoot off to the bathroom.

Siri crept in just behind me and scared the shit out of me.

"Shit! You could have said something, girl. Scared me half to death."

"Sorry, I needed to freshen up and ditch this condom. Plus I wanted to commend you on whatever you were doing up there. Dude is knocked out already and was moaning louder than me! You might need to teach me a few things."

"I aim to please. I will admit, he is the most vocal man I've ever been with so it might just be his nature."

"We should switch and find out."

"I know right!"

We laughed, but it was cut short by clouds of tension rolling in.

A shared thought loomed in our brains: *Is she serious?*

One of us had to say it, the quiet was resting uncomfortably between us. Guess it should be me.

"I mean, it's dark in there. Hell, they wouldn't know. Our body type is similar enough to pass off."

"That would be my most interesting diary entry to date."

Dual optical blazes lit with burning questions. Is that fair to them? Would they care?

I thought of Otto's not wanting to receive head in the cab and maybe it was more than just about the cabbie watching but rather a morality issue.

How would we feel if they did this to us?

I began to feel guilty.

But how often would guys think it was inappropriate that they signed up to get fucked by one girl, and ended up getting fucked by two?

Siri offered an alternative. "You know, if we told them we wanted to swap or do a group thing, they'd probably be down. Based on the conversation we had today, I'm fairly certain that Neven wouldn't care though."

"Hmm."

The thrill of secrecy still nagged at me. Knowingly doing it didn't provide the same thrill.

"I'll leave it up to you." Siri's burning eyes stared at me like she had her own preference as well. Kindred spirits on the same vibe since meeting. I wondered if her sentiments mirrored mine in this moment too. Hmm, what should we do?

Don't tell the guys? Page 121
Tell the guys? Page 124

Secret Swap

"Fuck it, we've just gotta be done before dawn and we can't fall asleep until we've swapped back."

Siri's eyes lit up. "I can't believe we're doing this!" she said with hushed excitement as though speaking of our act now would suddenly get us found out.

We crept back to our room, slinking like felines on the prowl. We momentarily bumped into each other in our best attempts to be stealthy and had to stifle giggles under our palms. We quickly collected ourselves and returned to our mission. Siri climbed up into my bunk and I heard Otto grumble as he stirred. I slid next to her partner who smelled amazing. I took his arm and wrapped it around me and nuzzled my ass against his crotch. He reached up and grabbed my breast and then stopped. My heart was pounding.

Did he notice the difference?

"Mmmmm," he moaned then mumbled something but I couldn't make out what it was.

"Hmm?" I tried to say with as little inflection in my tone as possible.

"Again?"

"Mmmmhmm."

I got on all fours and stretched into an extended puppy yoga pose. I felt him fumbling around behind me. I reached down between my legs to guide him in, and check for protection. He slipped into my tightness with more girth than my lover above me. I wasn't sure if he could detect a difference between me and Siri's pussy but he started grinding the fuck out of me. I was impressed with his skinny ass! He wasn't going to outdo me though.

I started throwing my ass back, making it slap against his stomach. Then I crossed my ankles to give him a tighter fit. He was holding his breath trying to refrain from making too much noise but I got curses out of him in about three languages. At one point he moaned, "Ohh, Siri," and I was so in the zone I nearly got mad thinking he forgot who I was! It's a damn shame she was going to get the credit for this. He placed both hands between my shoulder blades and rode my ass in a circular rotation. Neven definitely had a better stroke game than Otto.

I could hear Siri and Otto going at it as well. Seems a bit of jack rabbit action was happening. Neven's thrusts became hungrily fervid. I was trying hard not to make too much sound and risk blowing our cover, but he was a good lover. I buried my face in the pillow, but that seemed to entice him to want to force me to make sounds. He started smacking my ass and then he snatched me back by my hair.

"You like it?"

"Mmmhmm," I moaned, biting my lip.

"Say it."

"I like it," I whimpered.

Luckily he released my hair as that seemed to egg him on. He humped hard and fast until he stiffened with a grunt. He collapsed beside me and I quickly lay down with my back to him.

It was quiet in the bunk above me too.

My eyelids drooping with sleep deprivation, I hoped Neven would fall asleep quickly. Thankfully, he slipped into a light snore just before I did.

I lifted his arm from around my waist and stood up.

On tiptoe, I peeked to see if Siri was on the outside. She was. I poked her big bubble booty with my finger.

"C'mon," I whispered.

We snuck off to the showers, sharing our partner preferences buzzing with devious energy.

Sleepily climbing into our original beds, I felt like I made a new best friend. I hadn't ever shared something this intimate with anyone else.

I wondered if it'd be awkward at breakfast.

Double Trouble

"I want to swap, but I think we should just tell them we want to have fun together. I'm sure they'd go for it."

She looked slightly disappointed too, but we both knew it would sit better with us morally if we were upfront.

"So what are we going to say?"

"Just follow my lead."

I went back to the room feeling confident my go-with-the-flow plan would work.

I went straight to Siri's bed and woke up Neven. I pulled my partner-in-crime in behind me. Neven rubbed his eyes, surely to be certain he wasn't seeing double. He reflexively placed his hands over his dick.

"Who are you? What do you want? My wallet?"

"No, no, no. Nothing like that. We just hoped you'd like to have fun with us together."

"The both of you?"

"Yes." We beamed.

"What's the catch?"

"That my partner Otto joins us. You don't have to touch him or anything if you don't want."

"Does he have to touch me?"

"Of course not. Neither one of you has to do anything you're uncomfortable with."

He scratched his head, his eyes crinkling at the corners as he weighed the deal.

"Okay."

Next I woke up Otto. I kissed him slow and stroked his face.

"You want to have fun with me and my friend?"

"What kind of friend? A vibrator?"

"No." I laughed. "An actual friend."

I called to Siri. Her curls popped up into frame and she walked back a bit so we could see her eyes. "Does he want to?" she inquired eagerly.

"Well?" I stared at him for confirmation.

"Hell yeah!"

"Okay, but her partner Neven is down there. He wants in too. Not with you, just you know. We'll switch off and take turns doing both of you." I wanted to make sure I sold the idea after dropping the bomb about another dude.

"Cool. As long as he doesn't try anything with me."

"Everyone respects each other's preferences. If you both wanted to engage with each other we wouldn't care and if you don't, we don't care. As long as everyone is clear on the dos and don'ts."

"Alright."

"Come down here. It'll be easier this way and their bed is a bit bigger."

He climbed down, eyeing us all suspiciously. I guess it wasn't every day two beautiful women hatched a plan to sleep with them.

"I'll take this one for now, and you grab him." Both Neven and Otto laid across the bed sideways so their feet were still planted on the floor. I climbed on top of Neven as she climbed on top of Otto. Like the long lost twin souls we were, we rode them in sync, periodically touching and kissing each other. I grabbed Otto's hands and put one hand on my breast, the other on Siri's. Then I followed suit with Neven. Their arms crisscrossed grabbing handfuls of us both was the most they ever touched. Siri was an excellent kisser. We alternated kissing both gentlemen and each other. It was going surprisingly smooth given all the moving pieces.

When Neven started gyrating faster, I suspected he would be cumming soon. I leaned forward burying him in my breasts before catching his groove and fucking him back. He strained and grunted lowly when he came. Not nearly as vocal as Otto. Since we were finished before Siri and Otto, I fondled her nipples, kissed Otto, and smacked her ass with some encouraging words. The motivation worked for them both and soon they met Neven and me in the afterglow.

Now that we were acquainted, we could loosen up a bit. Through the night we switched partners and positions within sessions. The guys felt more comfortable to get a little rough after seeing how both I, and Siri, responded to pulling each other's hair, biting one another, and exchanging ass slaps. Before the sun came, each person in that bed had multiple times as well.

We fucked around and missed the tour, but I had my doubts that Siri would be disappointed. I know I wasn't. We created a bond for life that night. We also learned we only lived two states away back home. Might have to take this show on some local roads. Don't be surprised if you catch us in your city.

Fonder

After a longtime friendship became the relationship that would break me nearly beyond repair, I vowed to never let a friend become more than that again. I didn't believe in the "friend zone." I felt like you make your intention clear from the beginning. If I just wanted to be friends, I was going to state that. If I wanted more, I was open about that too. I didn't like the idea of stringing a guy along, knowing he was only doing those things in hopes of one day sleeping with me. More than that, I didn't like believing I had an actual friendship where someone valued me beyond my genitalia, but really they were patient predators waiting for an opportunity to get what they really wanted.

It never stopped Jamal from later teasing that I had him in this non-existent friend zone. I would tease back that he "girlfriend zoned" me. He'd never spoken up! Everyone knows closed mouths don't get fed. For months, he watched me go on a few dates and complain about not finding a "good guy."

Jamal and I had been friends who lost touch, but picked up right where we left off when we found each other on social media. We didn't work far from one another so we'd get together for happy hour and the like. One hazy evening, I even thought he was trying to play matchmaker and hook me up with his friend. I assumed we were on the same page. I genuinely cared for him and didn't want to lose another friend.

After a particularly stressful workweek, Jamal was going to put me in a cab, but my mission "drink the stress away" was a bit too successful and he decided to take the cab ride all the way home with me.

Draped in his navy cashmere pea coat that swallowed my much smaller frame, I locked my arms around his bicep and nestled up to it. He felt strong. He was rubbing my hair which felt like the perfect de-stressor after a week of occupational havoc. Here he was making sure I got home safely after I recklessly got hammered in public. He was a perfect boyfriend already. I wouldn't call it beer goggles or liquid courage but it's just when the epiphany hit me. I was going to tell him. I was going to tell him tonight.

"Jamal..." the rest of the words got stuck and I stared at him, blinking until there was just one of him.

"You okay, Callie?"

"Yes. I just..."

Before I could speak he kissed me, full and intense. My spirit swooned. Jamal was an excellent kisser! We arrived at my place much too quickly and there was a pause, a moment where the friend part of him waited for a respectful go-ahead. I nearly took my panties off before stepping out of the cab to give my approval.

His huge hands enveloped me as we made our way to the elevator. A quick ride up and then the stripping began. We didn't even make it to the bedroom. He just propped me up on my kitchen table and fucked me.

From that day on, he called me "Ducky." He blamed my lips, that evidently even in their resting position looked like I was trying to serve "duck face," for being too irresistible for him and he made the choice to dive in.

Fast forward two years and I was still glad that he did. I'd never been in love like this before and it was nothing short of amazing. We communicated well and had sex so hot I'm not sure it's legal in every state.

Unfortunately, we were about to face our biggest couple challenge to date. Jamal's job was going to require him to go out of state for almost three months. Since finding each other, we'd never spent so much time apart. I whined the entire time I was helping him pack.

"This is really, really, really, really stupid you know?" I pouted, asking rhetorically.

He answered sweetly anyway, "I know, babe. I know," kissing me on the forehead.

"Stupid Pittsburgh"

"Pittsburgh *is* stupid."

"Totally is!"

We were respectable Ravens fans after all. Going to the home of the Steelers was sacrilegious.

It was sweet of him to join me in my tantrum for a few moments. I felt like he'd really miss me too. He was going to be a solid four-hour drive away from Glenn Dale. That was with good traffic and weather conditions. It was too far to travel every weekend after a full workweek. I was so accustomed to him being there every day. I felt lost without him and he hadn't even left yet!

In the week before he left while organizing things he'd need to take with him, we also came up with a few ways to stay connected. He promised we'd have a date night and even continue to binge watch our favorite shows together.

I was never afraid Jamal and I would be broken by this, but I was not looking forward to our vivacious sex life becoming a scheduled bore. Jamal assured me he wouldn't let it come to that. When my man made a promise, it was clear he intended to keep it.

The end of that first week, he drove home. He didn't tell me he would, he just did it. I heard motion at my front door and my eyes shifted to the drawer where I kept "Sarah McGLOCKlan" in case any intruder wanted to be *in the arms of an angel*. I quickly realized it was my baby and went running to the door, nearly knocking him over. He tossed his black duffel aside and bent me over the couch into the wheelbarrow position.

The next weekend I wasn't so lucky. We video chatted each other and he shared his screen so we could watch a movie. We talked while both of us ate dinner and it almost felt like he was home. Until I started feeling horny and realized my fix was hours away. The same thought must have struck him because he asked me to take off my top and suck my titty for him. I giggled and blushed like he'd never seen me do that before.

"Come on," he insisted, grinning. "Let me see."

I hesitated then eventually gave in. "Okay."

When I pulled my shirt over my head, he howled like a wolf. I covered my bare breasts, laughing.

"Lick that nipple like me, Ducky."

"Okay."

Then came a flurry of requests: "Lick both nipples," "Sit back. Let me see you," "Spit on that titty and make it wet for me."

With each request he made, I got a bit of insight into what specifically turns him on. It was a benefit of this distance I hadn't expected.

"I love seeing your lashes flutter like that when your eyes roll back. That's when I know I'm hitting that spot."

Knowing that he watched me for indicators of my pleasure made me excited too.

That weekend I sent him a huge "Sunday dinner" of all of his favorites I made and had it shipped overnight in dry ice.

We had video chat sex, phone sex, and sexted often but I was missing the real thing after weather ruined our bi-weekly visit. After a phone sex session, I said to Jamal, "This helps, but I'm missing you, babe. My fingers can't fill me up like you. I need that."

He agreed it wasn't enough. But it would have to suffice for now.

My friend Camden and I carpooled and she spotted a package in front of my door before me. "You ordering dildos while your man is gone, honey?"

We both laughed. "Girrrrrrl, I need to! But actually I didn't order anything. I have no idea what that is."

"You know, if people stop seeing a man go in the house they might try something."

"Girl, you know nobody is thinking about me. Besides, if they are watching they see Jamal still comes home. They know better."

"You want me to stay here while you see where it came from?"

"I'm not worried. I appreciate the thought, but you don't have to. It may be something from Jamal."

"Okay then. I'll see you tomorrow. Be safe."

The box was lighter than I anticipated so I picked it up swiftly. I had no idea what could be inside. There were no indicators on the outside. I opened the box to find a dildo that looked like a replica of Jamal's dick with an attached suction cup. I had never seen such a thing. I called him before I even finished sifting through the box.

"Baby!" I squealed

"Yes, dear?" I heard the smile in his voice.

"You sent me something special today!"

"Did you open it?"

"I didn't look at everything. When I saw the dildo I stopped to call you. I was so excited. It looks... just like you! How did you...?"

"I made a replica of my Johnson in a silicone kit and added a suction cup."

"Oooooooh! Why a suction cup babe?"

"Because tonight you're going to feel me fucking you in the shower."

"Oh!" I shrieked. Jamal was never this vocal when he was at home. He would just do it.

As I rummaged through the package, I saw handcuffs with suction cups, a tube of red lipstick from my favorite brand, and some silicone lube.

"You bring your computer into the bathroom. Make sure you have on that red lipstick I like that you smear all over my dick. Take off your clothes like a stripper for me. When you climb in the shower, stay near the back. I don't want you slipping, but I want you getting wet. You hear me?"

"Yes," I answered shyly. Something about how bold he was being made me nervously excited in all the right ways.

He instructed me to switch to video chat to receive the rest of my instructions. I propped the laptop up on a few towels on the toilet to get the perfect angle. Jamal took over from there.

"Sit on the edge of the tub and play with her for me. Use the lube so she looks extra shiny and juicy. Open your legs wide so I can see. Before you turn the water on, lube up your gift and stick it on the wall facing out so I can see your face when you back onto it. Put the restraints on your wrists but don't stick them on anything just yet."

I coveted feeling Jamal's dick again so much.

"Now, look at the camera before you ease back onto the dick. I want to see that face." I followed his commands. "Yessss, that face when you feel me slide inside. I missed that. I didn't know how much until just now."

I held on to the edge of the tub, bouncing back onto the toy. With Jamal's voice and grunts, coupled with my imagination, I was able to lose myself and pretend it was the real thing.

"Tilt your head down so I can see that ass slap back against the wall and swallow my shit up." I held tight to the tub and on weakened knees I stood, releasing stress in a muffled yelp.

"Damn, that was sexy. Pull it out of you and stick it to the back of the tub so I can see you swallow it from the side."

I did as my man directed.

I reached back and spread my ass as I eased slowly back onto it before letting my cheeks go and slapping back against the wall.

"Fuck, Callie!"

I thought he was going to lose it when he started jerking so fast his hand became a brown blur.

"Now put your arms behind you and stick those cuffs to the wall behind you."

133

I'd completely forgotten about them.

"Now fuck me hard like you know you're mine. I sent you that dick because it belongs to you. Now you have to act like it."

His words sent me into overdrive. I was throwing my ass back on it like a porn star. No more commands came, just hard breaths and curse words. I felt orgasm number two surging. I was going to go for it. My enthusiasm must have sent Jamal over. I heard his telltale growl and curse. His climax exacerbated mine. He got himself cleaned up and I put on a sudsy show for him to add in the "spank bank" for later.

He decided to take his own shower and call me back. When he did, I was in bed. We had video chat pillow talk.

That night's topic of discussion included how unfair it was that smokers got to take multiple breaks because of an addiction. I would love to get paid to dip off multiple times to go enjoy things I liked that may have kept me cooler under pressure. Why wasn't I allowed to have a French fry break, or leave and grab a smoothie. Why didn't my massive taco craving count as an excuse to leave the building with other taco lovers? He said I should use that time to go have mini-masturbation sessions. I laughed, but he didn't.

"I'm not always that horny during the day, my love."

"Well what if I helped you along?"

"I'm listening."

"I could text you throughout the day and tell you to do certain things, and you have to do them."

"Like?"

"Well that would be a surprise. Will you do it though?"

"Okay! I'm game."

Surprise 1? Page 136
Surprise 2? Page 139

Clamp Countdown

The next morning I'd forgotten about it completely but he hadn't.

I woke up to a text that read, "Wear your adjustable nipple clamps."

I won them long ago at my girl's bachelorette party. We'd never even used them! Since they were the type that could be screwed tightly, I put them on the loosest setting and clamped them on. I had to admit, just knowing they were there turned me on. I got a text from Jamal at 11:17. "Tighten them."

I hurried to the restroom a few cubicles over and pulled open my shirt to tighten the clamps. I returned to my desk excited by our game.

At 12:30 it was time for my lunch hour. As soon as I finished eating, I received another text at 1:15."Touch yourself and tell me when you're about to cum. I'll count down when you can."

I went into the private restroom down the hall this time. As instructed, I touched myself and as I felt my climax building, I fumbled with my phone to inform him. He sent a 5, then a 4, then a 3. Then he sent, "Beg."

Fuck! "Please!"

He sent me a 5 in response.

No! He's starting over.

"PLEASE! Pretty please can I cum?"

He sent a 4.

I was watching my phone like a hawk.

3.

2.

I stared, heaving, waiting for permission to release.

"Stop. Tighten."

What?

What!

Shit!

I tightened the clamps and I didn't cum, but I wasn't happy about it either.

At this point they were really fucking tight. I felt like my nipples were engorged and throbbing.

By 3:00 I was stewing in my seat. The sexual tension was making me irritable and not particularly productive.

At 3:13 there was a text. "5"

I rushed to the bathroom with my phone in hand.

"4"

"3"

I sent an "I need to cum please don't stop" for good measure.

"2"

"Cum for me."

Those three words.

I rubbed away the tension as wave after wave of orgasm hit me so hard I had to curl my lips in and cover my mouth.

When I pulled myself together, I sent a thank you text to my lover.

He informed me that though I had cum, I was not to touch those clamps.

Time crawled by as it always does when you're anticipating something good. Nine years later, as it seemed, it was finally time to go home. I didn't stop to do errands, I didn't make any calls, I just got in my car and took the fastest route home ready to video chat and see what else he had in store.

He barged in the door forty minutes after me.

I couldn't believe he was home!

Without breaking his stride, he grabbed me from the kitchen and got me on the couch. He opened my legs and embarked upon sucking my pussy immediately. He stopped just once to say, "Tell me when."

I nodded.

He never asked before. I hoped he wasn't going to try that countdown shit again. I would flip him over and ride his face until I came and deal with the repercussions after. I gripped the back of his head pushing him into me, grinding against his face. His mouth felt so marvelous probing inside me as he sucked. I felt my climax brewing. I was nervous to tell him. I didn't want him to stop,

"I'm close," I whispered

"Remove the clamps," he replied quickly as to not lose momentum with the task at hand. He started slurping harder and faster as I unclamped my nipples.

The rush of the release felt so good, I grabbed his head with both hands and bucked against his face screaming uninhibitedly. My pussy was still pulsating when he jumped up and penetrated the welled pool of awaiting him. He pushed my breasts together and kissed my nipples tenderly. They were a bit sore from being under lock all day and his soft kisses were the perfect remedy.

He sputtered something I didn't understand, before I felt his release ooze inside.

He rolled next to me and asked, "How was work?"

Lit?

For spontaneity, he texted, "Cum for me."

Wherever I was, whatever I was doing, I had to stop and masturbate. I also had to send either video or audio proof of my compliance. Sometimes he said, "Just wake her up, but don't cum yet." He loved to pull that one when I was at work and not follow with "cum for me" until I was out of the office.

One afternoon he sent "Wake her up" and I didn't even leave my desk. I just slipped my hand in my panties and rubbed circles around my clit. It was enthralling to comply in a room full of unsuspecting people simply because my man had requested it.

About an hour later, he asked where his proof was, to which I replied I hadn't gone to the bathroom but had fulfilled his request at my desk so I couldn't make a sound. In the evening as I was getting ready for bed, he still hadn't told me I could cum. I shot him a text asking, "Anything you want me to do?"

He simply replied, "Nope." Perhaps I was being punished for my lack of proof. I went to bed frustrated but I had learned my lesson.

The next afternoon I asked, "Audio or video?"

He said, "I haven't requested that you cum yet. Neither." I was on real punishment! I slipped into a bathroom at work and pulled out my breasts to snap a quick picture. He replied, but still no request of what I was hoping for.

That evening, he asked for a panty pussy print photo and even after I sent, he still gave no orders. The following day, he sent roses to my job and the card read, "Not yet." As we sexted throughout the day, he mentioned that every time I looked at those roses, I was to think of how soft and silky the petals were, just like my pussy. He wanted an object that seemed benign right in my face to remind me of how badly I wanted to touch her.

By that evening, I called begging.

"Pleeeeeaaase!" I choked out.

"Who decides when?"

"You! But..."

"But?"

I sat quietly not knowing what to do next.

"I never said you couldn't touch yourself. I just didn't say you could cum. Have fun!"

Have fun? Okay.

I pulled out my Jamal-away-from-Jamal, swiped on that red lipstick he loved seeing on his dick so much and recorded myself deepthroating, gagging, and spitting all over it. I ran my lips all up and down on it, then rubbed my face against it. It drove him crazy to watch me make a complete mess of my face by being dedicated to getting him off. I sent it to him at work the next day. He wasn't going to rub one out at night and go to work refreshed. If I'm frustrated and cranky, you're frustrated and cranky. Give in!

I was on edge at work. I was snippy with co-workers. On social media I posted how cranky and grumpy I was. I started thinking about how he wouldn't know if I just went ahead and did it. But it felt like the same betrayal as cheating. I would be doing something I told him I wouldn't unless he said. I wasn't going to lie just because he was absent and it was convenient.

By day three, I was plotting how I was going to make him say it. I was going to video chat with him. If I said I thought I might squirt, he would be less likely to stop the show. Even if I didn't fulfill that, it would be an allowance to let it go. A white lie wasn't so bad. I needed it! I sent a text in the early afternoon.

"Webcam session tonight. I need to see you."

"I need to see you too, baby, but I can't video chat tonight. I'm working really late."

"We always video chat to say good night even if we don't do it!" I whined. I realized I was being annoying but my horny hormones were taking over. I was frustrated and disappointed. I missed my man. For the first time, I felt a pang of jealousy. Every day since he'd been away, we always video chatted good nights and good mornings. Now suddenly he had to work too late to say good night? Paranoia only distance and too much reality television can bring shifted my whole attitude. I wasn't even thinking about him giving the go ahead.

"Nah, we'll say good night. I just might not be able to chat like I know you want to."

I realized then how quickly I overreacted. That would have to do.

I came home to another package at the door.

This time there was lingerie and a printed note that read, "Send me your sexiest selfies in this, then maybe."

I yanked off my clothes, took a quick shower, slathered on some coconut oil and slipped into the sheer eyelash lace chemise he sent. I put the lipstick on he liked to see me in, tousled my hair so it looked like I had just had some wild, slutty sex with him. I sent a few photos. No reply. I sent a video bent over, smacking myself on the ass with the dildo before fucking myself with it. No reply. I knew he was working late, but normally he still responded to me. It was getting late, I was starting to worry.

Before panic could set in too much, my lover sent a text, "I'm a lucky, lucky man to have all that just for me."

"I miss you, babe. I was starting to worry."

"I know. I didn't mean to stress you out. But I know what could help alleviate that stress."

"Ooooooh, you're finally going to let me cum?"

"No."

My heart sank. "Not even with your toy babe?"

"No, Callie."

"Can I ask why?"

"Because I'm home."

Sure I had heard him wrong, I asked, "What!"

"Look out the window."

Upon seeing his car, I took off down the stairs, snatched open the door, ran to him and jumped in his arms with no regard for my barely-there attire.

The older gentleman seated on his porch smoking next door said quietly, "Must be doing something right, boy."

My robe was open, its belt dragging in the grass but I didn't care. There wasn't a space not covered with kisses on his face. I tugged at his pants as he tried to close and lock the door. "Ducky..."

"I can't wait another second."

He chuckled. "Alright, alright."

"Ducky, sit down here, and I'll come get you in a minute.

"But!"

He cut his eyes at me.

142

"Okay," I huffed, flopping back into my seat.

He just chuckled and headed upstairs.

He came back down faster than I expected.

He took my hand and led me up the stairs.

What I found was a spotlight in front of our full-length mirror.

Stuck on the mirror was the suction-replicated dick.

He handed me noise-canceling earplugs and told me he was going to heighten the sense that was usually the most often deprived in sex play and handcuff me.

"So I won't be able to hear you?"

"Barely. Don't worry. Your mouth will be stuffed. We're not going to attempt to converse. You'll know what I want. You always do. I just want a close up of me occupying two holes at once."

Gleaming, I rushed to the mirror. I popped the plugs in and adjusted the dildo to my height before bringing my arms behind my back so he could cuff me.

Under the spotlight in front of the mirror, I saw every detail up close.

I saw my water-filled eyes fuel my lover. I saw my breasts bouncing wildly about and occasionally slapping against the mirror. I could see the tremble in my thighs when Jamal hit my spot. I watched drool drip continuously down the mirror as he pushed my face against it so close my nose could feel the heat it soaked up from the spotlight. My eyes widened with panic the deeper I was forced to take his dick in both places. I witnessed the immediate relief when he let me come up for air.

I observed his reaction to all of it as well. I watched his eyes roll back and then burn with intensity. I noticed him grimacing as he curled his toes into the carpet. I could faintly hear sounds but they sounded like they were two rooms away instead of us being the ones responsible for them. I could hear my heart pounding in my ears above anything else.

Jamal tugged my hair and lured my head away from the mirror and back towards his shoulder. He sucked my neck and my knees weakened. With the cuffs on, I had to be careful. If I lost my balance, I couldn't catch myself. I really didn't want to be in the emergency room that night.

I spread my legs further apart to sturdy myself and the way my pussy opened up turned Jamal into a mad man. He turned us both around until we were facing the bed. He bent me over and, holding my arms like reins, fucked me silly. I hovered over the bed, arms burning and knees shaking. I came so hard I squirted on the floor, creating a puddle we both nearly bust our asses in before he rode my booty until he was satiated.

The.rapist

I always hated that demeaning kinks had a negative stigma. Everyone assumed the participant's background included some level of molestation, early sexualization, rape, or emotional trauma. They needed to make sense of this "condition." A condition that people were acting out as a result of said emotional trauma.

Frankly, this annoyed me for two reasons. Firstly, two mentally and emotionally stable consenting adults could very well have a healthy kinky sexual relationship without either party having a traumatic background. It's not as though vanilla couples have clean slates either. Dysfunction taints both pools equally. Secondly, and on a much more personal level, it made it that much more difficult for me to understand and accept how and why I liked what I liked. Though on a logical level I understood the aforementioned to be a cop-out, at least the correlation made sense as to why it fit into their lives. Without this, it was hard for me to establish what made me think and feel the way I do.

My parents had me at twenty-one so we did a bit of growing up together. My mother spoke openly and honestly about everything, including sex. Sex was never a taboo subject we skimmed over.

For the last two years, I had a steady boyfriend and our sex was normal. What Maxon considered kinky was fooling around for a few seconds in the garage at night before heading to the bedroom to have proper sex. It was an intimate expression of love, but it was predictable. His hand was going to touch this breast, suck it for four minutes, move to the other breast, then two stomach kisses led to cunnilingus which inevitably led to sex... in the missionary position. I was lucky to get doggy style once a month.

Maxon was fantastic on paper: great job, stand-up guy, thoughtful, romantic. The kind of guy that all your friends and mother say you're lucky to have because he's a "keeper." No one factored in passion. I didn't know if I was just confused about what a real man was and if the passion I sought was a thing of fairy tales, or if spark was a real thing: a tangible missing link from my otherwise perfect union.

When Maxon started asking about marriage and starting a family, I felt fear butterflies. Instead of excited fluttering, I felt I was in a sinkhole of monotony and no one would understand why I would want to pass up on perceived perfection. I needed an impartial outsider's opinion. I couldn't be sure if I was just having personal issues with commitment or if my ideals were even real.

Like me, my family and friends were too close to the issue to see. Maxon was a catch. As far as anyone was concerned, that was a fact. I didn't want to discount or discredit him, but I wanted something more. Before making a lifelong decision and sliding an anchor on my left ring finger, I looked up a therapist who was in my insurance network and found one who had an impressive medical profile with excellent online reviews. *Good on paper, yeah, not all things good on paper are all that great.* I knew that all too well. But I put in the call and made an appointment for the following week with Dr. Fallow.

Dr. Fallow's waiting room had a 360-degree fish tank that wrapped around the office, filled with a multitude of exotic fish. At the front desk there was a giant oblong tank filled with a handful of bouncing blue jellyfish. Fragrant fresh white peonies in a vase with a shattered glass finish near the sign-in sheet were a welcome greeting. On the coffee table there were hardcover books of scenic photography and collections of famous prints. The waiting room chairs were plush as was the carpet. I had to resist kicking off my pumps and sinking my feet into it. In addition to a water cooler, there was a hot cocoa bar in the corner complete with tiny marshmallows. It was clear Dr. Fallow wanted his patients to feel comfortable.

I expected someone to usher me in, but Dr. Fallow came out to greet me himself. The first thing I noticed was how strikingly handsome he was. I didn't think I had preconceived notions about therapists, but I didn't expect him to be so good-looking, or young.

"Are you alright, Miss Jackson?"

"Yes. Yes, of course. My apologies. I'm a little dazed from lack of sleep."

"Perhaps we'll begin with discussing what's keeping you up then."

"Maybe." I chuckled nervously.

I began to feel like this was a mistake. How could I be honest about my sexual fantasies with a man who could very well be included in them! I expected some old fogey with suede elbow patches on his tweed jacket, staring down at me over bifocals to take notes, not this fine ass man!

"So what brings you here?"

"This is a mistake," I blurted out.

"What is a mistake, Miss..." he peered over at the sheet in his lap, "Tentatrice Jackson?"

"Please, call me Trice. No one outside of family or work calls me Tentatrice and 'Miss,' well that just makes me feel old."

147

"As you wish. So what do you feel is a mistake, *Trice*?"

I watched his lips move to pronounce my name and I thought of how I'd love to make him say it in the throes of passion.

"This... this whole thing ,Dr. Fallow." I feel my face burning crimson. "Even saying your name makes me uncomfortable. In Italian,'fallo' means phallus. It's how my Nonna referred to a man's... you know. So calling you that makes me feel... inappropriate."

"Well if you'd prefer I can follow your lead and you can call me by my first name, which is Atlas, if it makes you more comfortable."

"Not really," I mumbled.

"No?" He tilted his head down to obstruct my view of the floor, forcing me to make eye contact.

I shook my head no.

"Why do I get the sense that you're not used to speaking up for yourself?"

I looked away. I don't know if it was some shrink sixth sense or if my erratic behavior was just that telling, but it made me uncomfortable that he pegged me so quickly. I felt naked in front of him, and not in the way I wanted to be.

"I... don't. I mean, I do say stuff. I speak up... when I'm sure about things."

"So do you feel uncertain often?"

I pondered for a moment before giving an answer, "No. Not often. Not about everything. Just... one thing."

And there I was, ready to spill it. He lured me in before I had a chance to bail.

"And what is that one thing?"

"My boyfriend."

His face tensed, brows furrowed, and he shifted in his seat at the mention of boyfriend. It could be wishful thinking on my part, but he seemed to have a reaction to my not being single.

"And what of this boyfriend who makes you feel uncertain?"

"He's fantastic in all the ways that are supposed to matter and he loves me, and I believe he's loyal and it's just... it's just..."

He waited patiently while I fought back tears.

"He doesn't touch... like, he won't...." I grunted searching for an accurate, but not-so-vulgar term. Then I thought of what this was costing me, "He doesn't fuck me. I want to be fucked hard, primal, passionate, triple x porn star fucked and he just, wants to make love looking into my eyes, Every. Fucking. Time. No pun intended."

The corners of his mouth were turned down and his eyebrows were raised in what appeared to be an impressed expression. He was hard to read, which I'm sure was deliberate.

"Have you communicated this to him?"

Hmm. I thought he was interested in what I was saying. He was likely proud of the confession, not the content of it.

"I've tried. But it seems we've reached the end of the road with that. He doesn't appear to want to leave his comfort zone. I've initiated some things but he becomes rigid and uncomfortable and we end up slipping right back into the routine. I don't want to feel like I'm pulling teeth either. I want him to *want* to do something different. I don't want to live my life feeling caged like this. I also don't want to go out there just to find what I'm looking for doesn't exist and what I had was the best you could ask for."

"If the best you could ask for left you dissatisfied, is it really the best?"

"I... I don't know."

I hesitated and stammered through every response. I had to ask him to repeat the questions multiple times because I was too focused staring at his bulging biceps through his button up. I caught myself searching for a print in his slacks a few times and had to scold myself.

"Mr., um, Atlas, you know why I said this was a mistake?"

"Tell me."

"I find you distracting and disarming and that combination is overwhelming."

"Disarming? I believe that's me putting my degree to work. Distracting? How so?"

Like most of the session, I refused to make eye contact.

"You look nothing like I expected. I didn't think you'd be so attractive and it's hard to discuss sexual things with someone who makes you feel sexual tension."

"I hope that I'm not doing anything that causes you to feel that I would behave inappropriately."

"No. I just mean it's difficult for me to express intimate things with you when I have images of doing intimate things with you."

I don't know what the fuck kind of truth serum was in that cocoa out there or what advanced course he took in disarming, but I was spilling out things without a filter in sight.

"I see. And so you'd prefer to see another doctor?"

"Don't you think that'd be best?"

"Well, if it prohibits you from being honest and getting the answers you seek, then yes. But it doesn't seem to stop your honesty from what I can tell so far. Perhaps it prevents you from having to deal with that uncomfortable feeling that rises when you try to discuss things with your boyfriend. Do you think switching doctors would be another way to escape that?"

"Possibly."

"I think you owe it to yourself to figure out the motive behind the switch and make your decision based on that. If you decide I'm not the right fit, I can refer other fantastic therapists for you."

I got lost in a twenty-second daydream about just how perfectly he could fit *in* me before responding that I would make a tentative appointment for next week as I mulled it over. If I decided I needed to switch, I'd give the necessary forty-eight-hour cancellation notice.

He walked me out of his office into the waiting room where I scheduled that appointment.

The next four days I thought more about what I was going to wear to my appointment than what I was supposed to be figuring out. It was a clear indicator that I should call for his list of recommendations and cancel our appointment, but I couldn't do it.

"So, Trice I'm happy to see you kept our appointment."

"We'll see," I muttered.

"How are things?"

"Things are okay, I guess. My fantasies have become more frequent."

151

"Fantasies?"

"Yes. I started having them a few weeks ago and now they're more persistent."

"What happens in these fantasies?"

"I think about a man. I can't see his face. I never see his face. He tells me to shut up and..." I immediately started breathing heavy. "Should I continue?"

"If you'd like."

"He rips my clothes off. I start to scream and he yells at me to shut the fuck up. He has a knife, and I feel the cold steel against my thighs and my heart is pounding. I think he might kill me. He cuts my panties off and snatches them off me."

I was writhing on the couch, nails digging into my thighs.

"He tells me I can't make a sound. So I bite my lip and close my eyes, preparing myself for him to have his way with me."

My eyes rolled in my head, thinking of losing all control.

"He binds my hands with tape and forcefully pulls my legs apart. He squeezes my ass, hard. Like my pain feeds him, and my satisfaction means nothing."

At this point I was trembling with desire and clutching the leather of his couch, nearly puncturing it. I let my head roll back without realizing it, as I seemed to have lost sense of where I was. I was rubbing my thighs and caressing my breast through my shirt.

"He's fucking me in a way that is so raw and primal. Mashing my head into the floor. Telling me I love his hard dick."

Slowly winding my hips, I felt my pussy pulsating. Juices were spilling out of my freshly waxed pussy. When I finally opened my eyes and remembered where I was, I noticed Dr. Fallow staring at me with a very noticeable hard on. I watched as precum stained his pants. Either he had thick nut or he was going commando. Both options caused me to salivate.

I raised my eyebrows and raised my eyes to meet his.

"What do you think that represents for you?"

"That I want to be taken and fucked with wild abandon. I actually fantasize about being abducted... often."

"Abducted? Explain please."

"I mean a man in a hooded mask snatches me off the street. He binds my wrists and ankles with zip ties and tosses me in a trunk to bring me to another location. He has a gun but I don't know if it's loaded. He tells me something like, 'I'm a good shot bitch so don't try anything fucking stupid.' When we arrive to where he wants me, he doesn't actually inflict harmful pain on me though. Maybe he ties me up and makes me cum more times than I may believe I can handle or something. Though... I would like him to bag me."

"Bag you? I'm not familiar with that terminology. Also, how would you know it was role play and not a true abduction?"

"Hmm, maybe we'd have a code word, something random like 'thorn.' A word you don't hear day-to-day. Or he could say my name. That tells me it isn't random. By bag me, I mean to wrap my head in a plastic bag while he fucks me. I'd want him to try to time it so he could puncture a hole in it over my mouth as I came. I love the idea of relinquishing complete control of my body, especially with something as essential as breath."

"There's still risk involved, Trice. A lot of risk."

"No risk, no reward. Fear is mostly your imagination getting carried away. I would like to experience what feels like real danger. Plus the adrenaline from fear coupled with your body's reaction to arousal is intense. I don't have to tell you fear and arousal are closely related in terms of the way they affect the body. Experiencing them together seems like double the rush."

"I can see how you would feel that way."

"Plus with stalking you as they gather information on your routine, your likes and dislikes... they're so enamored by you they can only focus on you. They watch your every move. Even the time spent away from you is spent obsessing over how to get away with taking you. They must have you, by any means. If it means breaking the law, so be it. You can't put a limit on someone's passion. For a person to lose control over you is kinky as fuck. Albeit a very dark version of it, but it turns me on driving a man that crazy."

"Rape fantasies are very common. It just represents your desire to not have to be in control. People who primarily have to be in control in their day-to-day enjoy relinquishing that power in the bedroom. I'm generally not concerned about it. A rape fantasy doesn't condone rape any more than horror films condone violence. This, however, has me concerned. You say you want to act it out."

"With a trusted partner. Just role-play."

"Well, our time is up."

"Grateful?"

"No, but that was quite a bit to digest. This session may need to be on the house for as much as

I learned from you today, Trice," he joked as he walked me to the door.

"I take other forms of payment, Doctor," I answered, raising my brows suggestively before departing and making my next appointment.

Take Doctor's Orders? Page CUNT
Continue Sessions? Page 163

CUNT

After seeing Atlas for weeks, my desire for him only increased. We attempted to work through it, but every session it occupied our space like suffocating humidity. In my most recent session, it seemed like he was avoiding talking about my issues at all. He asked few questions about Maxon or my internal workings, and was instead interested in my weekend plans. This "therapy" was going off the rails. For as unprofessional as this was, he may as well have been fucking me. But in trusting the process, I answered all his questions about my whereabouts and intentions. Perhaps they were part of some big picture I couldn't see.

I wrapped the session contemplating whether it was truly time to change doctors. Maybe if I wasn't his patient I could get the help I needed, and he might actually fuck me. I was having a difficult time trying to see why I hadn't just done that already.

Sunday night, I was rounding the corner of 18th on Avenue C mid-call with my friend Rosa when I felt something stabbing me in the back.

"Don't turn around, bitch, or I'll fucking kill you," he said, pressing his weapon harder into my back. "If you scream or try to fight I'll blow your head off."

My heart was racing. I felt tears burning.

"I'm not playing with you, Trice. Walk."

Adrenaline took over and somehow I planted one wobbly foot in front of the other.

"Now say goodbye to whoever's on the phone and if you say so much as one word other than, 'I need to call you back in a few minutes,' they'll never find your body."

I had a phone to my ear, but fear had drowned out her voice and I'd become every idiot in a horror film I screamed at. When it was time to save my own life, I panicked. My stunned idiocy may cost me my life now.

"Now," he growled at me.

"Rosa, I need to call you back in a few minutes."

I pressed end and he snatched my phone.

I tried to hold on to it and dug my nails into his hand.

If he kills me, his DNA is under my nails.

"Bitch! Try that again and painful thorns will be the least of your problems."

What? Painful thorns? What's that got to do with...? Thorns! This was Atlas.

"Atl-"

"Shut. Up. Or. I'll. Fucking. Kill. You."

It was him. I finally recognized his voice. For the first time, dread didn't plug my ears and I could hear him. He was fulfilling my fantasy!

"Keep walking."

He walked me to a parking lot and ordered me inside the trunk.

"At-"

"NOW!" he barked.

He hogtied me with zip ties and slammed the trunk.

We didn't drive very far, though I felt the distance using the knocking of my head due to potholes to count the miles. Even though I was 99% sure it was Atlas, what if I was wrong? What if he was fucking crazy and used my confession as an excuse to work out his own serial killer fantasies? Just because I knew him doesn't mean I was safe.

Why didn't I mention a safe word with my fantasy sharing? What if he took it too far?

He parked and pulled me out in an underground parking garage. He cut the ties on my feet so I could walk. I was tempted to run but what if he was just trying to do this for me? What if I ran and got him fired and this became a career-ending debacle? I didn't know if I thought this all the way through. But he probably had. Calm down, Trice. I'm sure if you shouted, "Seriously stop!" he'd quit. Just enjoy the fantasy. Breathe.

He walked me to a warehouse with a blue freight elevator. He pushed me into the corner and had me face away from him. He seemed to be very against me looking at him despite him wearing a ski mask.

When he pulled me out of the lift into the room, it appeared like it was bigger, but this section was closed off with wooden boards in various shapes and sizes like a last-minute makeshift barrier. Against the back wall was what resembled an electric chair. There were straps on the arms of the chair and at the ankles. There was also a big hole in the middle, which didn't make a bit of sense to me.

He stood behind me, unbuttoning and unzipping my pants. He gently pulled them down, which seemed oddly out of place given the circumstances.

"Step out."

I did as I was told.

"Sit."

I sat in the chair as he stood behind the chair, snipped the zip ties and unfastened my bra before strapping my arms down. Then he covered my eyes with some fabric to obstruct my vision. Then he walked to the front and strapped my ankles. My imagination took off. I didn't tell him much else about what I wanted. What would he do?

He left me alone just long enough for mild panic to set in again, then I felt something bulbous coming up through the hole in the chair. I tried wiggling a bit, afraid of what was coming into contact with my precious pussy. Then he turned it on. It was a vibrating wand!

My legs were wide enough for him to stand between them. He leaned forward, presumably leaning against the wall with one hand and used the other to rub his dick all over my breasts. I felt the heat radiating from his thickness onto my breasts as he stroked it slowly. As long as I'd waited to have Atlas touching me and I couldn't even see it! It felt damn good though.

He must have had some kind of remote to control the speed of the wand because I could feel the vibrations getting stronger. He leaned down, pushed my breasts together and sucked them. My legs trembled down to my tightly curled toes. He growled, pushing my breasts together in an attempt to titty fuck me. I was disappointed I couldn't tuck my chin enough to suck the tip. The positioning was a bit awkward so it didn't last long. He reverted back to stroking it himself and slapping it against my breast instead. He took the liberty of turning the speed up on the wand too.

At this point I was full on yelping. I didn't usually have so much direct stimulation for so long. It was a torturous pleasure.

I didn't feel him in front of me anymore, and I wondered what would happen next. Suddenly I felt what appeared to be plastic on my face. I gasped, sucking it in deep and he removed it. Then he replaced it, holding it on for longer that time. Then removing it. Each time he repeated, he would hold it longer. If I shook my head no, he'd pull it away. It was terrifying... and invigorating!

He turned the speed up on the wand again and held the wrap across my mouth and nose until it fogged up and my eyes were wild with the kind of tantalizing fear only an experience this unique can bring and before I could even shake my head, he punctured a hole in my mouth and out bellowed the longest, loudest orgasm I'd had in my life.

My chair was a soaking wet mess, and I cried, "Off. Off. OFF!" He snatched the cord out of the wall and let me catch my breath as exhausted tears streamed down my face. He unstrapped me, told me, "Find your own way home," and left.

Once I'd amassed enough strength, I dressed and walked out to the cool night air. I was disoriented and confused. I wasn't sure where I was. I pulled out my phone and checked my GPS. I wasn't that far from home. I grabbed a cab via app and made my way home. When I got home, Maxon wasn't there so I could shower and go to bed in peace. I was exhausted.

From the time my eyes opened Monday morning, all I could think about was the previous night and what I would say to Atlas during Tuesday's appointment. As the evening rolled around, Maxon came home to me cooking dinner and wrapped his arms around me. I didn't feel anything. I barely felt guilt for indulging in my fantasies. It wasn't fair to do this to him. Now that I knew the passion, creativity, and fulfillment I was searching for could be mine, there was no going back. I'd ride the week out, but this relationship was ending. I made minimal conversation and tried to avoid body contact as much as possible before bed. I was focused on my appointment with the only man I longed to see.

When I arrived in that familiar waiting room, I was vibrating with anticipation. Atlas stepped out to greet me per his usual. I stepped into his office, and the moment the door closed I grabbed him. "What are you doing?" he asked quizzically, holding me at arm's length.

"Sorry. I guess not at work huh?"

"Have a seat."

I plopped down comfortably.

"So what's new since last Tuesday?"

"Well, on Sunday my therapist gave me the best orgasm of my life."

"Who is this other therapist you have?"

"Are we not going to talk about this, Atlas?"

"What do you mean?"

I was becoming frustrated. "Sunday. It was you, and now you're acting like it wasn't."

"I have no idea what you're talking about."

"Right." I laughed sarcastically. "Of course not."

"How about a change of topic. What else interesting happened to you since I saw you Su-Tuesday?"

I noticed a mark on his right hand. Where I had dug my nails into my attacker.

"What happened to your hand?"

"Oh it's nothing."

"I'm breaking it off with Maxon."

"What led you to decide so definitively?"

"I had an experience that changed my life. It was inevitable anyway."

"What happened in this experience?"

"Oh, it was nothing." Let's see how he liked me minimizing shit.

"It caused a great shift in your life. I don't know if I'd call that nothing."

"Like I said, inevitable."

"So how do you feel about it?"

"Relieved."

He went through a line of questioning that gave me more closure than I believed I needed. He was good at his job but I simply couldn't continue to see him. I was tempted to sit there and spill fantasies with the hopes that he'd continue to anonymously fulfill them. But being there with him denying our encounter felt a bit like rejection, and I wasn't comfortable with that. It also seemed to cross prostitution and ethical lines. I thought I would revert to my original plan of switching therapists and see if Atlas would be open to fucking me without the worry of being fired or breaking some code.

The session wrapped and we had an awkward hug.

"See you next Tuesday," he said as we parted.

"Nah. You won't. But you know where to find me. Don't you?"

Risk

I decided to go braless in a black maxi dress with thigh-high side slits. I usually wore leggings beneath it, but I opted for flesh-colored panties this time instead. If I was going to feel uncomfortable, so was he.

No fish was exotic enough to draw attention away from my nipples in that waiting room. A woman with whom I assumed to be her young son look horrified at my get-up and I grabbed a book from the table to cover up. The room was usually empty and clearly I'd lost my entire fucking mind focusing solely on Atlas that I forgot about the reactions of others. When Atlas stepped out to greet me, he looked at me the way I imagine I looked at him the first time. It was very brief—for the sake of maintaining professionalism I'm sure—but it was a reaction.

His eyes fell on my pierced nipples that had to be visible after sitting in that chilly waiting room.

"You look good... to... be here. You know, happy. Happy, to be here."

"Indeed I am."

"Miss... excuse me, Tentatrice. Considering your initial concerns with attraction, I feel compelled to ask if your difference in attire is deliberate."

Was he calling me out?

"What do you mean?" I stalled.

"Well, when we first began our sessions you were dressed... considerably more conservative. I only mention it because I wanted to make sure that my suggestion to reconsider why you would switch doctors didn't send the wrong message. I never want to be responsible for the derailing of your mental health."

"You didn't send the wrong message," I said dryly. I decided then this would be my last visit with Dr. Fallow so I may as well have fun. "Did I?"

"What message were you trying to send?"

"You don't know?" I stood up and walked over to his degree. "Don't tell me your university skipped over this part."

"There is no school of Trice. If I want to know what you wanted to say, only you could teach that course."

"I could teach you. You want to learn?" I walked over to him, my breasts at his eye level.

He swallowed hard. "I'd like you to have a seat so we can chat."

"Am I not allowed to stand? Is that against a rule?"

"Well, no, not a rule per se."

"Shucks, I like breaking rules."

"Okay, you prefer to stand? I'll stand as well. We can communicate standing."

"What if I prefer that you sit, while I stand?"

"Miss Jack... Trice. This..."

"Okay, I'll sit."

I attempted to sit on his lap. He grabbed my waist and stopped me mid-squat.

"In the chair, over there."

"Fine."

"Thank you." He pulled his collar away from his neck, overheated.

I sat down and spread my legs so they peeked out of the slits. I pulled at my dress, mentioning the climate change.

"Trice. What is it that you want?"

"I want you. I want to know what it's like to do something out of character. I want to be taken and consumed and overwhelmed by passion. I want to know it exists and is not a figment of my imagination. I want you to say fuck this bullshit conversation and help me the best way you can, by showing me that this can happen."

"You know I can't do that."

"You can't? Or you won't?"

"Can't."

"Do you want to?"

"What I want is of no concern. You are here to help yourself. That is my job, and my only concern."

"You sure about that?" I asked, eyeing his hard-on.

"That is a matter of biology beyond my control. It has nothing to do with..."

"Nothing? That's totally unrelated? How can you help me if you can't be honest with yourself?"I grabbed my purse and left.

The following night when Maxon wanted to make love, I closed my eyes and pretended it was Atlas. For every soft stroke, I imagined it was a transition thrust until we got into position to do something nastier. I flipped Maxon over and rode him with my eyes closed, clasping my hands over his, guiding them, using them to aid my imagination of what I hoped Atlas would do.

I came harder than I had in months. Truthfully, I almost called Atlas's name.

The next morning, Maxon remarked at how amazing the previous night was and how connected we were. I felt guilty and angry. Guilty for obvious reasons, but I was angry with us both for how disconnected we were and how unnoticed it was. I had to take some responsibility for it, because I was why he didn't see a difference. Perhaps I had been faking it all along.

I saw Atlas's office calling and realized I'd stormed out without saying whether I would be returning or not. I figured I should at least answer and tell his receptionist that I wasn't returning.

"Hello?"

"Trice?" My eyes widened and I stopped in my tracks.

"Atlas?"

"Yes."

"I saw the number and assumed it would be your secretary, not..."

"No. I felt I should apologize personally."

"It wasn't your fault. I was out of line."

"You were being honest, but it was my responsibility to..."

"Oh, I was being a brat and you tried to redirect me."

"I should have...."

"You did what you should have."

"Hmm. Well, I was wondering if you wanted that list?"

That moment felt very much like a post-fight official break-up. My eyes began to fill.

"If you want it. I just felt I should be the one to give you an out. *If* you need it."

"Mmmhmm. I understand."

"Trice, you can continue to come. I'm just offering."

And I did. I returned for three more visits that were more forced and uncomfortable than meeting your significant other's parents after they've caught you having sex. We discussed the weather and our shared love of peonies. We tiptoed tensely around real subjects.

The night before what was to be our third appointment, I had a vivid dream about Atlas. He stared at me with his long-lashed pensive eyes and finally showed me that the same way he knew my thoughts, he knew my body.

He took me, right on his mocha-hued chaise, and everything I knew was missing was exorcised in self-assured relief and ecstasy.

They must have become real-life moans because Maxon nudged me asking if I was okay. I grumbled affirmatively and turned on my side. Maxon wrapped his arm around my waist as guilt pooled in my eyes.

As soon as I sat down to face Atlas, he began his typical line of questioning, answering all my questions with questions.

I sidestepped the facade because it was too much to do it there and at home.

"I dreamt about you last night."

"Interesting. Would you like to share what happened?"

"I dreamt you bent me over that chair." I got up and walked over to the chair, bending over it like I had in my dream and my imagination many times. "You told me I had to be quiet so I wouldn't disturb other patients in the waiting room or that were with other therapists. You buried your face in my wetness, holding on to both of my ass cheeks and spreading them to get your tongue deeper inside of me. Then you sat me on top of your desk."

I walked over, hiked up my skirt, and climbed on his desk, spreading my legs to reveal my plump lips clinging to my soaked panties.

"And instead of sweeping everything off of it, you did an even grander fuck it move, and didn't move a damn thing and just fucked me right on top of all this paperwork."

I masturbated myself in front of his face and I saw his erection growing as he sat frozen, unsure of what to do next.

"If you can honestly say you don't want to be the one to show me what wild abandon and passion feels like, that you haven't fantasized about me too, that you haven't wondered how sweet," I removed my inserted fingers and breezed them beneath his nose, "this nectar is, I'll leave."

His mouth agape, he sat paralyzed. "Wh-wh-what do, uh, do you um... you think that means?" He tried to hold out. One side of his internal struggle was winning.

"I think it means I'm tired of coming here and pretending that as I watch your fingers move to take notes on me, that I don't imagine them tugging at my nipples and stroking my clit. It means I'm as distracted by your lips and where I want them to suck me as I was the first day I met you. It means my subconscious is trying to act out what reality needs desperately." I never moved my hand from my clitoris as I spoke, moving my fingers in mesmerizing circles.

Doc caves in? Page 169
Doc holds out a little? Page 171

Remove the Period

He swiftly removed his tie and used it to bind my hands. He pushed me to the floor, mashing my face into it. He reached up on his desk and grabbed a letter opener. I felt the cold steel against my thigh before he cut my panties off.

I moaned, realizing my fantasy was coming to life.

He barked, "Shut the fuck up."

"Oh!" I whispered.

"Shut. The. Fuck. Up," he growled.

I felt the heat radiating from his dick between my legs before the pressure of his girth opening me.

"Fuck."

"Don't say another word."

I breathed in short bursts through my nose in an effort to not make a sound, but Atlas was fucking the sense out of me. Every suspicion I ever had about leaving Maxon was confirmed with each thrust. I needed this, and he was never going to give it to me.

Atlas was smacking my ass so hard it was stinging. He pulled me up by my wrists and tossed me on the chaise. I nearly rolled off because my hands were still bound and I couldn't catch myself.He propped me up and went back to pounding me out.

"I had enough of you taunting me with this..." he grabbed my face, "tight. Little. Cunt. Now you're paying for it."

He slapped my tits.

Again.

I held my breath to mute my orgasm.

I had never experienced anything close to this before.

"Shit!"

He was fucking me too hard for me to be quiet so he stuffed my panties in my mouth until he pulled out and sprayed all over my stomach.

Splash

He jumped up and walked into his private bathroom where I heard water running and some splashing. I guess he was trying to cool off. The water stopped and I had no idea what was going on the other side of that door.

I stood up and leaned against the bathroom door before resuming my masturbatory session. "Mmmm, Atlas." I fondled my nipples like I wanted him to. I even bent over in case he opened that door. I wanted him then more than ever.

Thinking of how I knew he wanted it, that his dick was begging for it as bad as I was turned me on so much. "Fuck me, Atlas, I need it," I crooned through the door. "Last night was my first time dreaming of you at night, but I've dreamed of you many times before. I know you know. I've sat across from you and thought about sitting on you and wrapping you up in my legs. I've wanted to climb on top of your face and grind my pussy all over your mouth. Force you to drink me and then flip me over and fuck me."

I heard the faint sound of heavy breathing on the other side of the door. He was jerking off to me masturbating and telling him my fantasies! "My favorite fantasy is where you try to analyze me but you can't focus because I'm deep-throating that fat dick I just saw through those pants. You try to gather your thoughts but the sound of my gagging distracts you and the sloppy wet suction makes it too difficult for you to focus. So you give in and you hold my hair and you fuck my face." I paused to hear muffled grunting and quick breathing. "I just want to make you cum, Atlas. Make you cum like I cum for you at night when I touch myself in the shower, and in bed in the mornings. It's so bad now I even touch myself to you on my lunch break. I'd rather consume you for lunch than whatever I packed. Nothing can be as filling or fulfilling as you Atlas."

He moaned, "Tentatrice," and I could barely continue.

"I go to the furthest bathroom and use the last stall. I tug at my nipples and wish it was you. I imagine you may get rough with me and pull my hair back. I put my leg up on the handicapped bar and I push my fingers deep inside me and summon you for orgasms I need."

"Ohh, Trice."

"It starts as whispers, and then as my orgasm builds I get louder and louder and I stop caring if I could be heard, 'Atlas, Atlas, Atlas!'" The sounds on the other side of the door sounded like the release of a conflicted man.

"Uuuuggghhhhhhhhh" he strained as he cum.

Knowing that finally he'd cum for me sent me over the edge and I creamed on my fingers crying out to him.

A few minutes passed and neither of us really knew what to do. I heard him washing up, then I heard paper towels ripping. Then just silence.

"I'm going to go. I was hoping to use the bathroom?"

He stepped out. Shame was written on his face as we awkwardly passed each other. I did a quick clean up and took a deep breath before walking out.

"So..." I let my non-question linger in the air.

"So?" he responded, as clueless as me.

He tried so many times to fight it. I owed it to him to never put him in this position again. This would be my last visit. I kept my next appointment and scheduled peonies to be delivered at that time instead.

124

My love worked from home, unfortunately I did not. I called out that day, but didn't tell him.

"Babe, you're running late"

"Truly, I am. You're right," I said, slowly sipping my hot morning tea.

"You don't look too worried about it," he said, chuckling. "I'm going to the office. Somebody's got to work around here."

"Hmm." I stood directly in his path, placing my palm on his chest "*I'm* going to get to work, right now."

He stared, puzzled, waiting for my follow up.

"I'm going to work on you. It's a very important day."

I walked him over to the whiteboard calendar on our refrigerator. He looked mildly panicked, like he may have forgotten an anniversary.

"Today is..." I removed the red dry erase pen and wrote on the day's date in all capital letters, "COCK WORSHIP DAY!"

He repeated after me with the brightest smile as I encircled the date,12/4.

"Is *that* what today is?" he asked, beaming.

"Is that a problem?"

"Hell naw!" He let his southern accent slip out a bit like it does when he's excited.

We both had a hearty laugh at his enthusiasm.

"So... what does that mean?" he inquired happily.

"It means exactly what it sounds like. I spend the entire day, worshipping your cock in every way you'd like. Starting with this."

Squeezing the honey I'd just used in my tea onto my tongue, I chased it with the tea, melting the honey just enough to coat my tongue. Kneeling very swiftly, I extracted my gift from Jason's pajama pants and with heat-laced honey, I worked to get the final ingredient to my concoction, fresh-squeezed Jay juice. The moment he felt my extra warm mouth and velvety tongue, his knees buckled slightly before he placed his hand on the marble island in the middle of our kitchen. He grabbed two handfuls of my hair and pumped into my mouth, losing himself in pleasure. We alternated being in control of the speed and depth.

Eventually, he pushed me up against the island, held my head steady and fucked my mouth to his heart's content. I wrapped my arms around his thighs for balance in my squatting position, completely engulfing him in warm wetness. He furiously thrusted in and out until he shot my honey-laced earnings down the hatch. Gasping, he rested his elbows on the island until he was empty and I was full.

When he finally caught his breath, he said, "And you plan to do this all day?"

"I didn't say 'cock worship morning' did I?"

"I luhh you." His country drawl was leaking again.

"Love you too."

He headed into his office while I showered. Soaping my breasts, I pondered which tactic to try next. Following hot with cold seemed like the appropriate selection. After toweling off a bit, I pulled a frozen fruit pop out of the freezer. The cool gust of air on my wet bare breasts caused my nipples to instantly harden. I stripped my cool pop, stepped on the pedal of the trash to lift the lid and tossed the wrapper in the trash.

I sucked my 'cicle like it was Jay, slurping loud enough for him to turn around and mouth "come on" with his hand over the receiver. He looked pained as if he didn't just have a round of sloppy top less than an hour ago. I pulled the pop out slowly, smiled innocently, and winked, bypassing his office en route to the linen closet. I pulled out the towel I typically use when I temporarily dye my hair, and a hand towel.

I pranced into his office and motioned for him to stand up. He stood, looking confused, trying to concentrate on his call. Holding the ice pop in my mouth, I placed the larger towel down on the floor and rolled his office chair on top of it slightly so most of it lay in front of the chair. Next, I covered the seat of the chair with the hand towel. Juices from the pop started trickling down my chin to my chest. I lifted my breast to my mouth and licked up the runaway juices.

"Umm, I'm sorry. Can you repeat that? I missed that last part." Jason stammered into the phone we'd both forgotten was there for a moment.

I held the pop in my mouth again as I used both hands to pull down his PJs before motioning that he could sit. I sat on the towel at his feet, popped both legs open, spread my lips and slid the pop up against my opening. I glided it up, flinching as the cold tip reached my clit. I brought it up and rubbed it around my nipples, sucking the juices off as they melted, making a sticky mess of my breasts. When I put it back in my mouth it tasted better now that it was flavored with me.

I fondled my breasts with both hands, holding the remainder of the ice pop in my mouth, letting my lips nearly numb into a cold ring. I sat up and placed my ice-cold mouth on Jason's throbbing hot cock.

He inhaled sharply, "Sssssssshh. Nah. No! I... my back... my back has been acting up," Jason tried to cover into the phone. "I just sat down. I actually should get my heating pad so I can focus. I'm going to do that, send those emails, and call you back Jim." He hung up before Jim could contest.

I held the ice pop against the underside of his penis, letting the warmth of it melt it down to his balls. I slurped beneath, licking up the juices and lapping at his sack. When my pop was halfway gone, I sucked it up to the tip of the stick and put both Jason and the pop in my mouth together. Juice was running out messily but I didn't care. When the last chunks of the ice pop fell away and melted, I slurped the sticky mess I created all over his dick. I pulled his feet from beneath him so they weren't planted on the floor, pulled the level on his seat and dropped it so I could bury him deeply into my throat. I stuck out my tongue so I could lick his balls, simultaneously jerking him off in my throat.

"G," he groaned softly.

I made my uvula vibrate and he shot out, surprising himself.

"Fuck!" he sighed. "All day?"

"Mmmhmm," I replied easing him out of my throat.

"Whenever I ask, or whenever you feel like it?"

"Both." I smiled happily.

"And how do I ask? Is there a special way?"

"Nope. Verbal... non-verbal..."

"Non-verbal?"

"You can be as creative as you wish."

"This is my favorite fucking day. My favorite. Ever!"

I laughed until tears filled my eyes.

I did let him get some work done for about three hours after cleaning up the sticky mess that I created.

I was headed to the kitchen to make him lunch when he turned and we locked eyes. He snapped his fingers and made a come-hither motion.

I dropped to my knees, crawled over to him, sucked and slurped until he filled me, wiped my mouth, rose to my feet and walked away as quietly as I came. I washed my hands, and prepared his lunch as I planned.

When I served him his panini, he stared at me lovingly. "You should call off more often!"

"You wouldn't get today's treatment every day, J."

"I know. But I love looking up and knowing you're here. Not to mention, you're damn good to look at, Giselle," he added, smacking my booty.

I headed off to the media room and propped my feet up to watch some Netflix.

Three episodes into my binge fest, Jason walked in. He smiled a knowing smile: the grin of a man who knows his wish will be granted before it is asked. I nodded, but held up a finger and asked him to hold on a second while I grabbed a ponytail holder. While digging in my purse, I heard my tin of mints and got an idea. I popped four in my mouth, tied up my hair and waved him over to me.

I assumed he saw me put the mints in, but by the look of shock on his face he was not expecting that sensation. I rolled the mints over and under his shaft, creating a cool, tingling sensation for the both

178

of us. He seemed to want to slow down and enjoy this session. He made love to my mouth slowly. He stroked flyaway hairs out of my face, stared down lovingly at me. He lost himself in my suction and I lost myself in the pleasure of receiving him. When I felt his telltale signs, I was surprised to feel him pull away. He jerked off over my face as I quickly realized he wanted to paint it. He squeezed out a small, warm load onto my lips and cheeks.

This time, he retrieved a rag to clean my face before I went into the bathroom to freshen up. We snuggled on the couch together resuming my binge session until it was time for dinner. We couldn't make up our minds what to have, and eventually decided to order a pizza.

"35–45 minutes," Jason announced when he finished placing the order.

"You know what we could do in that time?"

"Are you serious? I don't know if I have anything left!"

"I know! That's the fun part. Emptying you and filling me. Let's see if you cum before the pizza arrives. Let's try."

He threw his hands up surrendering to the suggestion. "Who can argue with that?"

I sucked him slow to ease up on the friction, making sure to use extra spit and lots of tongue. We had been going at it a lot all day.

I was humming a tune of pleasure, sending vibrations up and moaning all the way down. It turned me on to see him focused solely on receiving. This time his cum oozed out slowly, filling my mouth instead of shooting down my throat. It gave me time to savor his taste. I continued to suck as he writhed and flinched beneath me until he begged softly, "Stop. You almost got knocked upside the head, woman!"

I knew it was über sensitive after he came but sometimes I couldn't help myself.

The doorbell rang and we both shouted, "One second!" before scrambling to look presentable.

We'd decided on pepperoni as Jay claimed, I'd had enough sausage for today.

Time for dessert.

Dessert 1? Page 181
Dessert 2? Page 183

Cat & Mouse

I headed to the pantry in search of Fruit roll-ups™.

He turned to me smiling.

"What you finnah do wit that?"

"I'm gonna wrap this around your dick and suck it till it's gone or you cum. Whatever happens first."

I ripped it in half so I didn't have to wrap it around twice. I wanted it to be relatively thin so he could still feel my suction.

He raised his eyebrows and lowered the waistband on his sweats so his erection bounced out. I wrapped the candy around his member and began sucking.

After a few moments, he swiped his hand behind him searching for his computer chair. Once he sat, I could really get to work. He lovingly caressed my face and it inspired me to go even harder. There was only a bit of the sticky film left. It was more like a residue. I created extra spit so it wouldn't be so sticky. Jay loved it wet.

He grabbed me beneath my arms and hoisted me up onto my feet. He stood up and bent me over his desk. He adjusted my pubic mound right on top of the mouse. It helped me glide across the surface and added some clitoral stimulation. My man was a genius! I reached back, spreading my cheeks on my tiptoes, allowing him to submerge himself into the depths of me.

He clasped my waist and embedded himself inside. I clung to cords and paperwork I could only hope weren't important or irreplaceable. He pushed down on my small frame for leverage, pressing the mouse firmly against my pussy. In a stroke of luck, I'd swiveled on top of a cord and it created some necessary resistance and light vibrations as I rolled across. I rocked to the rhythm of our love, sweat droplets dripping from his brow onto my back.

"Gigi," he growled under his breath. I curled my legs back behind his, swirling my hips until his breathing staggered and with a final grunt, he uncorked and sprayed inside me. My seizing walls received him gratefully.

We lay panting, sprawled across the desk. I immediately thought about how I was going to need an apple cider vinegar bath to try to restore my pH balance after this stunt. I wouldn't have it any other way.

Hard On

I asked Jay to give me a few minutes to whip up dessert and to stay out of the kitchen so he didn't ruin my surprise. "When I say when, stand up, take off your pants and underwear, and close your eyes."

He looked at me like *what the hell are you doing now, G?* Though given the day's events, he didn't bother to protest.

I grabbed some butterscotch chips and chopped them up, tossed them in a bowl with some coconut oil. I popped that concoction in the microwave a few times until it was just right. I poured it into a mason jar and let it cool for a bit. A few minutes later, I stuck my finger in it and examined it. The butterscotch quickly went from glossy to matte and hardened on my finger. It was warm, but not too hot. Perfect! I told Jay I was ready.

He stood with his eyes closed, swaying slowly with anticipation. I stroked his dick and it stiffened quickly given the day's events.

"No peeking," I reminded him.

Then I held the mason jar in front of his dick and eased it inside.

"What the?" He jerked back a bit but not before he was coated to mid shaft with glossy butterscotch that dripped from his tip until it began to harden.

His widened eyes were full of questions he never asked. I dropped to my knees, set the mason jar aside and sucked the cast of butterscotch on his dick. I knew the tip was the most sensitive, so I enjoyed knowing that sucking that area would be muted by the coating, allowing me to dote on him for much longer than usual.

As the butterscotch melted and dripped over the both of us, it made quite a sticky mess. The

183

pieces didn't all fall away at once. Certain areas were exposed enough to feel skin, and I'd work my tongue in crevices I'd find, much to my lover's delight. His weakening knees told me I'd be having warm cream to chase my butterscotch soon. He gripped my hair into a sloppy ponytail at the nape of my neck and pumped into my mouth. Gagging and drooling, I steadied myself as he skull-fucked me. My reward came sugary, sticky sweet.

Bridal Blues

Treacy and I were best friends since the first grade. Well into adulthood, our bond continued to solidify. We chose the same college in Atlanta and we both moved back to Virginia after. My boyfriend joked that we were closer than sisters and she was on some single black female type of shit. I explained that her mom was hardly ever home growing up because she was working to provide a roof over their heads while her drunken father was out stumbling the streets, and as rumor had it, occasionally into another woman's bed. My parents just started making more food and accepted her in as their second daughter.

Sometimes her father, Mr. Dawr, would make his way to our house screaming for his daughter, but my father put a stop to it because it embarrassed and traumatized Treacy and sometimes he would hit on me. Treacy, or as we mostly called her, Tre, was mortified. I never let on that it made me uncomfortable. She felt bad enough.

She found love before I did. She and Cheyn met when we moved back and he immediately wooed her. They seemed like such opposites, but I suppose they do attract. He was a pilot and she was a teacher.

During her school breaks and all through the summer, he had her sending me postcards from all over the globe. I missed my bestie, but I was happy she found a man she could trust. I knew something was up when my boo Dub and I got an invite to fly with them to Paris. We'd only been together six months but he was willing to come as my plus one for this trip.

As I suspected, Cheyn proposed in front of the Eiffel Tower. She said yes and immediately

185

turned and asked me to be her maid of honor. It was my turn to scream yes. We dined in this amazing restaurant within the tower and sipped champagne until the sun rose.

Seven months later, and a month before her nuptials, Dub popped the question. Tre couldn't wait to share all her wedding planning secrets with me. Before I could even hang up the phone, she was at my door with matching plastic tiaras and bridal magazines. I ordered some pizza and we shared ideas until somehow we both knocked out on my couch.

We were awakened by someone banging on my door like the police. I tiptoed to the peephole and saw Tre's fiancé. I looked back at her and mouthed, "It's Cheyn." She was shit at lip-reading so I tried again but he started yelling, "Baby! Come here!" so I opened the door.

"Damn you look good."

"Are you drunk, Cheyn?" The question was rhetorical. He reeked of alcohol.

"And I'm grown too! Wanna see?" He grabbed his crotch.

I spun my head away from the door. I hadn't seen that look on her face since we were kids. Damn, history really does repeat itself.

"You should get him home Sis."

Her eyes welled with tears but she wouldn't let them fall. She grabbed her keys and left, yanking him to the car.

"Text me when you get in."

She nodded solemnly before disappearing into the driver's seat. He was still rambling and ranting about nothing.

When I spoke to her the next day, she didn't bring it up so neither did I. I also steered clear of any wedding talk. We gossiped about reality television and some mutual acquaintances we knew on social media. After some time, it seemed all was back to normal.

Six days before the wedding, Cheyn showed up drunk as a skunk again at their place—this time sans pants. They remained in the cab he had enough sense to take home. Dub quickly mentioned he had an early morning staff meeting and we should be getting on our way. I was frustrated and furious. My friend deserved better than this! Dub told me to stay out of it, but how could I? This was her worst nightmare coming to life. They were about to be married. Was she sure she wanted to commit to a lifetime of that? Did she want her children to suffer the same fate she did? If their wedding wasn't less than a week away, maybe I would stay out of it, but this felt like a time to interject. I made a plan to talk to her when I came home from work the next day.

I didn't hear from her the entire day. That wasn't unusual after an embarrassing episode. In this instance, time was not a luxury we could afford. I picked up some of her favorite snacks at the supermarket and a small bouquet of flowers before driving to her place. When I arrived, her car wasn't there, and there were no signs of her. I called her twice, but she didn't answer. I decided to take my ass home and call her later that night. Any later than that and I would be filing a missing person's report if I didn't hear back by the next day.

I called her mom on my way home. She hadn't spoken to her in a few days and she was excitedly yammering on about the wedding. She evidently had no clue what was happening. It didn't feel like my place to fill her in so I didn't. I pulled up to my house and Tre's car was there! I'm looking all over for this heifer and it turns out she's at my place.

I walked in and didn't see her, Dub, not even the damn dog. Where was everyone? I opened the bedroom door to find Tre riding my fucking fiancé.

Something New Page 189
Something Borrowed Page 193
Something Old Page 196

Something New

I pulled a chair from my nearby dining set and sat down and started live streaming the act happening before me. I tagged them in the video so everyone would know who was involved. All of our friends were replying with angry faces, sad faces, and asking if it was real. Some people were telling me to turn it off and beat her ass.

They were so engrossed in each other, they didn't notice I was there at all. He gripped her ass as she bucked furiously on top of him. When she leaned forward, he sucked her nipples. She choked him as she rode, saying things I couldn't decipher. He sat up to turn her over and noticed me. He tried to push her off and she turned, startled. All the color left her face when she saw me.

"Natalie!"

"Why are you stopping? My presence didn't stop you from fucking, why should it stop you from finishing?"

"Nat, it's not like that. This is the first time it happened. This wasn't an affair. I came here looking for you, and I started crying about Cheyn being drunk and how scared I was to marry him. When he hit on you, I lost it. Every man in my life has always wanted you instead. They always loved you. And... and... he just wanted to comfort me. Then he looked at me like he... like he could want me. The tables were turned and finally someone wanted me instead and I... and I..."

"You what, bitch?"

She was sobbing but I didn't feel the least bit sorry for her. I let her speak because I never wanted her to think she had a reason to try to contact me again. She had explained herself.

"I'm sorry, Natalie"

"Y'all really should have kept going. You have a nice audience here. I'm streaming and your boss doesn't seem too thrilled that his employee is a lying, cheating whore."

"Nat!" she cried, "I love you!"

For some reason her claim to love me was the last straw.I put my phone down on the chair, leapt over to her like a lioness on a gazelle and beat the shit out of her. She mainly tried to defend herself and didn't even really fight back but I didn't ease up. I punched her until my arms were sore. I kicked my sorry ass ex in the crotch and told him to be gone when I returned.

I hopped in my ride sizzling hot. Driving on autopilot, I fumed aloud, "Really? After I embraced both of you as my family? When your sorry ass daddy was fucking up, who was there? Me! When your mom was working and couldn't be there, who was there? Me! And him!" I was seething. "I held this mafucka down, helped pay his student loans, cosigned on a car for him, made sure he was fed and fucked all the time and you repay me like this? My so-called best friend. All the people you could have fucked and you choose my best fucking friend? This is what we're doing now? Okay. Okay! Noted. Fucking noted."

I had my destination. Dub's best friend Slade lived across town. Lucky for me, he was also single. I wasn't trying to cause collateral damage. I pulled up behind his house drunk with vengeance. He opened the door grinning. Dub clearly hadn't filled him in yet.

"Wassup, Nat? Where's Dub?"

"Slade, your friend is trash. I'm going to get right to the point. I came here to fuck you. He pissed me off in the worst way imaginable and to get back at him I'll do things to you I've never done to anyone and you've likely never had someone do to you. Lust alone couldn't bring out an inner whore like this. If you pass, you'll miss the opportunity of a lifetime. And before you answer, might I inform you that as someone who was as close to him as I was, trust me, *you* don't owe him a fucking thing."

"Natalie, come on man."

"Is that a no?"

"You don't want to do this."

"Oh I do. I definitely do. I'm just trying to figure out if you want me to get on my knees and bend backwards so you can look down and see yourself gliding in and out of my throat until I swallow your nut. You know, before I suck it hard again and ride you until my pussy walls suck generations of kids out that dick."

"Your pussy, suck generations of kids...?"

"I got that Chinese finger trap, snappah. Fuck with me."

He hesitated, but then grabbed me and tongue kissed the hell out of me.

I stripped, and got down into the camel yoga position. He stood behind and tugged my hair back to shove his dick in my mouth to begin making good on my promise. Turns out, Slade fucked better and his nut was sweeter. When it was all said and done, I was contemplating how we could do this again. Slade must have been equally impressed but he turned to me and asked if this was just a one-time deal. I told him it didn't have to be. Dub was gonna be sick if this became a thing. Fuck his feelings though. Just the thought of him was making me sick.

"I'm going to run to the bathroom."

As I was washing my hands, I heard a knock at his door. I nosily slunk to the door to find my weak ass ex standing there with some of his belongings.

This was too good.

I opened the door pants-free with tousled hair, wearing one of Slade's shirts. "How's it feel?"

His eyes grew wide before becoming pained slits. Couldn't tell you what happened next. I closed the door on him and that chapter of my life, and climbed back into bed with Slade.

"Dub was here. He knows. I think he's gone. If not, I can think of some fun ways to distract ourselves from any attention he tries to get from either of us."

"Hell yeah."

We commenced to round two, and three and...

Something Borrowed

I backed out of the room before I was noticed. I went back to my car and pulled off. I wasn't sure what my destination was going to be but I couldn't stand being there, feeling betrayed by the two people I loved most.

I ended up at her house. I wanted to set the bitch on fire. I had a spare key to her place so I walked right in. I had no idea what I was going to do, but I felt like I wanted to ruin something that was important to her too. I looked in her closet and saw the garment bag that held her wedding dress. I was going to set this bitch ablaze. As I was lugging it to the front door, Cheyn came in. Hmm. I had a better idea.

It wasn't uncommon for him to see me in his house so he just asked if everything was okay. I told him everything was fine. I brought the dress back into the room and slid it on. With zero bias, I could say it looked five times better on me than her. I pressed record on my phone and set it up on the vanity. I called Cheyn into the bedroom. He stopped in the doorway confused.

"What are you doing, Natalie?"

"Just trying to have a little fun. Do I look good in the dress?" I spun around so he could see how it gripped my ass snugly.

"Beautiful. Is that your dress?"

"It is now. You'd fuck me in this dress right?"

He looked terrified. I could tell he was afraid to answer. It did seem like a set-up. But drunk lips speak a sober mind. I knew he wanted me.

"Just once, sweetie. It'll be our little secret."

With no further convincing, this scumbag was ready to fuck.

I lay on the bed and lifted the dress so he could suck my pussy. I grabbed his face and buried it inside me. I fucked his mouth hard. Then I flipped him over and rode his face until it looked like a glazed donut. He tried to grab me and turn me over, but I stopped him.

"You want to fuck me?"

He looked at me as if to say, of course. I repeated the question. I wanted him to say it.

"If you want to fuck me. Say it."

"I want to fuck you."

"What's my name?"

"Natalie."

"Say 'I want to fuck you, Natalie.'"

"I want to fuck you, Natalie."

"Nah. I don't believe you."

"I do!"

I stroked his face tenderly. "Beg."

"Damn, Nat, let me fuck. I'm throbbing right now. I want you so bad. I've always wanted you. Every time you came over or we went out to dinner I just wanted to grab you and fuck you right there. I used to think I chose the wrong girl. I fantasized about this so many times. Please, please can I fuck?"

"Fuck no."

I walked out with him still on his sorry ass knees, mouth sticky wet with my juices, and likely a deeply confused mind. I quickly swiped my phone and clothes before exiting the house. I never wanted him, and I didn't want him believing I did. I knew they didn't have condoms in the house and I wasn't trying to risk getting pregnant or something else. I just wanted to get my rocks off in her house at her man's expense wearing her wedding dress. I also wanted her to know that I had the opportunity to fuck her man, but I didn't, and moreover I wanted

194

her to know that he desired me and always had. I knew this would break her, but I gave it about as much thought as she gave fucking my man. I couldn't press send on our impromptu video fast enough.

Reap what you sow, hoe!

Something Old

"You bitch!"

"Sis, I can explain!"

The nerve of her to call me sis while on top of my man! I picked up a chair from my dining set and hurled it at the both of them. She ducked and he caught the worst of it.

I saw red, and it was more than just the blood gushing from Dub's mouth.

I tackled her and stomped her ass into the floor. She crawled to the corner and balled up until I tired of kicking her.

"Fuck you and fuck you. I want you both out of my fucking house!"

"Nat! Baby, Natalie!" he tried to call but I was digging in my nightstand drawer. Both of them knew me well enough to know what that meant.

I took the safety off and cocked my .45. "If I see either one of your fucking faces when I turn around, I'm going to assume this was a suicide mission."

They damn near killed each other clamoring to make it out the door at the same time, wrapped clumsily in a sheet. It would have been comical under any other circumstances.

Long after they were gone, I teetered between infuriated and deeply hurt. I had no one to turn to. My man and my best friend were who I told everything to. I decided to call my mama. As soon as she heard my voice, she knew something was wrong. When I was finally able to get the words out, she was fussing and cussing so loud I had to pull the phone away from my ear.

She drove over to my house and drew me a bath with calming oils. She brought some leftovers with her, which included some of my favorites. My mama's baked macaroni and cheese could probably solve many of the world's problems. She tucked me into bed—in my spare bedroom, because fuck that bed now, and climbed in with me. She stroked my hair with my head in her lap and let me cry until I wore myself out.

In the morning over mama's cheese and spinach omelets, pancakes, bacon, and hash browns, my mother continued to fume about the level of betrayal we both endured. She looked at Tre like another daughter. She couldn't believe she would do this to me.

"Believe it, Ma. I saw it with my own eyes."

"Should have let that slut stay home alone and hungry waiting for her drunk ass good-for-nothing Daddy."

"Mmmhmm. If we knew then what we know now..."

We had a Tre bashing session with mimosas until Mama had me giggling again. She told me she was going home after lunch but would be back the following day. After tight hugs and goodbyes, I hopped in the shower, hoping the piping hot water could wash away the ache within. It was futile. I broke down and sobbed until I was so weak I had to sit on the edge of the tub. My entire life had fallen apart and I didn't know up from down.

After lying in my bed staring at the ceiling for hours, I found myself enraged. I was hurt by them both, but I had given Tre many more years of my life. How could she? To think I was on my way to cheer her up and this is how she repays me. I was fuming. I couldn't lie there anymore. I had to do something, anything. I got dressed and hopped in my coupe.

Initially I was on a ride to nowhere, but the angrier I got, a destination became clear: Tre's dad, Mr. Dawr's house. This was his fault. He ruined her, he was responsible for her poor partner selection, why she was triggered, why she was envious of me, all of it. I sat in front of his house oblivious of the hour. I knocked loudly on his door the way he used to during his drunken rage.

He opened the door looking panicked by the sight of me.

"Is everything okay? Is Tre okay?"

I showed up disheveled, at a late hour. His questions weren't unwarranted.

"Everything is fine," I lied.

"Okay. So what brings you here?"

I wanted to vent. I wanted revenge. I wanted to cry.

"Would you like something to drink?" he asked before sitting next to me on the couch.

I shook my head. "Tre and I got into a fight. You fucked her up. You know that? Do you realize how badly you fucked her up?"

He nodded, regretful.

"And it was me. Me and MY family who picked up the pieces. Do you understand that? I spent my life protecting her and that was YOUR job, not mine."

"You're right."

"But I'm done. I'm done protecting her."

"I understand that."

"You used to hit on me all the time. Was that just the drunk ramblings, or do you find me attractive?"

"You're very attractive, but as you know, I'm sober now. With a sound mind I can't say acting on lustful thoughts with no thought of consequences is something I'm prepared to do."

"But if it's a secret, there are no consequences."

"Listen, Natalie, I-"

"You owe me. I need a man to touch and hold and fuck me and make me forget what my life has become on account of your daughter who behaves the way she does because of you."

"You're right. I do owe you, but this isn't the way."

"It's the only thing I want. It's the only thing I'm interested in." I mounted him on the couch and pushed my D cups in his face. "Lie and say you don't want to so I can prove you wrong."

He had his arms outstretched across the couch, fighting his natural urges. I grabbed his wrists, planted his hands on my ass and started grinding in his crotch.

"I can *feel* you want it," I said, referring to his stiffening erection, "Let me taste it."

"Natalie," he murmured.

He was only wearing pajama pants so they came down easily. Once I had my mouth on it, I knew I was going to get everything I wanted.

I sloppily sucked and jerked his full dick. I was pretty surprised by what he was packing. I climbed back into his lap to ride him but I kept thinking of how his daughter was riding my man. So I turned around and rode him with my back to him. He pulled my hair so he could reach my neck before sinking his teeth in.

"Hurt me."

"What?"

"Hurt me!" I cried.

So he bit me harder.

"Yes, and scratch me. Fuck me. Hard."

He pushed us both up and then bent me over the other side of the couch and fucked me hard like I asked. He couldn't see my tears. All I wanted was something to make me forget and even this wasn't working.

"Harder!" I yelled. If I couldn't feel pleasure, I needed to feel pain. I needed to feel something aside from this burning ache inside.

He held my hips hard and jackrabbit fucked me until he came. He fell back on the couch and almost immediately fell asleep.

I sat next to him, burying my head in my hands. I grabbed my bag and started searching for my phone. I was going to take a picture and send it to Tre.

Before I could get a good shot, I had a video call coming through. It was her.

Real time reveal was even better.

I answered.

"Natalie, before you hang up I just want you to know how sorry I am and I..."

"Me too."

She didn't expect that.

"Did you say you too?"

I plastered a fake smile on my face, my voice dripping with feigned innocence. "Yeah. I understand. Sometimes you just can't turn the dick away."

Then I panned out to show her butt naked, dick drained daddy laid up next to me.

"Daddy!" she screamed, and he stirred. I hung up and put the phone on airplane mode. I collected my things and drove to a hotel. I sure as shit didn't want to be anywhere I could be found. I wanted to enjoy my revenge in peace.

Peace would be elusive over the next few weeks. My physical health had joined my mental in being upset. I always had a nervous stomach so it wasn't unusual for me to be queasy if my emotions were in turmoil, but this was different. While describing it to my mother she said, "Let's hope you're not pregnant."

"Nah, Dub was out of town just after my last cycle, and we know who he was screwing after that."

"Well good. We don't need another him running around. Couldn't be somebody else though could it?"

"No Ma, I haven't... um. I've got another call. I'll call you back in a few."

I looked through my calendar. I was late.

"Fuck!"

I snatched out shampoos, conditioners, flat irons, hair dryer, drain cleaner, all kinds of shit under my bathroom sink to find a pregnancy test I knew was back there. After peeing on the stick, every thought crossed my mind in those agonizing two minutes. I went over all the people and events that led me to this moment.

I hadn't heard from Tre at all. As far as I knew, she hadn't even told anyone what I'd done. She knew she'd be forced to explain how she was the catalyst. There was nothing left to say. No words could make a difference, except for the word staring back at me on the test.

"Pregnant."

Th-eat-er

Our guests left in pairs following the illuminated aisle to the exit in the darkness.

You couldn't have told me that when we decided to have an in-home theater we'd be hosting erotic shows.

Brian originally wanted a huge projection screen for a man cave. I convinced him to forgo it to have a stage since he's quite the thespian, as are our friends. We'd have improv night and stand up shows and charge five bucks to cover light refreshments. We could always pull a screen down and use a projector to watch a movie if we wanted to. This offered us two options.

During an improv set, there was a silly scene that emulated sex. I looked at Brian and said, "We should have people come and do that. I bet they'd pay more. Hell I'd pay to see that."

We laughed but later that night he brought it up again. "How would something like that even work?"

"Well we'd have to allow for it to be anonymous. Instead of a sign-up sheet, they'd put their email in a bowl on the way out if they wanted to participate next time. We'd recommend they arrive with their faces covered, park a block away and walk so their cars weren't recognized, and most importantly make it a judgment free zone. They could act out whatever they wanted as long as it was between consenting adults."

He chimed in with ways to get people who might be interested in being our exhibitionists and voyeurs.

Next thing I knew, we had the light back on and pens moving swiftly as we worked out the kinks.

"This could actually be something." I smiled, staring at our notes.

Tribulation? Page 204
Brush Up on Me? Page 208

Tribulation

When we told our friend Paula what we wanted to do, she gasped excitedly and said, she'd love to join us.

"Uhh, we were talking about with someone else, or if you wanted to watch. It wasn't an invitation to join us."

"Ohh." She smiled sheepishly.

"I mean, we hadn't even discussed performing ourselves."

Honestly, the idea hadn't even occurred to me until that moment. Brian and I were no strangers to the swinging life, but in this new circumstance, I'd only envisioned myself as a voyeur.

I called Brian in from the other room. "Yes, Elena, my love?" he responded sarcastically as he entered the room.

"You ever think about us performing in the theater?"

"You and Paula?"

"Me, and you... and Paula."

"I'm in if you are." He kissed my nose and returned to whatever he was doing.

"So Paula, what do you have in mind?"

Suddenly, her voice was hushed, like she was nervous to share. "I like, um... tribbing."

"Tribbing?"

"You know, like scissoring."

"Ohhh, so Brian doesn't really have to be involved."

"No, but either is fine."

"He enjoys just watching. I'll leave it up to him."

"Okay." Her voice was still just above a whisper. She wouldn't make eye contact.

"Girl, how you planning to rub your coochie on mine, but can't look at me to talk about it?"

She laughed so hard it was silent before she snorted holding her belly, wiping tears from her eyes.

When she collected herself, she nodded, "I can't even argue with that."

From then on, she was open and forward about her desires. Brian eventually decided he would be joining us.I told Paula she was free to fuck him, but his cum belonged to me.

She had no problems with the terms.

I thought it'd make for a better performance if we did some extra bonding prior to the show. The day before, we got waxed together. The morning of, we got mani/pedis. We decided to rock wigs for the show. I chose a long wavy blonde wig, while she opted for a layered merlot-hued bob. I had masks for us, but Paula felt like we didn't need them. She really was feeling bold; I liked it.

I managed last minute guest set up and greeting with Brian, while Paula set the stage for us. Once our voyeurs were seated, I found myself surprisingly nervous. At swinger parties, it wasn't uncommon to have people watching you, but they were usually engaging in other ways, or would watch for a bit then move on to something else. I'd never been the solitary main attraction. Well, lights, camera, and...

The lights were glaring and I made a note to change them for the next couple. Paula had made two play areas for us. We walked out together holding hands. Our small crowd applauded. I hadn't anticipated that. Paula pulled me close and we made our way to a fluffy area full of pillows and blankets. She had me face her with my back to the audience, and she lay next to me stroking my hair. My heart stopped thumping in my ears and I was able to calm and focus on her. She kissed me until everything else fell away. We lay there grinding and wriggling on the pallet with no regard for the eyes upon us.

She slipped a hand under my top, then between my legs. We undressed one another before she mounted me. Our hips began to sync up, gyrating so our clits lined up for mutual enjoyment. The warm steady friction felt incredible. The more aroused we became, our bodies created additional lubrication so our wet lips slipped between each other's. Moans from the audience reminded me of their existence, but nothing could distract me from the pleasure of her soft body on mine. She leaned forward to suck and kiss my breasts.

Brian had joined us on stage and eagerly undressed and joined us. He knelt behind Paula and I felt her warm exhale on my neck when he slid inside her. He smiled at me and I returned his loving gaze and grin. It took a few moments for us to realign so everyone felt good, but once it did, we moved like a well-lubed machine.

He pulled out of her and entered me. Paula adjusted by turning so one of her legs was beneath mine. She held my thigh up to get her closer friction and grant Brian deeper access. The synergy was fantastic. We kissed and I relished each set of her lips pressed against mine. I smirked internally thinking this position just may provide a blended orgasm. My man affirmed how well he knew my body, serving calculated strokes that encouraged my impending peak. Paula moaned in my mouth as it appeared hers was near as well. I held her soft booty tightly as she thrust her pelvis against mine. I sunk into an abyss of pleasure as my blended orgasm hit like a tidal wave I never desired to return from. My moans echoed through the theatre as others joined the erotic symphony.

Brian pulled out and tugged Paula close, pushing into her. Her twitching body clutched mine as she came. I could see in Brian's eyes he was close. I still wanted his cum but I didn't know if we'd be able to rearrange in time. I gently moved Paula to the side detaching them but I was late. Small drops cascaded on my tongue. I wasn't angry, just disappointed. I playfully smacked Paula's pussy, causing her to flinch and squeeze some nut out. I scooped out the rest with my fingers and sucked them. I heard a collective gasp from the audience. What? Hadn't they ever had cream pie before?

Brush Up on Me

For our first show, even Brian and I didn't know who was going to perform. The only thing we knew is there'd be a group of performers. I was excited to see what kind of show they were going to put on. I wondered if it'd be kinky, or sensual, or silly. I wondered if they'd take the art aspect really far or focus on putting on a show. I hoped they immersed themselves in the experience and that our observations were an afterthought.

The night of the show, Brian and I sat front and center. The other seats were filled with equally excited spectators.

At curtain up, the stage was framed with tube lights emitting a steady black lit glow. Two women walked out from opposite sides of the stage wearing white lingerie that glowed in the light. They also had glow in the dark lipstick and nail polish.

Moments later, three men appeared on stage with white boxers. One of them was sporting an exceptionally noticeable dick print. They assembled together and brought out a table and set it upstage. On the table from what I could see were bottles of paint and possibly some brushes. There were other items, but I couldn't suss out what they were just yet. They moved like they had done a bit of orchestrating their movements to create fluidity and make their transitions look fun instead of chaotic. I could appreciate that.

The men pulled off their boxers and their erections were engulfed in glowing mouths, while being jerked clasped with nails shining brightly. One of the women's keyhole fishnets were ripped, and seeing no regard for clothing really stimulated me.

Another woman who was nude save for a white headdress walked on stage and they all flocked to her with their bottles of paint in hand. Some painted her with a brush, others used their fingers. One of the women stopped painting the newest member altogether and instead began painting herself. Then she rubbed her paint-covered body against hers, smearing everyone's work together. The consensus seemed to be that that was the most effective and fun way to paint each other.

Brushes were tossed in lieu of bodies brushing up against one another, their slick bodies gliding over each other. They appeared to be one gyrating mass of moaning, painted limbs. It was very erotic. Out came the glow in the dark condoms and I must say that watching the glowing rods disappear and reappear was my favorite part. Eventually the glowing, writhing, moaning heap lulled. The hush of group satisfaction was a work of art.

As we bid our guests good night, we left the space so our performers could take down the set and exit, maintaining the anonymity.

When Brian and I stepped into our theater, we found our guests had left us a souvenir. It was a canvas our guests pressed their bodies against to make an abstract piece. They signed with their thumbprints in the shape of a circle. How thoughtful! Maybe I'd hang this in the hall that lead to the theater the way cinemas do with movie posters.

Kinky Crank

After complaining to Solana for months about how bored I was with the dating scene, I couldn't really be mad at her for dragging me to BDSM Speed Dating. I had no hope of finding a life partner. It was just a refreshing change to what became a monotonous droning on about your accomplishments and dreams between lonely awkward people hoping to connect for longer than two weeks and ditch the single life for good.

Folks who've been committed a long time romanticize the dating life. "You're free to fuck anyone." Yeah, but finding someone you *want* to sleep with that also *wants* to sleep with you and not have a complicated relationship surrounding it is nearly impossible. Unless you're one of those unicorns who can truly do no-strings casual encounters, who also miraculously draws those same people to you, in which case you should go play the lotto, you lucky bastard.

This seemed like a way to break up the aforementioned monotony and have some drinks and laughs with my homegirl who was also tired of the single life. She claimed it was a fun, pressure-free way to meet some interesting folks.

As soon as you arrived, there were six podiums with huge tablets. I mean, the tablet had to be about 42 inches. They were like TV screens. On it you were asked a series of questions that would determine where you fell on the kink spectrum. It printed out a little receipt of your results at the end that you were to hold on to until they were ready for the speed rounds to begin.

Drinks started to flow and it wasn't long before people were mingling and creating idle chatter as their inhibitions lowered.

A woman entered the room and commanded everyone's attention.

"Okay, Sirs and Madams. I'm going to ask that you split into two groups. If you scored higher than 60% as a submissive, masochist, prey, or brat, I need you on this side of the room," she said with her arm outstretched to the left,

"and if you scored higher than 60% as a dominant, sadist, hunter, or tamer, please go to this side of the room," she requested, outstretching her hand to the right. "Don't worry if one of the things I mentioned isn't above 60% or three of them are but one is far lower. Just go with the majority please. Thank you."

People began moving like cattle. Interestingly, it seemed as though people who had gravitated towards each other were being pulled to opposite sides of the room. I wondered how much they shared about their preferences up front or if they were drawn to folks who were best suited towards them.

In any case, I made my way over to the Sub side. According to my results, I was 93% submissive, 70% prey, 64% brat, and 54% masochist. This seemed accurate. As long as the other participants were honest, I was likely to find someone who I was at least sexually compatible with. This might be fun for more than a laugh.

Once we were separated, they had all of us ladies sit on one side of a long table. All the gentlemen that were in our group were to follow her to the other side. When she returned a few moments later, she had all the males from the Dom

211

group. She explained that we'd have five minutes with each man before a bell would ring. Each of us was wearing a number. If we liked a guy, we'd write down his number on the note pad in front of us at our station. If they liked us, they were to write down our number. At the end of the night you'd have a list of the people who chose you with contact information of their choosing.

It sounded simple enough and it wasn't nearly as intimidating as I thought it'd be. Knowing how shitty my memory is, I decided to give each number a star rating on a 1 to 5 scale and try to jot down a few notes about them so I could remember who was who.

The bell to commence was rung and a ruggedly handsome man sat down in front of me.

He jumped right in, "You ever done this before?"

"Nope."

"Me neither. What got you in the door?"

"My crazy friend."

"So you're here with someone?"

"Yeah, but her crazy ass is over there with the Dommes."

"Ahh. I see. That's smart to come with a friend. I'm here alone."

I'm not sure what else he said but I couldn't wait for his time to be up. Maybe he was a Dom that needed to warm up, but this was speed dating. You've got to microwave it a bit.

The next two weren't all that interesting either. It was as if they were afraid to come on too strong or not afraid of anything. There was no middle ground. I just wanted to chat with a normal fellow who liked spanking and choking and shit.

So far it'd been 25 minutes into it and I'd had five dates. There were only 12 men on this line-up. I'd have to do something to get these guys comfortable or at the very least begin doing ridiculous things to entertain myself until this was over.

Number five slid into my station after the bell rang and began asking me questions about what I was doing later.

"Uhh, I'm not sure, I'll have to see what my friend is up for."

"Come on. Ditch her and leave with me. All the other girls here look okay, but it's clear you're the hottest one. If I wait until the end of the night, you'll have forgotten all about me and I'll miss out on the opportunity to tie you up and stuff your throat with my cock."

"Is that so?" I said coolly.

"Don't tell me you're scared of having my stiff eight inches crammed down your throat."

I grabbed one of the oversized dick shaped lollipops adorning the table, unwrapped it, and pushed the entire thing deep into my throat.

He grabbed himself beneath the table. "Mmphh. Yeah, you dirty bitch. I knew you could handle it. My cock is thicker than that though. It won't be that easy for you."

I pulled the lollipop out.

"I can gargle peanut butter with this golden throat, Daddy."

I caught the peripheral views of the previous gentlemen 1–4 looking perplexed by what he must have said to get that kind of reaction out of me, and a few glances from 7–12 who suddenly became more interested in me than the woman sitting directly across from them.

"I would leave here with you right now. Ram my cock in all your holes, you filthy bitch. You'd like that huh?"

"Oh you know it. I'd get on my knees and..."

Ding!

Time was up, thank goodness. I made a note on my pad to avoid #5 and gave him a zero star rating. I had no interest in having his cock rammed anywhere.

Number 6 slid into the seat; his dark eyes were beguiling.

"Hello," I squeaked out.

His voice rumbled like thunder and commanded even more attention than his presence, which was saying a lot. "Good evening. I have a list of questions varying from G-Rated to X-Rated, feel free to skip as many as you'd like."

"Finally, sounds interesting."

"Coffee or tea?"

"Tea."

"Cats or dogs?"

"Dogs."

"You know any other languages?"

"Spanish, French, and I'm learning ASL."

"What food do you crave most often?"

"Pizza!"

"Top three favorite movies?

"Closer, What Dreams May Come, and A Bronx Tale."

"Scariest thing you've ever done?"

"Ziplining in Costa Rica. We were up super high."

"Where's the coolest place you've ever traveled?"

"Cuba."

"Where would you travel with a group of your closest friends and family?"

"Mauritius"

"Where would you travel with a spouse?"

"Bora Bora."

"What's the first thing you would do if you woke up as a man?"

"If it were temporary, I'd just be peeing and cumming into any and everything I could get my hands on. If it were permanent, have a good cry to mourn my womanhood and then become an advocate for women since men tend to listen to other men more than women."

"Into being degraded or humiliated?"

"Very much."

"Leather or lace?"

"Lace."

"Hand or paddle?"

"Hand."

"Spreader bar or cuffs?"

"Cuffs"

"Silk ropes or ties?"

"Ropes."

"Safe word of choice?"

"Fuchsia."

"Fuchsia?"

"My second favorite F-word."

"Shall I assume Fuck is the first?"

"Nope. Flick." I accentuated the L in the word.

"Cheeky."

I looked back and grabbed a hunk of my ass.

"Very."

He resumed his line of questioning.

"Spit or swallow?"

"Gargle it so he sees, then swallow."

"What was that stunt you pulled with the lollipop for?"

"You noticed?"

"Isn't that why you did it?"

"I did it to entertain myself. I was bored."

"I'd love to bore you, but I think you'd find it impossible."

"I'm inclined to believe you. This has been the most interesting part of my night thus far."

"Good. I aim to please... at all times."

"Well..."

Ding!

Oh well, that one went entirely too fast.

"It was a pleasure to meet you, number 9," he said, extending his hand, staring into my soul.

"The pleasure was all mine, number 6."

He shifted to the next girl, but I couldn't keep my eyes off of him. I felt bad only half listening to number 7 but I was shamelessly eavesdropping on 6's conversation with the next girl.

He asked her different questions. Her answers seemed boring to me, but I had no idea what he liked.

Poor number 7 just stared at me hopelessly. He'd seen me deep-throat a lollipop for number 5 and I couldn't stop staring at 6. He probably felt like it was his fault. I tried to redirect my focus back to him, beginning by asking a few questions.

"So do you like to travel?"

"Nope."

"Are you close with your family?"

"Not really."

"What brings you here?"

"Was hoping to find an openly kinky chick."

"Any luck so far?"

"Not really."

"Hmm."

We spent the last minute in complete, excruciatingly uncomfortable silence.

Ding!

Thank goodness.

Numbers 8, 9 & 10 were interesting, but not really what I was into physically.

Number 11 took a methodical approach and asked to see my tablet readout.

He was 100% Dom, 100% hunter, 97% Tamer, 75% degrader and 0% masochist. On paper, he was my pussy's prince charming. He was friendly, but you could sense the intensity in him was just beneath the surface.

He looked over my sheet and smiled. "You're very bratty."

It was my turn to smile. "Very."

"I would tame that right out of you. You'd be a good girl for me."

"How so?"

Ding!

I wanted to kick that damn bell. The timing was always off. It was always time to move on when things got interesting and never time to go when I desperately needed an out.

I wrote down 11 with 5 stars and a few notes.

12 slid in and he was very funny but I got more of a friend vibe from him. Nothing about his demeanor made me want to remove clothes, let alone submit. People were different behind closed doors though.

When it was all over, the organizers sent us to our respective areas to tally up matches. We were going to receive our results by text or email, whichever we selected at the beginning of the night.

Solana found me, gripped my hand and led me to the coat check swiftly.

"What's the matter?"

"Girl, this place is filled with a bunch of nut jobs. I liked one guy. The rest were super creepy. I don't want to linger and have to reject them on the spot.I want out of here."

"Okay."

We walked down the block to wait for our cab. It arrived in under five minutes much to Solana's relief. She climbed in the back and before I could set one foot in the vehicle, I felt a hand grab me.

Number 6! "I know we're supposed to wait. I hope you don't find my urgency invasive. If you do, you can just go with your friend and not look back, but..."

"Celeste, come on!" Solana interjected.

I looked to her, then back to him.

He continued, "See me? Later? Cash in on one of the only times *I've* ever begged for anything."

"I'll take your number."

"You'll have it already. I chose you."

Being this forward and breaking a rule created to prevent shit like this from happening would normally be off-putting, but I could tell he wasn't that guy. He just couldn't bear the thought of me not choosing him. He was a man accustomed to getting what he wanted, and he wanted me.

"So what are you asking for exactly?"

"I'm asking if you chose me; if you'll see me? If..."

"Celeste!"

"Damn Lana, give me a sec."

The driver scoffed and grumbled.

"I chose you too. I'll call you when I get home."

"Okay."

I climbed inside the car and he leaned in before I closed the door and apologized to everyone for the wait.

As soon as I shut the door, Solana started, "I told you they were some creeps. We should have went a few blocks over before requesting a ride. Well, at least you had attractive creeps."

"Not all of them. He wasn't a creep though. I liked him."

"Of course you did." She rolled her eyes. "Just be careful. That was a bit much for me. Respect the boundaries, Sir, even if you're fine."

"He was fine though." We high fived, cackling.

Our phones pinged simultaneously. The text results were in. Apparently I was a big hit. Everyone chose me except number 7. I wasn't surprised. I bet a lot of it had to do with that stupid lollipop stunt. They ranked them in order in terms of compatibility. Mine was: 11, 6, 10, 9, 8, 4, 2, 1, 3, 12, 5.

I was surprised 11 came in first place and not 6. Maybe he should get the first date. Make 6 sweat a bit. Oh but he'd have my number by now too. So much for that plan. Who should I go out with first?

11? Page 220
6? Page 223

Show and Tell

I decided to see how accurate the test results were. I hit up number 11. It said his name was Vincent.

He was available for dinner the following night. We made small talk, but regular conversation was choppy. Things only became fluid when sex was the topic of conversation. We were clearly sexually in sync, but not as aligned in other capacities. He may have been my pussy's prince charming, but he didn't arouse my other senses. The shit he was into and the way he looked made me want to abandon my dry spell and take him for a spin. In perfect time with our sexual synchronicity, he cut to the chase.

"Is your pussy as pretty as your face?"
"You should look at her and tell me."
"I have a fun way to see her up close and personal."
"Why are we still here talking about it?"

We grabbed the check and a short ride later, we were at his place.

It was very stereotypical kinky: paddles, whips, chains, cuffs, etcetera. There was a table beside some contraption I wasn't familiar with though. Maybe Vincent wasn't so standard kink after all.

"So I see you're already eyeing it?" he inquired from behind me.
"What is that?"
"It's how I'm going to get my close up. I can show you better than I can tell you."

That was all I needed to hear to spring into action.

In a flash I was wearing only a zealous smile. "Show me."

"Climb on the table."

In the time it took me to get situated on the table, he was undressed as well.

"Lie down. Face up. Head towards me."

I followed instructions.He rounded the table and stood near my feet.Then he clamped each ankle with a thick metal cuff.

He stood beside the contraption and slowly turned the attached crank.

I felt myself begin to slide towards him. "Oh!"

"Don't worry, I'll go slow."

He cranked until my body slipped away from the table and I was upside down. With each crank, my legs were pulled further apart. I was hanging like the letter Y.

He stopped and stood in front of me, gauging if the height was right for him to insert himself in my mouth. I wasn't down low enough. It didn't help that we had a substantial height difference.

"I knew it'd be pretty." he remarked gazing between my open thighs.

"All the blood is going to rush to my head like this!"

"Then I suggest you make me cum fast."

He cranked me into position and stuffed himself into my mouth before bowing into me.

He hooked his arms under my thighs and gripped my ass tight so I wouldn't sway too much.

I hugged his thighs, sucking until my nose was pressed against his sac. When I swirled my tongue and then began to hum, I felt his knees weaken.

He wasn't about to be outdone so easily. He nursed from me like my nectar was healing.Shaking his head back and forth fervently completely engulfed, I nearly lost consciousness. He was right. I had better get him off fast. He released one of my legs to grip my hair. He stood on tiptoe to gain some leverage and pumped into my mouth. He cradled my head, pile driving my throat. He hadn't abdicated his responsibility to get me off either. My thighs quivered and I would have been full on thrashing had he not been gripping me so tight.

I would have warned him I was a squirter but my mouth was full. Thankfully my spraying turned him on and inspired him to do the same. He lifted my head up so I wouldn't choke, and hastily turned the crank so I'd feel the earth beneath me again.

He leaned against the table, staring at me down on the floor. Before he even fully caught his breath he said, "Now, we've got to do 96."

"Is that you hanging up this time?"

"Nope, it's completely different."

"How?"

"I can show you better than I can tell you."

222

'Lest you forget

Due to his forwardness, I assumed 6, whose real name I learned was Sabian, would want to jump right into sex. That wasn't the case at all. We ended up linking up that first night and going to a diner for breakfast. He ordered chicken and waffles. I had a stack of chocolate chip pancakes. Afterwards, we drove up to Hoku Overlook. He took some blankets and lined his trunk's bed with them, and we hopped in the back and did some star gazing. He had an app on his phone that located constellations and gave some astronomical information about them. We made out under the stars like teens, just tongue kissing and light petting. It felt sensual and innocent. It was a wonderfully romantic evening.

Our second date, we went to a park. We sat on the swings and learned about each other's family. He came from a large close-knit family. I had one brother, and my parents were divorced and couldn't stand to be in the same room. He was the middle child and lamented about being neglected. I teased him for "classic middle behavior." He told me I'd see when I was around them. Then he paused like it was too soon to mention meeting family. I lightened the mood by telling him they'd probably like my freckled face more than him. He seemed to relax after that.

"I like that freckled face," he smiled.

"Meh, I've never cared for them. I used to get made fun of for them."

"I want to kiss every one of those freckles."

"We'd be here all night!"

"And?"

He began kissing my face, slowly drifting to my lips. Another long make out session ensued but ended before becoming sexual. It was refreshing. I was enjoying getting to know him. He ended the night with a tender forehead kiss, saying, "'Lest, get some rest." I loved that he had a pet name for me already. My friends shortened Celeste to Cee, or something completely unrelated. He was the only one to call me Lest. I loved seeing the way it rolled off his tongue.

Our third date, he brought me to one of his shows. He was part of a band named Ryot. As the lead singer, his stage name was Ryot. They were good enough to be signed, but preferred to keep their day jobs. Music was just a passion of theirs. It showed on that stage. The night I came, they were doing an acoustic version of all their fan favorites. He sat on a stool, strumming his guitar, belting soulful ballads and I was in awe of him. I stood in the first row swooning like a groupie. He may not have been pressuring me for sex, but I wanted to toss my panties on stage and myself on top of him. That night was looking like the night.

They closed the show with Sabian announcing a new song. Hell, they were all new to me. I was sure I'd love it too. He shared with the audience that the name of the song was "Lest you forget."

My heart palpitated. I didn't want to make some vain presumption, but it seemed like this was not a coincidence and this song was going to be about me. I tuned back in to have my assumption confirmed:
Under wild circumstances
Love has given second chances
Moment I saw your freckled face
Beaming under starried space
I knew, I knew

Early on, yes I know
No telling how this thing will go
The stars will recall that fateful night
Remind you, if we ever fight
I see perfection in the things you fret
Lest, you forget
Lest, you forget
'Lest, don't forget
'Lest, don't forget

Tears streamed down my face, and apparently right into my panties, dissolving them. If there were any lingering thoughts on if we were doing it that night, there weren't anymore. I met the band and sped through small talk. I wanted out of there and into his bed, or couch, or shower. I was in heat and ready to put the fire out wherever. I whispered in his ear, "Your place, or mine?"

"Mine." He smiled wide.

We made the short drive to his place and it was impressively clean. It was fairly minimalist, but seemed to suit him. He had some interesting art on the walls I'd ask him about some other time.

"I'm going to tie you up."

I smiled approvingly.

In his bedroom, he had a black accent wall with a quote in some other language on it.

Once I was naked, he used some leather straps to tie me to the bedposts. He walked away after retrieving a candle. He struck a match and the scent of sulfur filled the air before being replaced with Jasmine.

"Is that for mood or are you going to put wax on me?"

"Both. This is a massage candle. It doesn't get as hot as regular candles. You'll like it."

I watched him close one eye, trying to drip with accuracy. First drop landed square in the middle of my nipple. The next was a bit off center.

He let some pool in my navel. It was still warm enough to warrant a slight wince, but it felt good. I found myself closing my eyes, preferring to anticipate where the next drop would go. Writhing beneath his calculated spills, I caught a glimpse of my shadow dancing on the wall in the flickering light. He let it drip inside my inner thighs. He began at my knees and worked his way up. I was afraid he'd try it on my pretty little pussy.

As the wax stiffened just outside my opening, he grabbed his stiffening member and rubbed the tip on my pulsing clit. It was thick and radiating heat. It caused me to squirm more than the wax. I ached for him desperately. I arched my back, trying to will him to enter me.

"You want it?"

"Yes!" I whimpered.

"Say it."

"I want it!"

"Again."

"I need it. Please! Sabian. I want to feel you inside me."

He plunged deep, kissing my gasping mouth. With long, fluid strokes, he moved his hips in slow waves that immersed him in my wetness. My thighs trembled as he reached a space within me that had been untouched before.

I cried his name out towards the starry skies that belonged to us now.

He replied with feral growls, unleashing his creamy spunk.

Once he untied me, he told me he was making new constellations connecting my freckles with wax, and naming them after places we'd been. "This one is Hyde. Not only because you cannot hide your beauty, but that's the name of the park we went to on our second date when I knew you'd be mine. I actually knew the moment I met you, but after you were willing to see me I thought you might actually have me.

"This one," he tilted me gently to one side, "This one is called Ryot's belt. This is where I'll aim to smack with my belt."

"Like Orion's belt?" I giggled.

"Precisely. You'll be sure to preface my name with the 'o' without reminder then?"

"Of course," I answered happily, wriggling in his lap. "Why candle wax?" I inquired.

"We light candles on cakes and altars and many things we love and celebrate. Why should your body be any different?"

We spent the rest of the night making love and constellations.

From that moment on, I never looked at him, or my freckles the same again. For it was impossible not to love them both.

Lest I forget.

Drilled

I didn't have a high threshold for pain. So when I suspected I might have a cavity, I asked to be squeezed in immediately. I didn't know how long it takes for things like root canals to become necessary, and I wasn't interested in finding out the hard way.

I'd recently moved to the opposite side of town so I asked my co-worker London if she knew a good dentist nearby. She spoke highly of Dr. Zahn so I looked him up and begged to be squeezed in as soon as possible. His receptionist said Thursday at ten, and I jumped at the opportunity.

After I got over the first nauseating wave of antiseptics and chemicals consistent with every dentist office invading my nose, when I opened the door I walked over to the receptionist Wynter behind the glass sliding window so I could sign in.

In return, she gave me a shitload of paperwork to sign relieving them of any responsibility should they fuck up, as well as paperwork to tell them any ailment every branch of my family tree might suffer from or thing they might be allergic to. They requested my insurance card, photo ID, a vial of my blood, and my first-born. Always a joy to be a new patient at any facility.

I spotted an outlet at the end of a row of chairs and sat next to it so I could charge my phone while I signed my life away. I put my phone on airplane mode so it would charge quicker. Once I filled out my stack of forms, I searched through the array of magazines on the table. I found a magazine my parents got me a subscription for as a kid and thumbed through it for a walk down memory lane. I gasped when I got to the hidden pictures page, recalling my efforts to find all the items with my mom when I was five. That part was my favorite. I was so engrossed in finding a flashlight on the page I didn't hear my name being called.

"Tahliah?" she sang again.

"Oh my goodness, I'm so sorry! I was so caught up..." I quickly wrapped my phone cord around my fingers, popping it and my phone into my purse.

The smell was stronger in the back and threatened to give me a headache. I hoped I could keep it at bay. I had to take a few x-rays and then I sat in the chair, bibbed and waiting anxiously. When he came in, he looked surprised to see me.

"You know, Tahliah is not a common name, or so I thought. I have another patient by that name and assumed it was her and... well, never mind. What brings you in today?"

"I think I feel a small hole in my tooth but I'm not sure."

"Which side?"

I opened my mouth and pointed up and to the left.

He took a small mirror from his tray of tools and said, "Let's have a look inside."

The moment he leaned in, I felt his penis thickening up against my chest. He backed away quickly and I could tell it was purely accidental, but hellooooo doctor!

I was sporting a 36H cup. My girls bump into things more often than they don't.

He didn't acknowledge what happened verbally, but he tried to look from another angle.

Same problem. Only that time I pushed my chest out further, brushing up against him. I didn't see a band on his finger, why not have a little fun?

He peered into my mouth for much longer than I'm sure he had to, softly grazing his growing erection across my breast. My nipples hardened, not one to miss the stiffening party.

"Willeaux & Brooklyn are ordering from Ji's Pot, you want something?" Wynter asked, peeking her head in, waving a menu.

"Well!" he declared, "It looks like you may be getting a cavity. Nothing a quick filling won't solve." He was breathing heavily, eyes wild and flushing more each passing second. "Wyn, I think I'm good. I plan on taking a long lunch today so I can run out if need be. Thanks."

Her inquiry forced us to think about what had been going on. I thought it best to keep it patient related and not draw any attention to what was happening.

"Do I have to get a needle?" I wasn't a big fan of needles. A needle in my mouth sounded like a nightmare. My legitimate fear was enough to break the tension.

"You don't *have* to get one. Most people generally do, but it's a relatively pain-free procedure."

"I'd rather not. Can I get it today?"

He stared at me like he was mentally answering yes, and not in reference to the filling.

The lingering question ballooned, filling the room.

"Yeah... yeah, umm, I'll just have Wynter get us set up and I'll be right back."

Wynter came in, laid out a few things and stepped out quietly. I had filthy thoughts sprinting back and forth in my mind about Dr. Zahn.

When he returned, he closed the door before getting to work. He leaned in and I could tell he was waiting to see if I brushed back or hunched my shoulders to pull away. I pushed my bust against his thickness, my silent acceptance to our blatant disregard for doctor/patient acceptable behavior.

He maintained a steady graze of his throbbing cock against my breast. The carnal part of me wanted to rip off his pants and my shirt and feel the heat of his warm thickness become fully enveloped in my plush mounds while I sucked the tip. But there was also something so incredibly tantalizing about this slow pace and its prohibition. He took his time working in my mouth, moaning softly as he did. A small puddle formed in my panties as my arousal became so intense I could no longer fight the urge to touch myself.

I quietly unzipped the side zipper on my trousers and slipped a hand inside my drenched panties. Once I found my sweet spot, I let out a soft "ahh" that made Dr. Zahn look down to see what was going on. I saw his eyes roll back before his head did the same. He shook his head back to his senses and focused on the inside of my mouth. But he was pressing against my breast, getting more friction and grunting softly.

I wanted to unbutton my blouse and give him some visual stimulation and myself some skin-on-skin contact. I was afraid that that would be too hard to conceal if someone walked in, but I was wearing a bib and the door was closed. Fuck it. I was going for it.

As I shifted the bib aside, I could see him using the overhead mirror to watch me. I unbuttoned one, he bit his lip. I unbuttoned a second, he stopped working in my mouth altogether. I pulled one breast out just enough to see nipple and most of my areola spilling out on top of the cup. The instant his eye made contact with my pierced nipple, I thought he'd cum right in his pants. I slid my hand back into my pants, keeping the other free just in case I needed to slide the bib over.

At that point, he was bent over so far he was nearly mounting me, rubbing his crotch over my bare breast.

He couldn't think clearly enough to do the routine procedure anymore. He was barely maintaining the "rouse." He was just pressed against me, grinding my breast. I knew he ached to pull his dick out as bad as I wanted him to, but that would be too much to try to conceal if we were caught.

At one point I had to grab it. It felt like it was calling my name. At first touch it throbbed, and I stopped caring about being caught.

Just then we both heard the knob of the door begin to turn and I quickly covered myself with the bib and pulled my hand out of my pants. It was Wynter again but she couldn't see me. My back was to the door and she only popped her head in again. "Dr. Dewhymn is on line three. I told him you were with a patient, but he said you guys have been playing phone tag. Wanted to make sure it wasn't urgent."

"It isn't."

"Okay. You want this closed?"

"Yeah, the drill in room two was bothering her."

"Okay."

We both heaved a sigh of relief, but realized we couldn't go on like this.

"I'm pretty much done but I..." I could tell he was searching for the words to express his desire.

I shook my head no. "I have to..." there was something about saying it, acknowledging it, that was too much. The vocalization somehow made it inappropriate.

"How?"

"Lock the door."

"It doesn't"

"Push something against it!"

I don't know what had come over me. I wasn't normally that demanding, but I wasn't normally that aroused either.

"I'll tell Wynter we have to discuss something private and... I don't know, when the blood rushes back to my head maybe I can think of something."

"Okay."

Option 1 Page 234
Option 2 Page 236

Cheat Code

He delivered some story that he decided would suffice and rushed back into the room.

"Okay."

"I should warn you I have quite the gag reflex."

"Not a problem. An old dentist's trick is to push a pressure point in the middle of your left hand to suppress your gag reflex. Watch." With a re-gloved hand, he inserted and pressed my tongue in the back of my mouth near my uvula. Naturally, I gagged. Then he tucked my thumb in the palm of my left hand and closed the other fingers around it to apply pressure to the spot. Then he repeated the action. I didn't gag!

"Now for a bonus we can use the topical anesthetic we use prior to the Novocain needle. It won't hurt at all. Promise." He rubbed some on his index and middle finger and pressed it on the roof of my mouth and swiped some across my tongue. "I doubt we'll have a problem now!"

I needed every trick in the book. His print was divinely deceptive. He was packing even more than I thought! He held it in his hand and rubbed it across my bare breast. "I wanted to feel this so bad. Shit. They're so soft...."

My hand was back in my panties, pushing the button.

He rubbed the head across my lips and asked what I'm sure he requested of his patients often. "Say ahh!"

He slid inside and I squeezed my hand tightly, amazed by how deeply I could take him with my new cheat code. He ground into my mouth slowly, holding my head like we had all the time in the world. Every so often, he'd grope my breasts adoringly. He was so gentle. I wanted to feel that touch while he stroked inside me. I pulled him out of my mouth long enough to make that request.

He agreed. "Bend over."

He pumped the chair up till it was the perfect height for me to kneel in so he could enter me. He slid in and I gripped the arm of the chair to stabilize myself. His girth alone was enough to make me weak, but the length made me put all my core strength to use.

He humped me slow and held my waist firmly. He was in so deep I felt tears brimming in my eyes. Each stroke massaged my G-spot and I was struggling to remain silent. Quick bursts of air through my nostrils and biting down on my curled-in lips were mostly doing the trick, but it was impossible to be completely silent. His dick was amazing. Each time I came, I was a dripping mess all over his chair. I felt his pace quickening and I knew he was going to cum soon. We were already being insanely reckless, but the least we could do is pull out. It felt so good that the faster he pumped, the further away my "pull out" seemed to be.

His grip was getting tighter. I had to do something or it was happening. "Cum on my face," I requested. He pulled out. I quickly turned around, and he jerked a thick, creamy load of nut on my cheeks and smeared it over my lips. Thank goodness I was wearing a bib!

Instrumental

He returned with deviant intent in his eyes. He was no longer interested in maintaining facades.

"Get naked," he commanded.

Instead of undressing as well, he stood by the door watching me. It wasn't until I stepped out of my panties that he walked toward me, palming my bottom when I bent over.

Briefly, he pushed his finger inside me. He sniffed then sucked my juices, grinning his approval. He began prepping the area like he was about to work on my mouth. His bustling lasted about two minutes, but it was long enough for me to begin feeling foolish standing there stark naked with him fully clothed.

When he finished he asked me to sit. I sat on a little pad he created on the seat. He told me to lie back and relax. He sat on the small rolling stool nearby before delving face first between my thighs. He buried himself deep into my folds, nuzzling before licking softly. He suckled my clit gently, coaxing my orgasm with precise deliberation.

I heard some shuffling around. I peeked down to see Dr. Zahn fumbling with one hand on the nearby dental tray. It didn't ruin his attentiveness to me, so I went back to relaxing and receiving. He used one of those metal instruments to hit my nipple ring, creating an odd vibration that I could only describe as a sensual tickle. He repeated this on both nipples while never breaking stride with his tongue. I was very impressed with his multitasking skills.

Suddenly he pulled his mouth away and I felt cool water cascading over my lips. He parted them so the water could have direct access to my clit. He was using the air and water syringe as a sexual tool!

236

He slowly raised the temperature and pressure. It was like a mini showerhead, caressing my hot spot. He switched the temperature back to cold, heightening my senses. Then he covered my pussy with his warm mouth again and it was so sensitive I could barely stand it. He used his thick tongue, pressed it hard against me and licked my orgasm right out of my body. I held his head, shuddering with rapturous aftershocks.

He knocked a tray of probes to the floor while grabbing for his own. Holding tight to my hips, he pushed in and I gasped on entry. Instead of covering my mouth, he shoved his fingers inside it. First, fish-hooking my cheek, next caressing my lips with his thumb, then he pushed his fingers deep into my mouth for me to suck. I gagged.

"Sorry," I choked out, "my gag reflex is bad."

"Not if I also choke you on the outside."

He gripped my neck and then pushed his fingers inside my mouth again.

It worked!

He began to release my neck until I clasped my hand around his.

"Harder," I whispered.

He grinned diabolically while clamping on my throat. He knew then he didn't have to be so gentle with me.

He braced my thigh and started banging me hard and fast the way I love it. My juicy breasts were bouncing so hard they were hitting me in the face. With each thrust he moaned softly. They turned me on. I rolled my hips, using my pelvic floor strength to suck his dick with my pussy. I gripped his ass, digging all ten nails into his flesh. His legs began to tremor and his breathing was erratic and heavy. I bucked beneath him, fucking him from below. He couldn't hold out any longer. I assumed he'd pull out, but he held me tight and came deep inside me, twitching and jerking until he rested in my bosom nearly out of breath.

"For someone so afraid of needles, I'm surprised you have these done. These nipples weren't pierced with magic dust."

"I got them on a dare."

"You, daring? Never would have guessed."

We got up and pretended to be well-behaved adults as best we could.

He walked me down the hall to the front desk and asked the receptionist to schedule my follow-up soon.

He tried to look professional and innocent as we said our goodbyes but that deviant spark in his eyes remained.

I couldn't wait to see it again.

In just one visit he cured my fear of dentists. London was right. Dr. Zahn was good!

Babydoll

"Communication is key." We hear that phrase so often that I believe it's lost its message, and just became a thing we mimic or only understand logically. I don't think we apply it emotionally, or put it in action as an essential need for a cohesive experience with our partners. Such was the case for me and Barnett.

There was an unspoken emotional distance and our conversations seemed more forced with each passing day. He would lie next to me in bed and if his skin brushed against mine as he tossed and turned, that was the only way I felt him. I didn't know if his sex drive just took a nosedive and he was embarrassed or if he simply wasn't attracted to me. I made some hints and tried to make some advances sometimes, but the rejection pulled us further apart. I daydreamed about being his plaything: a virtual blow up doll. I wouldn't have to figure out what he wanted, he would just take it. He would hungrily ravish me until he was satisfied. I didn't know how to fulfill him on my own anymore.

The day I walked in on him fucking a fake pussy, I was immediately enraged. Here I thought he was struggling with erectile dysfunction or something but he had no problems fucking, he just didn't want to fuck me.

I stormed off silently to the top drawer of my nightstand. "Here." I returned dangling my handcuffs in front of his face. "You want to feel like you're fucking an inanimate object? That gets you off? Hmm?"

He looked intrigued but still nervous. Unsure if the question was rhetorical, he waited to speak.

"I like feeling used. You can absolve yourself from all responsibility of achieving my pleasure in any capacity. Your sole purpose will be to get off with my body as you see fit."

I undressed quickly & lay beside the bed with one cuff secured around my small wrist. "The moment I hear that second cuff rasp closed I'll be your fucking *Toy*," I said seething, enunciating the word toy. My name is Latoya and he affectionately referred to me as "his Toy." I was going to be all the toy that he needed.

He approached slowly, unsure if this was one of those crazy woman tests he was about to fail. He took the risk anyway. He secured the second cuff.

I let my eyes glaze over, a silent admission of my physical transition to be just a plaything. He swept my hair into a makeshift pony, wrapping the excess tresses around his hand to get a good grip. I didn't make a sound as I opened my mouth wide, inviting. For a few moments he watched, waiting for a quizzical expression to flash across my face about the delay or what he was going to do, but I remained expressionless. Drool flowed freely from my lips onto his penis cascading over his erection.

"If you're going to replace that toy, you will be treated as such. It's bigger than not thinking of your pleasure. It's not thinking of you as a being who needs breath or time restraints. I'm going to make you regret offering yourself up as a replacement."

He shoved my head down into his lap while lifting his pelvis upward. Thrusting vigorously, he placed his other hand on my head, pushing down until my lips were on his pubic mound. I made no sounds as I struggled for breath. He jerked off in my throat, waiting for me to choke. Tears gushed mercilessly from my eyes but I wouldn't break.

When he yanked me off his cock, he waited for a gasp but I uttered no sounds, not even a groan. My chest heaved up and down as I caught my breath, but I refused to show signs of a struggle.

He eyed me with one brow raised, evidently impressed and turned on by my dedication. I hadn't seen that look in his eyes since the first night he fucked me.

"Normally I'd think about waiting until I saw your chest relax so I'd know you caught your breath. But you don't have to think of toys, babydoll."

So he filled my mouth, drowning me with his dick. My head bobbed up & down while he simultaneously humped my mouth. His eyes began rolling back, a sign that he'd be cumming soon. I prepared to take his load in my mouth and relaxed my throat. But he pulled me off his dick suddenly & the suction of my mouth made a pop like a freshness seal on a juice bottle.

He threw me back on the bed, spread my legs. He spit on his fingers before pushing them inside my already soaked pussy. He yanked me towards him by my full thighs & plunged inside me. He fucked me in deep, hard strokes. He was grunting like a beast as he pushed in & out of me. He wrapped his hands in my hair again. He called me his fucking slut &told me that my fat ass pussy belonged to him. That I belonged to him. He gripped my ass as if to remind me that was his too. His fingers were sinking into my pillowy ass, just as he sank deeper into me. He couldn't hold out any further.

"Ugghhhhh" I could feel the cum shooting out into me.

I blinked back into focus after my eyes rolled down from ecstasy as I transitioned into the woman he knew. He stared waiting for my response, gauging if this was too far, if I viewed him differently.

Breathlessly he broke the silence first. "I don't think you've ever said anything as insanely erotic as not making a fucking peep."

A bright smile spread across my face. "I wish we'd done this sooner."

That day became our kinkiversary. We got a new lease on our sex life. All along I wanted to be a fuck toy and he wanted a life-size doll to fuck. We had the same fetish, but were too afraid to communicate about it. We couldn't stop talking about it and even found others like us. I was never drawn to being a particular kind of doll, I was more intrigued by the idea of relinquishing complete control to my partner. He didn't have a favorite kind of doll to fuck, so we had different styles for different moods. Each of the "dolls" had names so when he was in the mood, he'd tell me to get "dolled up" and say the name of whichever doll he was in the mood for.

When I was not "in play" I kept a dildo pacifier in my mouth, a dong in my pussy and a plug in my ass, sitting as motionless as possible on the toy chest beside our bed. I had to keep my holes open and ready for Mister.

If he wanted Anne, I knew I had to transform into a rag doll who was going to be roughly tossed about. If he called for Kathy, I knew he wanted a pull-string doll. In lieu of a string on my back, he would flip me over, remove my frilly cotton bloomers and stuff my ass with anal beads and pull them out one bead at a time, and the only phrase I was allowed to utter was "Yes, Sir." If he requested China, I knew he wanted me to be a porcelain doll. I wore abnormally long lashes with my big circle contact lenses, very bright ivory foundation and powder, heavy pink blush, draw on lips in the middle of my lips so they looked tiny and delicate instead of my typical full pout.

I actually started to prefer that one to some of the others because I loved seeing the transformation from this perfectly placed makeup to a beautiful smeared mess when he was finished with me. I stared at myself in the mirror for a bit, reliving and imagining each moment that led to this disarray of chaos reflecting back at me before cleaning myself up. Other times I got to have more movement. When I dressed with a giant wind up key on my back, I marched stiffly but as he wound me up, I evoked nights I spent in my favorite dancehall spot back in the day, where I'd tick and wine until the sun came up, and put those moves to use to grind robotically in my lover's lap or wherever he chose.

When we hosted Dolly tea parties with our other Dollification friends, he was a ventriloquist host and had me sit in his lap after all our guests arrived then push his hand up my ass. Some made requests to play with his doll. If he was willing to take them up on an offer, such as asking if they could cum on my face, he expanded his fingers inside my ass and I knew to nod my head yes before opening my mouth to be used.

That evening, I sat on the wooden toy chest beside our bed with all holes plugged waiting until Mister arrived home in roughly a half hour. I wondered who he'd call upon.

Marionette Doll? Page 245
Blow Up Doll? Page 247

Get Dolled Up Marion

This particular scenario required a lot of set up but the payoff was definitely worth it. Barnett used ropes to tie my joints: elbows, wrists, knees, ankles and hook them up to the ceiling using a pulley. They were tied in such a way that from his seated position, he could control my limbs. He also used a special red rope that wasn't attached to any of the others to tie around my neck.

Once I was all tied up, he sat himself in his big black chair. I stood in front of him, waiting for him to move me as he wished. Usually he took turns pulling each string to remind himself which was attached to each limb. I flailed about clumsily trying not to laugh at how silly it felt. Once he was certain he was re-acclimated enough with the strings, he began using them for our pleasure.

He lifted both of my legs up and pulled his chair closer so he was directly beneath me. Then he dropped me into his lap in the straddle position. He allowed my right arm to dangle by not making those ropes so taunt so I could insert him inside. He yanked my arm back up so quickly after I completed the task he nearly smacked us both in the face with my hand. I held my breath to stifle my laughter. He pulled my knees and ankles up so I was spread eagle. I couldn't do any movement of my own but that was fine by him.

He wrapped the ropes around his hands to keep me in that position while he cradled my ass and fucked me spread eagle in the air. He let my arms relax and drape around his neck. He began tugging the red rope, yanking my throat towards the ceiling. Watching my veins bulging, eyes watering, and my light gasps for breath turned him on. The more my air was restricted, the more my body tensed. My pussy clenched up and milked him.

He released all the ropes, allowing all my limbs to embrace him. There we stayed, clinging to one another until our limbs tingled, alerting us to climb into bed.

Get Dolled Up Heiran

I hadn't been Heiran in a while. I was looking forward to it. For her, I donned a full body latex suit that included my hands, feet, and face that resembled a blow up doll. There were rubber holes in the crotch, ass, and mouth. For this, mental preparation played a larger part because I had to be completely still and put myself in the mindset that he could and would use me in any way for any amount of time that he chose. It was less about being able to move mechanically or doll-like. I had to pretend I was filled with air to the fullest extent. No talking, no moving, nothing. I kept my eyes and mouth wide. The hardest part was trying to maintain a vapid expression when one, or more, of your holes was being pounded out. Perhaps that is why it was one of my favorites. It was reminiscent of how this whole thing started, me lying motionless and slowing my breathing, trying my very best not to be anthropomorphic in any way.

As Barnett went off to prepare in whatever ways he does, I gathered my suit and lube to be the ultimate blow up doll. I rubbed some nipple stimulating cream on beneath my suit. It would be my own secret challenge to remain doll-like while my already sensitive nipples' sensation was be heightened.

It appeared I wasn't the only one who wanted to kick it up a notch. Barnett came in wielding a wand. He knew that was my weakness. We usually only used that when we weren't doing doll play. I couldn't fathom staying still using that thing. My expression must have conveyed my thoughts.

"That's right. I'm putting my doll to the test. I'll be a little lenient, but not much."

I focused on mentally preparing myself to attempt to endure intense pleasure and maintain a stoic expression.

He couldn't wipe that smug look off his face. He was prematurely looking forward to punishing me for failure to remain aloof. I was determined to do my best to prove him wrong. I silenced my floating doubt and fell into a meditative state as I sunk into the bed. I stretched out my limbs, preparing for use.

He wasted no time in testing me and shoved the wand between my legs. I let my vibrations remain internal, careful not to let on how good it felt. He was more frustrated than impressed. I held on, my watering eyes and soaked pussy the only evidence I couldn't contain. He increased the power and my eyes were twitching uncontrollably but I wouldn't let the rest of my body move. I refused to make a sound. He switched the wand off, mounted my throat and shoved himself in my lubed mouth hole. He aggressively pile-drived my throat. I didn't budge. He climbed off, grabbed a pillow down near my ass, then set the wand on top of it. He flipped me over on top of it, turned the wand on, and pushed into my ass crack. He didn't go into the hole right away because he knew the teasing would incite me to squirm.

According to him, being inside my lubed, latex plump ass was a pleasure all its own within the confines of the tight hole the suit provided. My body trembled without permission.

Don't.

Don't.

I chanted internally, determined not to break character.

He grabbed my throat from behind and growled, "Give me."

His voice, the grasp on my throat, that wand, his request, any number of them may have been the culprit that did me in. Maybe all of them. I answered the call of my body to express its desire. I cried as I convulsed. Gasping breaths that steamed up my latex suit gave way to feral grunts and growls. I thrashed and screamed. I rode the wave of ecstasy until it exhausted me. Whatever punishment he would dole up would be well worth it. I unleashed every backed up emotion and freed my deepest erotic joy. My love unzipped me slowly and in the cool air that met my dewy skin, I anticipated hearing what my punishment would be.

He swiped away the hair sticking to my face, leaned in and whispered, "Thank you." I sank into a renewed sleep.

Hell of a Dilemma

I met Omari on what had to be the hottest day in Chicago.

Though I was armed with a cool slushy drink, I'd spiked it with vanilla flavored vodka for an extra kick.

It was also a good way to day drink and openly walk the streets without judgment, or conviction.

The sweltering heat was causing my thick thighs to rub together and make my seersucker romper creep up into my crotch.

I felt the sun baking my shoulders to a warm golden brown as beads of sweat trickled down my neck.

I was supposed to be meeting my co-worker at "the bean" in Millennium Park, but I'd just received a text that said she was running about forty minutes late.

I was slurping the slushy on a nearly empty stomach, which isn't a good idea even on a moderately tempered day.

Just as I was thinking she was going to have to link up with me during the dessert portion of the meal, Omari approached me.

His smile was disarming. "Excuse me, Miss..."

I was so lost in his chestnut eyes and lashes twice as long as mine I didn't hear a word he said after that.

"Should I assume you're a tourist and that is why my question perplexed you?"

"No. I'm sorry. I fear this sun is baking my brain. I spaced out. Could you repeat your question?"

"Well it seems as though the smarter option would be not to ignore that, and get you out of this heat."

"I was thinking that very thing myself. I was supposed to meet someone, but they're late."

"Your boyfriend? You know how it is in the Chi. Maybe I shouldn't stand too close."

"No, I don't have a boyfriend. I was waiting for a co-worker, a woman, her name is Trinity." I'm not sure why I was oversharing and babbling. I'd seen plenty of fine men in my 27 years of life.

"Hmm. And what is *your* name?"

"Lucy. My name is Lucy."

"Is that the fake name you've come up with to go along with your red hair? I'll change my name to Ricky if I have to."

"No." I chuckled, "Lucy is my real name. This is also my real hair, and actual hair color. Cheers to recessive genes!" I said, holding up my slushy. You don't often see brown girls with red hair, I'd give him that. "My mother was on the fence about what to name me. I was born at dawn and so originally she was going to name me just that. But Lucy means pretty much the same thing, and I had a head full of copper colored curls, and there you have it. So Ricky, what does everyone else call you? Namely, your mama."

"Well my mother calls me Tonk but that's a story for another time. My name is Omari. Would you like to get out of this heat?"

Trinity hadn't replied back yet, and I was feeling a buzz. Perhaps that was the very thing that made me take Omari up on his offer.

"I have reservations for a spot nearby."

"Sounds good to me."

We took the short trek to the restaurant where I planned to dine with Trinity. A cool blast of air conditioning welcomed us as soon as he opened the door.

The bubbly hostess asked if I had a reservation.

"Yes, under the surname Furr, like fur on a kitten."

"Yep! I see you right here. Follow me!"

She panned the room as though she was looking for someone before grabbing two menus and leading us just a few feet away.

Someone came along with a pitcher of ice water and filled our glasses almost immediately. Perhaps I looked as overheated as I felt. I snuck a glance at myself in my phone to be sure I hadn't completely unraveled. Thankfully I was holding up surprisingly well.

"So, Omari. You know my full name, what I do, a co-workers name, and why my mother named me this way. How about some reciprocity? What do you do?"

"I'm in a bit of a transitional period right now."

Sounds like he's unemployed.

"I was actually a registered nurse, but I'm in seminary school to become a priest."

I broke into a fit of laughter. When I opened my eyes, he was staring at me with an expression that read confused and bordered on offended.

"Oh! You were serious? Really? I just... I didn't know there were any Black priests, and I definitely know you can't date. I just thought... So how did you end up... Really?"

He seemed relieved that my questions were rooted in ignorance and not a question of his competence.

"Well I always felt this call to heal. That's why I became a nurse. But after having an accident of my own, I realized that the internal work—often times

252

your faith—was as big a part of your recovery. Sometimes, more so than physical therapy."

"Wow. So you had a life-altering accident and left a career in medicine, to follow priesthood?

"Yeah."

"That is... not what I expected you to say. So, not to toot my own horn here but I thought you were interested in me. Am I imagining this chemistry?"

"Well for starters, I'm not a priest just yet. I'm still learning to work on my desires obviously. Chemistry is natural and yes, I feel it too. To be honest, I've been deeply into my studies and mentoring this youth group at the church. I haven't had much of a social life. When I saw you today, I had to approach you. I was called to. I was just hoping to converse with you, be close to you, to drink in your smile."

Well heaven help me, a priest in the making had me blushing.

"So what happens after this? Can I still talk to you? I don't know the rules."

He laughed and that disarming smile enchanted me. "Of course we can still talk. I'm allowed to have friends."

"Friends you're called to and whose smile you want to drink in?" I said, mocking him.

"I've read nothing that says those specific things are against the rules."

"But you are supposed to be celibate, correct?"

"Yes."

"How do you do that? I mean, if you were always a virgin I could understand more, but how do you do it after you know what it's like?"

"Well a bishop will not even entertain ordaining you if you don't have a desire to be with women. It shows you're a healthy man. But it's not about suppressing those desires, but rather redirecting that energy to focus on your vow to the church."

"Do you get a night to get it all out of your system before you go off and marry the church? Like a Fat Tuesday bachelor party type of thing or something?"

He laughed heartily. "Not that I'm aware of, but that's a great idea."

My phone rang and it was Trinity. She was finally available.

"Sis, I had to eat without you, but you can join us for dessert."

"Us?"

"Yes, I met this gentleman named Omari and he joined me for lunch. I was starving!"

"Fine. I'll catch up with you another time. I want all the juicy details later."

"Bye Trinity!"I redirected my focus back to Omari. "Would you like dessert?"

"On one condition."

"What is that?"

"That we each choose one for each other. Write it down and show it to our waiter, and you close your eyes so I can let you taste it and I'll do the same."

"Can't say I've ever done that before. I'm down."

My options were crème brûlée, cheesecake, caramel cheesecake, devil's food cake, red velvet cake, and flan. I wanted the crème brûlée for myself, but I was ordering for him. He struck me as more of a red velvet kind of guy. We made our selections and

254

sent our waiter off after sharing our little game with him. When he returned, he told Omari to close his eyes before setting down his cake. I fed him a spoonful and he guessed it right away.

"I was hoping you chose that!"

Then the waiter had me close my eyes before setting my dessert in front of me and Omari gave me a spoonful.

"Crème brûlée!"I opened my eyes before he could confirm. "This is what I wanted! I can't believe you picked what I wanted."

We finished our respective desserts while I continued to ask him more questions than I probably should have. He never seemed annoyed, but rather extremely patient with my inquisitions.

Before leaving the restaurant we exchanged numbers and used them often over the period of a few weeks.

One Sunday night, he confessed his desire for me was increasing. He wasn't sure he could be around me.

I knew from the beginning I wanted more than a platonic friendship with him. I also knew from the start he was unavailable in that way, so I suppose I set myself up for this disappointment.

We had a "date" coming up for that Tuesday after his youth group class. I still very much wanted to see him.

"Can I still see you Tuesday?"

"Well yeah, but I don't think it should be as regular you know. I'm seeing you too frequently. I know I'm sending the wrong message and it's not fair to either of us."

My heart was broken. I had fallen for him quickly. Trinity had tried to warn me three times not to get too emotionally invested. Against my and her better judgment, I leapt head first. I was hell-bent on having Omari. Which way was best?

Plan A? Page 257
Plan B? Page 260

Hail Mary Pass

I met him at the church in my favorite fiery red dress. I deliberately arrived ten minutes late so I wouldn't chance running into any of the kids. The fact that it wasn't for young eyes was proof of how slutty this dress was, but I foolishly wanted to pull out all the stops if I was going to convince him not to cut me off.

When he saw me, he didn't speak. He stopped mid-stride. He looked at me like I personified every sin I secretly hoped I did.

I pulled a devil horn headband I had from an old Halloween costume and popped it on my head.

He laughed and that smile melted me.

"What? I needed something to hold up my halo." I batted my eyes innocently.

"Your halo, if you had one, would be filthy, and glowing red brighter than your hair and those horns."

I chuckled surveying the space. "Is that a confessional?"

"Indeed it is."

"I've never had confession. What's it like when someone confesses to you?"

"Oh I don't know. I'm not there yet. I've only given confession."

"Oooh, can I confess to you?

He reluctantly walked over, but I could tell he didn't really want to.

"I don't know, Lucy."

"Oh come on. At least I'd get to say I took your virginity in some way."

He exhaled deeply, but walked in.

It was darker than I imagined. You really couldn't see much through the lattice screen.

"How does it start?"

257

"You say 'Forgive me Father for I have sinned.'"

"Forgive me Daddy for I have sinned."

"Lucy!"

"Okay, okay. Forgive me Father for I have sinned. What next?"

"You say when your last confession was. For you, just say this is your first confession."

"Okay. This is my first confession. I'm in love with a man I cannot have. I want to honor his principles and support him, but that means sacrificing my own heart. I've never felt this way about anyone and I don't know what to do. The thought of letting him go brings me to my knees."

I sobbed softly.

"Pray while you're there. I... he may feel the same way, but has made a commitment. Like any other relationship, loyalty is important."

"I know it's selfish, but I want him. I want him to choose me. He doesn't have to do this. He can be a nurse again, and he can teach the youth group, and I'd wear stockings in a pew beside him every Sunday if it meant I could have him. If I could taste the body and be filled with his spirit the way I do in my dreams at night. If he would help me, heal me, save me..." I sobbed again, not so silently.

I didn't even hear him get up. When he opened the door, he startled me. He stepped in and, shrouded in the darkness, held me.

Everything in me knew it was wrong but I leaned back to unfasten his belt.

"Lucy. Come on."

I worked fast and stuffed him into my mouth while he was partially flaccid. I sucked it fully erect until he stopped standing there motionless and began gyrating into my mouth. I sat him down and hiked up my dress and straddled him.

As I lowered myself onto him, he clutched my body close and cried out so loud it echoed.He hungrily sucked my breasts he ripped out of my dress, and pounded into me vigorously. He fed me his tongue while palming my ass like two giant basketballs.

I don't know the last time he'd touched a woman this way, but it was evident in his touch and thrust it had been a long time.

"Cum inside me, Omari," I requested softly.

He couldn't help it if he wanted to. I could feel him unloading. His dick throbbed with the release of each spurt of thick nut he shot out. His convulsions eventually slowed as his breathing normalized. His face planted in my bosom, I felt the shift in energy. He felt guilty.

"Omari."

He wouldn't look up.

I thought I would feel victorious. I was overwhelmed with shame and guilt. I'd made a man betray God and fuck me in a confessional inside a church, while wearing devil horns! I was on the fast track to hell.

"I'm sorry," I whispered.

I stood up and fixed my dress. I put my horns back in my purse.

I walked out into the light of day feeling like everyone knew what I did. I walked around the corner and requested a cab to pick me up and take me home.

I had been baptized in my desires, but my absolution would be invalid.

I never heard from Omari again.

Lent a Hand

I was plotting on Omari. I had a diet that included mostly citrus fruits, lots of water, cranberries, and completely laid off red meat and alcohol.

I was going to throw him a Fat Tuesday Bachelor party of one. We were supposed to meet at the church after his youth group, but I invited him over to my place instead.

As soon as he walked in, I handed him a handful of Mardi Gras beads. I had alcohol and all kinds of junk food along with a thick juicy steak on the menu.

"What the hell, Lucy?"

"It's your Fat Tuesday Bachelor Party! We both agreed it should be a thing, and now it is."

"And these?" he asked, raising the beads.

"I think you know what those are for."

He tossed one in my direction and I flashed him. He turned his head quickly.

"You are serious! Are you insane?"

"Just enough to be fun."

He ate the steak and tried to refuse the whiskey, but I wouldn't have it. He claimed he hadn't had a drink in months. I told him that the point of this party was to do a bunch of shit he shouldn't.

"So what's for dessert? I know you have something up your sleeve."

I grabbed his hand and guided it up my thigh. He resisted a bit at first but I pushed him in before he could protest.

"Tell me it's not the most delectable dessert you've ever tasted."

He licked his fingers and agreed. I sat on the table in front of him and opened my thighs. "Until you're full."

He descended, sucking and slurping like he was trying to do precisely that. I scooched to the edge of the table, and he pushed my thighs apart so my pussy lips spread on their own. He milked my oyster until I came so many times I had to beg him to stop.

He snatched off his pants and mounted me there on the table. He was pounding so hard I heard glasses and dishes crashing to the floor, but he didn't even look up. He just continued to devour me.

Even if I hadn't cum, his passionate eagerness was quite the turn on. He fucked me ravenously until he was gratified. In the post-coital glow he chuckled, "I knew the moment I saw you..."

"What? That I'd be trouble?"

"Nope. I knew you'd save me. In one way or another you'd save me."

"Save you?"

"I was about to do something I clearly couldn't handle. You were my test, and you showed me that I wasn't going to be able to devote my life that way. I needed to know. So I needed to find the one who could pull me away from it if that was possible. You're my blessing."

"You're not angry with me?"

"No. I'd be angry with myself if I was going to be angry, but I'm not. I'm grateful."

That would come to be "our story" and how Fat Tuesday became our wedding anniversary.

It's Written All Over You

You couldn't have told me that my walk through the concrete jungle that landed me in front of MARX was going to be a life-altering event. I stood under the MARX sign. The X's crisscrossed needles and colorfully painted background drew me in. I was in need of employment. According to their sign, they were in need of a receptionist. I figured it couldn't hurt to stop in.

Twenty-three years young, I walked in fresh-faced, probably looking as green as I was. My deep blue layered bob framed my face. At 5'9", I'd always been all legs, which I accentuated with my suspender tights beneath my black mini skirt. All eyes were on me and I imagined they assumed I was a walk-in appointment.

All of them looked up but one.

A man who I would later come to know as Scales greeted me. "Good afternoon, can I help you?"

"I saw the sign out there," I replied pointing to it as if he would somehow be unaware, "and I was interested in applying for the position if it hasn't already been filled."

"You can fill anydamnthing you want."

That was the first time he looked up, the man that would change my life. Then he spoke, "What's wrong with you man? The lady comes in to apply for a position and you reply what can be considered sexual harassment. You're supposed to make her comfortable to entertain the idea of working here, not scare her off. If you weren't my cousin..."

He stood up and walked over to me and for the first time in my life I was frozen. My feet would not move from the red and black checked floor.

I couldn't say there was anything about him that was conventionally attractive by societal measures. He wasn't a pretty boy or model type. He just looked strong and capable, like a leader. It was his energy more than anything that drew me to him. It was palpable and I wanted to drink him in. He had wide, round protruding eyes and a full goatee, with a mane of short well-kept locks. He had a full sleeve of tattoos and many others placed along his body.

"I'm Marx, yes with an x like the sign."

"Oh I assumed it was because people were getting marks of some sort."

"That too."

"So you own this place?"

"That's what the bills say."

"Nice."

"And you are?"

"Robyn."

All the chatter that was happening when I walked in had ceased and it seemed as if we both noticed it at the same time.

Marx looked around to convey that they should at least look busy. When his eyes landed on Scales, he remembered that he intended to apologize for him. "You'll have to excuse Scales, he doesn't know how to handle himself around beautiful women and it causes him to act like an animal."

"I'm the youngest of six and the only girl. Animalistic behavior is not foreign to me at all. I can handle it."

His compliment didn't go undetected, but that's another thing with having several brothers, they teach you game early.

"Good to know, you'll need that as much as this place needs a woman's touch."

"So, the position is still available?"

"Yours for the taking."

"Consider it snatched."

"A few pieces of paper need to be signed, but it's really simple work: answering the phones, making appointments, greeting walk-ins before Scales has a chance to scare them off."

"Sounds easy enough. Do I look over and sign paperwork now, or should I come back another day?"

"I can give you the papers to look over and sign tonight and you can bring them in and start tomorrow. We're going to have a busy weekend, a few of the Cowboys are coming in to get work and I could use the help as soon as possible."

"As in the Dallas Cowboys?"

"Yeah."

"Ugh. I guess all business is good business."

"I'm team Greenbacks. I'm a Giants fan, but they don't keep the lights on in this place."

"Fair enough."

"Your team?"

"Giants for life."

He chuckled like men do when a woman is as enthusiastic about sports as they are.

"Alright, Robyn. I'll see you tomorrow around..." he stared at the clock like it should define the hour, "noon. That work for you?"

"Noon is perfect."

———

My first day as an employee, I noticed it looked more like a barbershop than a tattoo parlor.

The floor resembled a giant chessboard. My desk was behind a glass case that housed after care materials and jewelry for different types of piercings. Beside the desk was a small waiting area with tattooing magazines on an oblong black marble table. There were poster rack displays mounted with tattoo examples sorted by category. In the main area there were five stations, and a section in the back with three private rooms.

What was initially light flirting quickly developed into a relationship without the mentioning of a title. Everyone knew. Initially the other guys teased me for how I blushed whenever Marx spoke to me or how I scowled when a customer wanted work in an intimate area that meant she had to go in the back to a private room. On those days, when my jealousy undeniably shot daggers at Marx, he would later take me back in the private room after hours and spread me open over the chair and leave his marks on me. His signature move was to pull my hair back so hard in the doggy style position that we could kiss upside down. He passionately pawed at me like the wild Leo he was.

During lulls at the shop, I'd ask him millions of tattooing questions and he'd joke, "You want an apprenticeship or you want to answer phones?"
To which I replied, "I just want to know."
One night he covered my eyes with his hands, his dual cologne concoction all the more noticeable and arousing, and we shuffled like shackled prisoners to the back room. He lifted his hands. "Surprise!"

I saw the area prepped like he was about to give a tattoo and two oranges. I hope he hadn't decided to give me a tattoo as a surprise, or that oranges were his idea of romance for that matter.

"Umm... thank you?"

"Come. Sit." He pulled me to a stool to have a seat. He sat in a chair behind me and explained what was still not obvious to me. He was going to teach me firsthand about all the questions I asked.

He talked to me about sterilizing the area, why everything was laid out on the tray and the importance of clip cord covers. Then he explained we were going to tattoo the oranges. He told me that most machines these days have a digital read out to tell you if it's properly tuned, but if you've done it a while, you'll know the pitch the vibration is supposed to make.

"Like with me?"

He smiled a knowing boyish smile. "Just like that."

Even with his steady hand aiding me from behind, my lack of artistic talent was evident in my inked orange. It made for a great laugh though.

At night I would doodle on him as he watched TV. I'd find a space not already covered in tattoos and fill it with loving words. Once, as he napped on his stomach, I wrote an entire poem on his back. He would draw masterpieces on me while I lounged in bed reading. It was relaxing and I loved the idea of him leaving his mark on me. I started buying eyeliner pens because I preferred their smooth texture on my skin, even though they didn't have the same staying power as some of our other writing tools. It was a perfect way for us to deepen and solidify our bond.

266

Deepen? Page 268
Solidify? Page 272

Suds Away Sins

Marx wrote on my stomach just above my belly button, "Beauty is eternity gazing at itself in a mirror. But you are eternity and you are the mirror." I asked him if he just made that up. He confessed it was written by his favorite Lebanese writer Kahlil Gibran. I asked him why he chose that, and he revealed he was his father's favorite and as he got older he grew to appreciate him as much. He chose that quote for me because sometimes he wanted me to be able to see myself through his eyes. If I could perceive myself through his gaze, I'd never need another mirror again, he claimed.

We discussed childhood and ended up in a space of deep secrets. I confided that when I was fourteen I was bullied by a senior in my school. He was popular and beloved by our peers and teachers alike. He would call me ugly, a maggot, pencil legs, stupid cunt, pretty much any demeaning thing that popped into his head.

Just before spring break, he cornered me in a back stairwell and raped me. I never told anyone. Not my friends, not my parents, not my brothers, no former lovers, and I never alluded to it in the three years we'd been together. I cried softly in his arms till sleep lulled me away.

I woke up with telltale puffy-ass eyes to find a note that told me to take the day off, with pay. The perks of your man being the boss. I wanted to do something nice for him, so I went out shopping for some ingredients I'd need for his favorite meal, grabbed him his two favorite colognes that he wore together as I noticed he was low on both, and a video game I knew he'd like. He got home later than usual but was very grateful for his gifts. We began binge watching our latest addiction on the couch.

"I've got an idea. You have anymore of those eyeliner pens?"

"Yes."

"I'm going to blindfold you and write on you front and back."

"Uhh, ok."

I dug out the pens and he went off to collect whatever he needed for this deviated version of our scribing routine.

He stood me in front of our full-length mirror and blindfolded me. I wasn't sure why I had to be in front of the mirror if I couldn't even see, but I guess he wanted to have a big reveal.

He initiated the night's session with writing on my face. That's something we rarely did.

It was so relaxing feeling the pen glide over my body I really wanted to lay down as I usually did, but he requested I remain standing.

When he started on my back, the pen didn't feel the same and I could smell the odor of solvents associated with markers and not pens.

"Are you writing on me in permanent marker?!"

"Stay still!"

"Grrrrr." I didn't know what the heck he was up to.

"I'm almost finished."

I heaved a sigh of relief.

"Okay. Now there's two parts to this. Just trust me."

Great. Now I was really anxious.

He started to remove the blindfold. I was mortified.

On my face he wrote in all capital letters the word "ugly." Across my stomach he wrote "maggot," on both arms, "stupid cunt," on my legs, "pencils."

I was wailing. How could he take a moment so private and use a loving practice we had to make fun of it. I shoved him away from me.

"Robyn, calm down. Listen to me. Listen to my voice. Remember I told you there were two parts. Look at your back."

Sniffling, I turned to my back and craned my neck around to see what he'd written.

It said "beautiful" across my back, on my legs he'd written the words "strong," on one arm he wrote "brilliant," on the other, "creative." On my lower back he wrote "SURVIVOR."

The tears returned without the rage and shame this time.

"Baby, I wrote the words on the front with eyeliner pens so you could see them on you and see that they don't belong. We're going to get in the shower and I'm going to wash them off of the beautiful, strong, smart, capable woman I love. The words I wrote on your back are how people who have your back, like me, see you. I wrote them in permanent marker because I wanted you to be reminded of them for a few days. That's what's real. That's what matters. That's what stays."

I sobbed loudly, quietly, and really, really ugly as I shed fourteen-year-old me's pain. I was going to cry every one of her tears and leave them there, never to burden me again.

My lover carried me to the bathroom and turned on the water. "I can't stand those words on you one more minute. Come on. Let's get this off you."

I cried healing tears in the shower.

He toweled me off and put me to bed.

The following morning, I looked at myself backwards in the mirror.

Marx was still in bed watching me stare at myself.

"Babe, I think I'd like to keep this one," I said, pointing to "survivor" written on my back.

"Keep?"

"Yeah, could you ink this on me in the shop?"

He smiled brightly. "We can do it before my first appointment."

That day, before any other artists or appointments arrived, my love went over his letters from the previous night and permanently inked SURVIVOR on my flesh.

Menial Matrimony

One morning, I woke to find he had written "cum slut" on my lower belly. I didn't wash it off. I got dressed and when I got to work, I showed him it was still there. He said that he intended for me to leave it on all day. There was an inexplicable thrill in knowing I secretly had a dirty phrase on me.

He did it again the next day, I found "fuck" beneath one tit, and "me" beneath the other. I hoped that was a reminder to self for him to titty fuck me later. Again, I didn't wash it off. Soon this was part of our routine. I'd wake up, carefully climb out of bed as to not smudge where he could have written on me, and stand in front of our full-length mirror to find what he'd written. That morning's surprise? "Fuck Toy" on the backs of my thighs.

I dressed in thigh highs and a circle skirt with my white button up I tied at the waist like a bad catholic schoolgirl. I was hoping he'd get a peek at his scribing on my thighs each time I leaned over at work.

I deliberately bent at the waist and spread my thighs when I "accidentally" dropped my pen upon noticing he was near me alone. He didn't say or do anything. He just turned around like he had something to do. I suppose he wasn't in the mood for my shit or maybe he had to prep for a client. Though according to the book, he didn't have an appointment for another hour.

"Robyn!" Marx barked from the back.

I hoped he wasn't going to tell me I went too far. This is his place of business after all.

"Aww shit. I know that tone. Somebody's in trouble," Scales teased.

"Shut up Scales," I hissed. But I was concerned. I walked nervously to the back.

He was sitting on the table looking at me very sternly."Close the door."

I quickly did as I was told.

He rushed me before the door was locked."Fuck. When you bent over just now, I almost tackled you out there on the work floor."

My relief was quickly replaced with excitement.

"Bend over so I can use my fuck toy."

I leaned against the door and spread my legs like I was going to be strip-searched.

He ran his fingers up my leg until his thumb was pressed against my opening. I pushed back so it penetrated me. He sunk it in deeper before pulling it out and sucking it. He pulled my hips back so my legs were further apart and unfastened his pants.

We normally had more foreplay but there were no gentle touches or soft kisses to speak of.He yanked my hair back like he always did, and kissed me. I could taste myself on his tongue. He let go and bit my shoulder. He tugged my breasts out of my bra and pinched my nipples. He rubbed my clit as he pressed my body against the door with his.

The harder he fucked me, the louder I was inclined to get, but I was trying not to reveal what was actually going on.

He wasn't making it easy.

Marx covered my mouth and fucked me even harder. Even my muffled moans were loud.

He pulled me away from the door and pushed me onto his table. He lifted both my legs from behind and pounded my guts out until he finished.

I'd never seen this side of him on the clock before, but I loved it. I floated out of that room and back to my station, trying not to let on too much but

I was busted. Right away, Scales looked at me and said loud enough for everyone to hear, "That was one hell of a punishment you got back there!"

My burning red face revealed what my lips wouldn't. I rolled my eyes and went back to my desk.

Later that night I arrived home after running a few errands to Marx having turned our living room into a tattoo station.

"What's this all about? Got a secret high profile client?"

"Yes."

"Oh really? I was just joking. Who is it?"

"You."

"What?"

"I wanted to put something permanent on you this time."

"What?"

"You trust me?"

"Of course."

"So you can see it after I'm done."

"After!" He nodded. "Where?"

"On that juicy fat ass."

"How big?"

"Bigger than small, smaller than medium."

"What if I hate it?"

"You won't."

"*If* I do?"

"I'll cover it with anything you want."

"Fuck. Alright."

I walked to him, lifted my skirt to tuck in my waistband and straddled the chair. He smacked my ass and then caressed it.

"You almost fucked around and delayed this ink with all that ass."

We shared a laugh. Then he got to work.

I watched a show on my phone to distract me. Otherwise I'd be tempted to look and ruin the surprise.

Halfway into my second episode, he announced he was finished.

I hopped up quickly and he asked me to wait a minute. He would get our handheld mirror so I could have a close up view.

He returned at the pace of a sloth as I hurriedly waved him over. Patience may be a virtue but it was not my forte. "Let me see!"

He handed me the mirror and I twisted my torso and hovered the mirror over my tender flesh. At first sight, I gasped. It was followed by a high-pitched squeal.

"I love it! I love it!"

"I told you that you'd love it." He beamed proudly, watching me enjoy my new work.

About a year and a half prior, at my urging, he had me registered with a SLRN code to make me his official registered slave.

I never wanted to get married.

I felt this suited our unorthodox lifestyle much better. It turned me on to be owned by my Dom, and paperwork of my willful enslavement meant more than some marriage certificate to me.

My tattoo said Marx and the X transitioned into a soundwave that then became thicker lines that turned into my SLRN barcode.

Below my barcode was my registration number, 052-106-210.

"And check this out."

He pulled out his phone and opened a barcode scanner. He scanned my ass!

My registration certificate popped up.

"That's not it either." He scanned the sound wave and it was his voice saying, "Mine."

I hopped into his arms showering him with kisses. "This is perfect, baby."

"I can't wait until it's healed and I can cum all over it."

"We don't have to wait to have sex though."

"We sure don't!" he agreed before popping on a quick bandage and pulling my hips back, smacking my non-inked cheek.

Cumming To

Typically the urgency that wakes me is restroom related, but that morning, the hunger for Joe awakened me and would not be suppressed. I did slip out of bed and stumble into our cobalt blue en suite and relieve myself with the hope of returning and waking up my lover for a bit of morning sex. Before climbing back into our bed, I removed Joe's gray boxer briefs that I often slept in. He said he liked the way my ass and thighs looked in them. I was sold. They were comfy and turned my man on? Less I had to spend on lingerie. Joseph slept soundly usually, but if he was exhausted, he could likely sleep through a tornado. Sometimes, I used that to my benefit.

I lay on my stomach with one hand between my legs, parted my lips and gently pressed a finger on my clitoris; I slid the other into his boxers to hold his sleeping member. Even flaccid, a handful of my man's thick dick would cause my clit to throb against my finger. I stroked it ever so slowly and delighted in it thickening up. Feeling the blood rush to form a squeezable partial chubby had my clit thumping. I loved feeling his body respond to my touch. In turn, my body's juices began to flow. I couldn't resist inserting my fingers.

If you've ever done the pat your head while simultaneously rubbing your stomach thing then you know how difficult it can be to have your hands performing juxtapositional motions. Trying to stroke up and down with one hand while encircling your hot button with the other is the sexual equivalent of that game. And the lighter the sleeper, the harder it is. Due to this challenge, I found it best to gyrate my hips and let them keep the rhythm instead.

As I rotated my hips, my lips spread and my fingers slipped in and out of my wetness. Even in dreamland my love is in sync, stiffening the wetter I get. Still careful not to wake him, I moaned softly through my nose as we throbbed in tandem. I wanted to ease myself down on top of him but I needed him to take me that morning. I woke up with a very specific craving. I removed my hands and turned on my side. I placed the two fingers that were just inside me beneath his nose. He smirked in his sleep! My heart melted. I tried to rouse him and his smile was quickly replaced with a frown. I knew he hated being woken up, but I had to try.

With a huff that blew my bangs up over my head, I turned and lay flat on my back, conceding to resume my secret dual masturbation session. First, I returned my fingers inside me and got them really wet, then I used my other hand to gently lift the covers and place my juicy hand back on his slightly softened penis. I didn't want to waste my juices all over the sheets fumbling for his erection. The moment my hand was back on him, he thickened up to full attention. For a moment, I thought he was waking up and I stopped, but he just turned his head away. I waited until his breathing was a soft snore again before I began to stroke him. Having to wait while he begins to soften in my hand and my clitoris throbs begging for stimulation is a tease like no other. Each time his erection returns, it's stronger. When I squeezed him gently, he throbbed back and it sent a current through my entire body.

It was getting harder and harder to keep a slow masturbatory pace being that aroused. If I wanted him to fuck me, or at the very least ensure my orgasm without pissing him off, I was going to have to do something else. With Joe being 6'7", we had to have a Cali King bed that swallowed up my 5'2" frame. In this instance, I could use it to my benefit because there was enough room for me to lie across the bed vertically.

I pulled the covers back on my side of the bed. Then I turned and planted one foot near his torso, and the other above his head. I scooched my booty down so that my pubic region was a few inches away from his face. Knowing that he could wake up and catch me at any minute turned me on. At times I couldn't help my moans. It was such a rush. Remembering the effect my scent had on him, I made sure to push my fingers inside and pull them out so that it not only served as an excellent lube for my clitoral stimulation, but it made it easier for my scent to waft over and rouse him like a fresh pot of coffee.

When I finally felt him stir, I looked down and he was rubbing his eyes. When he opened them, he stared at me confused then rubbed his eyes again. I put my head back down and continued to fondle myself so he could be sure what was happening. I didn't look down again because I had to focus on myself. If I became distracted by him, I may feel compelled to put on a show. Most normal masturbation isn't as exciting as porn to watch, but authenticity is best. Besides, if I had to wait this long to get him to notice, maybe he should wait to have to fuck me.

Surprisingly he didn't pounce on me. He just watched, rather intently I suppose, and if my peripheral vision served me right, stroked himself a bit. Instead of being distracted by his potential voyeuristic expectations, I used the fact that he was watching me to stimulate myself further. I began wondering what thoughts were in his mind as he stared at my body. If seeing my sex throb reminded him of the way it feels when he's inside it. If hearing the smack of my wet lips separating to finger fuck myself made his pulse race. If the scent that woke him made his heart pound like mine was.

I rubbed my clit feverishly, bucking my hips so close to his face I could feel his facial hair on my thighs. I was squeezing my pierced nipples beneath my black ribbed tank. I stopped momentarily to open my lips as my orgasm neared. I wanted him to see the juices pooling inside me. I heard him moan and my legs trembled. Now brimming with juices, the sound of his arousal sent me over, and with a triumphant orgasm, my juices spilled out.

Before they could reach the mattress, he caught them with his tongue and ran it all the way up to the center where he sucked directly from the source. He drank from me like I was a cup of his favorite java. But just for a moment, because then he gave me what I wanted all morning, to fill me with a cup of Joe.

He came in late & I had a plate for him in the microwave. On its door was a note that read, "Heat up dinner. I've taken a sleep-aid. Don't wake me. Make me cum."

Okay, so let me fill you in on the note.

The previous night we had a chat about a theory I have regarding my secret.

Every boyfriend I'd ever had, I tested my theory on. In the early days of us being sexually active, I'd go to hold their dicks after they fell into post-coitus slumber. They'd always wake up. Some would just stir, others would jolt awake abruptly & slap my hand away, one way or another they woke up. Then, as our relationship became more solid I'd try again, and 99% of the time they'd sleep right through it. The only exception: when we were fighting. Then they'd rouse a bit like they used to in the beginning. So, my theory was that a man trusts you if even in his subconscious state, he allowed you to touch his most intimate parts.

He laughed calling it "deeply flawed" and had the nerve to claim most dudes probably just faked it but always knew I was touching it & hoped I'd do more. I retorted that "I'd agree, except I watched their chest move while listening to their breath. I watched their eyelids. If your eyes don't move or your breathing rhythm doesn't break for a moment I'm inclined to believe they stayed in that state of sleep. *You* always do."

"You've done this to me?"

"Of course! But you already knew that, seeing as how you're actually awake right?"

He cut his eyes at me."How many times have you done this?"

"To you, or ever?"

"To me."

"Couldn't tell you."

"What? Why? You just hold it and then what?"

"Touch myself."

He balked at my admission."You're serious?"

"Yes. And when our relationship is really good and in sync, mmmph..." I bit my lip. "It's so good. You throb in my hand. Veins bulging as you pulse in tandem with me. Precum oozes out and I use it to lube your dick as I stroke slowly. I have to be careful not to wake you. This balance between being so excited my heart is pounding into the mattress while still grinding on my fingers fast enough to cum, but slow enough so I don't disturb you is thrilling. Sometimes if your breathing slows, I know you're close to waking so I wait a bit. I feel you soften and shrink in my fingers. I give it gentle squeezes as soon as your breathing returns to your sleeping rate & then he wakes back up. Once it's stiff again, I go back to my session. When I feel myself about to peak, I bury my face in the pillow to muffle any sounds I can't mute on my own because I get off so damn hard."

"Damn. Makes me wanna... take a nap!"

We fell out laughing.

"What made you even think to do this?"

"It's a way of getting off that involves your partner, but allows you to be completely selfish because it's all about your pleasure. Plus, I've also always wanted to have someone do it to me."

"But according to your theory, you wouldn't even know."

"Wouldn't care. As long as he told me he used me to make himself cum, I'd have a great time thinking about it later. Besides, you know I got that chloroform coochie. Once I put it on you, you knock out. Unfortunately I'm also a light sleeper and don't think I'd make it through."

He chuckled. "You think these guys would like being used by you in this way? If they knew?"

"Yup. I always had a way of getting answers about how they'd feel about something like that without revealing what I intended to do first."

"What if I didn't like it?"

I rolled my eyes. "Then I'd stop of course, but I don't see that happening, Mr. Nap Time."

"So if I fondled you in your sleep and told you about it..."

"Mmm." I moaned louder than intended.

"Really?"

"Really," I said nodding & widening my eyes for emphasis.

So that evening, he crept into our bedroom and try as he might, he kept waking me up. Now I'm not particularly happy about being woken up, so for it to happen repeatedly just made me groggily shove his hands away and contradict everything my conscious mind shared. Eventually he just gave up. On nights he tried without me using a sleepaid, I woke up before he even started. Poor thing. He really wanted to give me what I wanted.

Just before our anniversary after a particularly long week, I took a sleeping pill around seven. He came rushing in ready to shit, shower, and shave before heading out for a night with the fellas. At some point in the twilight hours, he came stumbling in drunk as hell. He snatched the sheets off me & tore off my boy shorts, fucking me in about twenty positions. He kissed me so deeply, I could taste enough cognac to get me secondhand drunk. He flung me around more aggressively than he ever did sober. Though I loved it, naturally it wasn't something I could sleep through. Rough groggy 3am sex was the closest I came to my fantasy.

For our anniversary, he surprised me with a trip to Mexico. I was so excited. I hadn't been since my college days in Cancun with my Sorors over spring break. I'm sure that precedence had no relevance in Puerto Vallarta with my man. He planned a few excursions and some chill days. There was also a surprise for me I was excited to know about, but he wouldn't break no matter how much I nagged. I just hoped it didn't interfere with my anniversary surprise for him. What could his be?

Surprise 1? Page 285
Surprise 2? Page 287

On the Roof

Shortly after arrival, we were able to acquire some green to smoke. We took it up to our rented terrace to spark.

It wasn't the best grade of weed I'd had, but it was enough to relax me and give me a happy buzz. We listened to some music and danced barefoot singing disrespectfully off-key, especially at the decibel with which we were making so much noise. Between songs he asked if I was ready for my surprise. Of course!

"So I got this gas mask and some of that laughing gas shit oral surgeons use when they have to take out your wisdom teeth."

"Where the hell did you get that from?"

"You can get anything around here if you got enough money. I was thinking we could try it and I could finally fuck you when you're semi-conscious like you always wanted."

"That sounds amazing. Can we try it right now?"

"Whenever you feel ready."

"I'm ready right now!"

Eventually I faded away to a space where my mind experienced things like a delayed strobe light. Every time I came to, I was cumming. I woke up sweaty, heart racing, my skin rippling with goosebumps from being groped and fondled. I didn't always wake up in the same position and it excited me to have no recollection of how I ended up there and to know I was positioned in such a way because he desired it. I wasn't sure if it was the gas, the green, or the Mexican heat, but everything felt magnified. All the foreplay: licking, kissing and touching that led to the intense orgasms, I was able to sleep through. Spasming walls, thrashing thighs, and pounding piledriving are hard for even a drugged mind to remain dormant.

I slipped in and out of consciousness as he slipped in and out of me until the blazing Mexican sun ran us inside for shade and cool showers. Knowing the effort he put in to making my fantasy come true was the best anniversary gift I'd ever received.

On the Rohypn

We spent the afternoon doing an assortment of water sports: parasailing, jet skiing, windsurfing —and as terrifying as it looked—I let him convince me to use one of those boards that resembles a snowboard that uses some type of water jet that shoots you like 45 feet into the air. Then for a few hours we lounged in our cabana and relaxed.

"You want to have a few at *Kahlo* before heading upstairs to our suite?"

I lifted my oversized floppy hat and eyed the bar attached to our hotel he was referring to. "Sure. Why not?"

I wrestled with whether to head upstairs shower and change before going to the bar, but after a full day, I knew we'd both only last for about two drinks maximum so it seemed silly to do all that just to leave in a half hour. As I scanned the crowd, it appeared by their attire that that was the consensus everyone had come to. I sat under a wooden sign hung up with a rusty nail that said "Paradise is here." I made a note to ask Joe to take my picture beneath it with my legs spread suggestively when he returned with our drinks. I was still giggling at my corny ass joke when he returned from the bar.

"What's so funny?" he asked incredulously. He seemed paranoid instead of amused.

"I was laughing at the sign. What happened at the bar that got a stick up your ass so suddenly?"

"Nothing. I think I'm just getting tired. What's funny about the sign?"

I shared and he chuckled then we not-so-discretely snapped the picture. Other attendants seemed to find it amusing too.

Out of the blue, I felt very faint. I couldn't tell if it was from spending all day in the sun or if this bartender was hustling for some serious tips, but either way I was ready to go.

"Take me upstairs now."

"You okay?"

"I don't know but I think I need to get out of here."

"Okay. Let's go."

We hurried through the crowd and everything seemed to whisk by in a blur, though I seemed to be in slow motion. The last thing I remembered was the loud ding of the elevator and the shutting of our door. I woke up the next day groggy and semi-disoriented. I was never one to suffer from hangovers but if this was the price of partying like a 25-year-old when you're 35, I would gladly make adjustments. Joe lovingly doted on me all day. He gave me a "hangover concoction" with a black pill and filled me with copious amounts of bottled water.

Massage therapists came to our room for an evening couples massage and it was divine.

By nightfall I felt 85% normal. I asked Joe what he wanted to do and apologized for wasting a day away.

"You didn't waste the day. In fact, I planned for this day. A day devoted to just taking care of you."

"Well isn't that sweet? Thank you, baby."

"I also planned for us to watch a movie tonight. You think you can manage that?"

"Sounds perfect."

He turned on the TV and sat next to me, exuding nervous energy.

"Is it something scary? I don't want to watch a scary movie while we're in a foreign place with unfamiliar sounds and shit."

"Nah, just watch."

"You just watch! You're busy staring at me and not even looking at the TV."

I was staring at a white wall and then Joe came into frame.

"Oh my gosh! Joe! What is this?"

"Watch and see."

"Briar, First and foremost I want to thank you for these last five years. In this time I've enjoyed growing with you, learning about you, and learning from you. One of the things I learned about your freaky ass was how you like to fondle people in their sleep and your desire to be taken and used while you slept through the entire thing."

This seemed like an odd start to an anniversary video. So much for sharing this with people when we get back home.

"I tried many times unsuccessfully at home to give you that as you very well know. Refusing to be defeated, I did some research and studying to be able to deliver your biggest fantasy. Truthfully I was nervous as hell, and often morally conflicted, but hearing you talk about it and reading from all accounts of other freaky-ass sleeping beauties, I convinced myself to go through with it.

At this point I was really puzzled. What was he getting at? What was he going to do to me that we hadn't tried?

"I hope you're okay with it and know that my intention was to surprise you with what I believed you desired, so..."

I looked to him for an answer. He just tilted his chin towards the television for the answer.

289

"I roofied you."

"WHAT?" I jumped up from the couch.

"Sit down," he said through the TV.

And it dawned on me that he knew me so well. He knew me well enough to know I had jumped my ass up when he said that.

"I know it sounds bad, but you said you wished you could have lived out a fantasy where a stranger had done that to you and how you knew it was the only way to sleep through the experience. I struggled with feeling like I was doing something wrong. I wanted to talk to you about it but I know you. I know the authenticity would be tarnished even further by knowing it's happening. I'm already not a stranger. I wanted to stick as true to your fantasy as you've described many times during our pillow talk. I monitored you closely. I had a doctor on call close by just in case. The "hangover concoction" and the activated charcoal pill was a gift from her. I made sure you had plenty of fluids and scheduled our massages for today to relax your body as well as your mind after enduring this. I'm aware it was dangerous. Shit, we had to come to Mexico just so I could get my hands on some. I hope you see this for the act of love that it is and not a way for me to take advantage of you sharing something with me."

I turned to him slowly, "Can you pause it?"

"Go ahead and talk. I know you need to. I'll give you a minute," he said from the TV.

My mouth dropped open. "Am I always this predictable?"

"Certainly not. That's why I made this message."

"Why did you make the message instead of just telling me?"

"You'll see."

"Okay. Hmm. Well, I am shocked, I'm not going to lie to you. I'm super caught off guard but this is fucking amazing. I can't believe you went through all of this to make my fantasy come true. Knowing you orchestrated all of this for me is... actually a massive turn on. Tell me all the details. What did you do? Where did we do it? How did we do it? What happened? I want to know everything."

"By now..." I jumped, forgetting he hadn't paused the video but he'd left space for us to chat, "you've shared how you felt and asked me 100 questions in four seconds. If you're still watching this, this act has been well received and I'm breathing a sigh of relief. It's my first full breath since I decided to do this months ago. Give me a minute. Okay. Now I knew you'd have questions. I thought I'd take the liberty of what I hope to be elevating your fantasy by adding something to it that you hadn't considered could be a possibility because of the nature of who it'd be with. Since I'm your husband and not some random stranger, I wanted to offer something they wouldn't."

"You didn't?"

He smiled broadly.

"You didn't!" I shrieked excitedly.

"Without further ado, our version of Sleeping Beauty."

The video faded out from him talking to seeing him help me into our room. I snuggled up close to my lover, excited to see what happened next. There was something about how endearing and attentive he was making sure I was okay. He lay me down gently and removed my clothes. Then he gave me a sponge bath. He lathered me up and wiped me down from head to toe. There was something soothing and sensual about watching him take care of me this way.

Then he rubbed me down with lotion. He carefully turned me on my stomach and craned my neck to the side and checked my breathing before continuing to moisturize me. He lotioned my back, my ass, my legs, and rubbed and kissed my feet. He went back to rubbing my ass up and down, spreading it, lifting it from the bottom, kissing it. I was winding my hips and squeezing my thighs together watching him. He took his penis and rubbed it on my ass, then smacked my cheek with it hard enough for it to wobble. He stood behind me, lifted my cheeks up and slid inside.

We sighed in unison.

I watched him pull my hips up, my upper body slumped, and fuck me hard enough my eyes fluttered and opened. I said something unintelligible that I had no recollection of. He turned me over and kissed and massaged my breasts, licking and sucking my thick erect nipples. He mounted me again, rubbing his cock over my pubic mound and around my lips before pushing it inside me. He was slower than I would have imagined. He cradled my head and kissed my lips as he came. He was lovingly tender though I wasn't coherent. It was beautiful... and hot. I wanted him so badly I straddled him on the couch. I picked up where the video left off. Kissing him passionately, his hand behind my head, I gyrated in his lap as we removed each other's clothes. We went on to have the most gratifying, ardent making love session I had ever experienced.

Tea With A Twist

This place was serious about following high tea etiquette: how to hold your cup and saucer, where to place your spoon after stirring, etc. They had a fabulous selection of china, glassware, and cutlery, including specialty honey-dipped teaspoons that were to be selected for your meal in addition to the meal. The restaurant's decor was very traditional with elegant tablecloths and vases filled with fresh, bright flowers. We were handed menus in the waiting area upon arrival, post checking in with the hostess.

The menu was called ～ Tea Table ～. It was divided into intimidatingly intricate rows and columns. The first section had what each tea was traditionally good for: energy, de-stressing, digestion, antioxidant boosts, nausea. Next, those flavors were divided into tea bags or full-leaf varieties. The following section was mostly a recommendation. If you were going to have salads and seafood, it suggested a certain tea flavor, for a savory meal a different tea, savory food with sweet baked desserts yet another recommendation, and so on.

Specific tableware from a list of eight options were also to be selected according to your meal. If you were having your tea with a twist, there was another table of recommendations. For example, which alcohol to pair with your sweet tea, or what food to have with a blackberry tea sangria. The flip side of the menu was just a listing of all the food, beverage, and condiment options from fresh hand-squeezed lemonade, sweet tea, loose tea, flavored milks and creams, and mini mason jars of their homemade jam. Most items could be purchased in the attached store as well. In addition to their jams and honey spoons, high-end teapots and specialty leaf teas—including their special hybrid teas—were available for purchase.

I ordered a white peach bourbon tea, and a classic cucumber sandwich with a lavender scone. I added some rainbow macaroons and lemon bars for the table. Our dessert came served on a vintage, floral-printed, three-tier, fine bone china cake stand with gold banding. Dressed in our frilly best, we had a fantastic brunch. We vowed to make this a more common occurrence prior to departing. I could see why so many women I knew raved about the place. It was refreshingly different, especially in this area.

The following day, my friend and co-worker Fawn inquired about my visit to Tea With A Twist.

"So..." she sang, her voice full of expectation.

"So..." I sang back, confused.

"How was the... you know...?"

"No. I don't know." I stared at her, confused.

She looked defeated. "Fine. Don't share."

"I have no idea what you're referring to!"

"I wanted to hear about your tea outing!"

"Oh! It was divine. That place is really nice. Join us next time."

"Girl, stop. I mean how was the..." she scanned the room for eavesdroppers, "*special* tea?"

"I had a white peach bourbon. I highly recommend it. It was deceptively sweet. I didn't feel the head swirls until I stood up."

"Why is this like pulling teeth with you? You want to wait until after work to tell me?"

"Tell you what, girl? I just went to have some tea! That's nothing to gossip about."

"I thought you said you went to Tea With A Twist!"

"Yeah. So? The tea spot. On 12th and Broad."

"Yeah! Me too! Tea With A..." she motioned with her hand for me to fill it the gap, "Twist."

"Yeah, they serve their tea with different alcohol. That's the twist."

"Oh my goodness. You really don't know?"

"Know what?"

"It's called Tea With A Twist to spell out TWAT, you moron. If you ask for the Newdah Tea, they take you in the back and you can pick from a whole host of bad bitches for some dessert... for an extra fee of course."

"You're full of shit."

"You think that place is packed... for tea? I shouldn't have to tell you lesbians aren't that into teabagging."

She fell into a raucous laughter as I sat there stunned. All this time I thought it was a quiet little sophisticated spot for femmes and it was really some kinky ass underground prostitution ring where you could order some cooch!

"So you just ask for Newdah and they take you in the back so you can... suck on random twat?"

"Or she can suck yours. But yeah, basically. Nobody you were with ordered that?"

"Hell no!"

"Well damn. You mad?"

I did get pretty loud. "Confused I guess. It's just... everyone knows this?"

"Well clearly not everyone."

"Have you..."

"I'm scared to do it. I was trying to live vicariously through you."

I sucked my teeth. "So how do you know if it's real?"

"Oh it's real. I've heard enough stories."

"Maybe they're all making it up. Maybe it's like a lesbian urban legend."

"Nah. I believe it."

"Believing and knowing are two different things."

"Well then go and know, Miss Private Investigator."

"Come with me."

"I just told you I'm nervous about that type of shit."

"You don't have to do anything, just come with me."

"B.B."

"Pleeeeaaaasssse." I smiled hard and batted my lashes.

"Fine." She rolled her eyes.

We were going to get some TWAT.

This time I sped through my dining experience because I was eager to get to the special. Fawn had found some bravery and decided spectating alone wouldn't satisfy her appetite. When our waitress returned with the check, she asked if we wanted anything else. My heart was pounding.

"I'd like some of the Newdah tea."

She smiled brightly before turning to Fawn. "And you?"

Fawn blushed before answering, "The same."

"Perfect. I'll take you to back to the desserts area in just a moment."

As soon as she walked away, paranoia set in.

"Girl, what if this a like a sting operation and we're about to go to jail? You want this shit on your record? Do I really want to explain to future employers I was caught doing this bullshit?"

"Stop it! We would know if that was happening by now."

"How?"

"The same way we knew about the secret menu item."

"I just learned about it from you! I will kill you if this goes south. They better send us to different prisons or I'll shank your ass on the yard."

She laughed. "Slow down, big Bertha. When did you get so damn gangsta?"

"You think this is funny but I'm going to leave. Fuck this."

As soon as I stood up to bail, our waitress was standing beside me. "Ready?"

I scowled at Fawn before submitting to my own curiosity. Still spewing threats through gritted teeth to my partner-hopefully-not-in-crime, I walked back afraid of what I would find.

She stopped us in the hall. Fuck! We were about to go to jail. I knew it.

"We ask for payment upfront for obvious reasons. Look over this, and initial here accepting our terms. We accept cash, and all major credit cards. I'll be back in a moment."

No wonder they served alcohol in their tea. I should have downed more before coming back here.

The black leather holder she gave us was a list of services as well as things we couldn't do to the ladies, and our understanding that the women could ask us to stop at any time if they felt uncomfortable and we were to comply. When she returned, we agreed and paid for our selections.

Turns out we picked things on opposite spectrums. I wanted to taste what was on the menu, she was going to be dessert.

Bridgette experience? Page 299
Fawn experience? Page 301

Boba Tea

On a life size three-tier serving tray, nearly identical to the one they served us sandwiches on earlier, were women sitting with their backs against the stand in the middle, their feet hoisted in stirrups at the end of each tier. They were all blindfolded. When I entered the room, it spun ever so slowly so I could see all the women. On the top tier were decadent chocolate ebony women. The middle tier was adorned with gorgeous Latin women, and the final tier had beautiful white women with hair in every shade.

I was immediately drawn to this thick, buxom Black woman. Her skin had this luminous glow. It wasn't from being slicked down with oil or some other lubricant. This was a rich inner glow that radiated from within. I couldn't see her eyes, but I wanted to. I wanted to know what she was doing here. What made her want to sign up for being tasted by strangers. I wanted to know things about her I had no business knowing.

"Her. I want her." The serving tray stopped spinning. My eyes were transfixed on her.

Two men pushed over what resembled an adult high chair. It was adjustable, and once they secured me inside it, they jacked me up to the proper level.

I didn't know how to begin. I didn't want to startle her. "I'm sorry. I don't know your name. I'm going to touch your leg so you know I'm here."I stroked her calf gently. It was softer than it looked and fuck, it looked soft.

She bit her lip responsively. She removed her feet from the stirrups and wriggled down into my lap. She spread her heavenly thighs wide. I rubbed my hands over her ample bosom. I felt compelled to dive into her cleavage and motorboat those melons, so I did precisely that. I slowed down and nursed her nipples, licked around her areola, sucked each mound separately, then together.

She stroked herself as I did this and sometimes I just watched and enjoyed her pleasing herself. Other moments I pressed my body against hers, feeling how sticky sweet she was on my skin. She searched for my hand and guided my fingers where she wanted them. She masturbated with my hand and it was the most erotic thing I had ever experienced. I couldn't deny tasting her any longer.

She was more delectable than she looked. I slurped as she held my head tenderly and undulated against my mouth. She was more intoxicating than any alcoholic beverage on their menu. I drank from her and felt healing for wounds unknown till that moment. Her moans grew louder, and her thick thighs tensed around me. She held a tuft of my hair and rocked her hips until she covered my mouth with pearl milk tea. My new favorite dessert.

Cooch Hooch

There were four oversized teacups like many amusement parks have. Two cups were occupied with several women seated in them; one had only one woman inside. The last remained empty. I peered inside as the hostess explained what I was failing to make sense of on my own. Each woman I saw was seated upon the face of another woman. That woman, she explained, pointing, had paid extra for a private cup. She said I could as well, but most people preferred sitting together and, with permission, enjoyed group touching.

Though initially, a group felt intimidating, a woman in the teacup invited me with a smile and I knew I'd be joining them for tea. I stepped in the cup and a woman who, prior to my arrival, was just providing supportive touch to the others relocated to a new position, craned her neck and patted her lips as an invitation. I was frozen. Then the woman who smiled at me motioned for me to take my seat.

I lifted my shimmery gold tulle skirt and planted my ass squarely on her face. I was received by a warm tongue. I re-situated myself until we were properly aligned.

The smiling woman who lured me in was seated beside me. She stuck out her hand with a quizzical expression. I nodded so emphatically her smile broke into a full laugh. She caressed my thigh in a way that felt more nurturing than sexual. It was a warm introductory touch. It helped relax me. Reading the calm in her face, it was easy to forget that she too was gracing the face of a woman.

We synced up our gyration like a choreographed dance. Our partners beneath us stayed in tune as well. We linked fingers and let our lips and breath cover each other. I nibbled her

301

exposed throat and she clutched my thigh as she ascended. I basked in her glory, as I felt my own looming in. She fondled my nipples and I clawed at her back as my body stiffened as my cup runneth over.

Fucking Falconry

The life of a mistress is not something you plan.

You just... end up there.

There are many roads that lead to this path of self-destruction, none of them excusable. I know for me, it was feeling defeated.

I'd had so many failed relationships no matter what I did. I read seven hundred self-help books, meditated, had heart-to-hearts with my best friend, asked my older brother for advice, changed my approach, stayed true to myself, stayed celibate for a year, signed up for three websites and had a roster for dating, and the only thing they all had in common, besides me, was that they ended up being a loss.

A loss of time, energy, ill-invested emotions, a total fucking waste.

I'd had just about every game run on me while trying to be honest and, heaven forbid, seeking the same in others.

I was called accusatory when the effects of that string of bullshit induced paranoia.

I was cheated on countless times, lied to, been the other woman thrice without knowing, and had a boyfriend of two years have a baby on the side.

Everyone was cheating, but me.

You can call me bitter, or lonely, or an adulterous whore, but what I wasn't going to be, was wasting time with liars.

The luxuries are plenty as a mistress.

You get more honesty than you get being a main girlfriend, which means I didn't have to worry if "my" man was cheating. He wasn't mine, and at least I knew what I was in for.

The hush money perks don't hurt either.

Hawke didn't like using cards because they were traceable, so he used to withdraw stacks of cash from his savings account each time we got together. We made love on a bed of green dead presidents before using them for my shopping spree.

I didn't have to worry about another potential impending heartbreak. Our ending was inevitable. There was a security in knowing it was going to end, so you set certain boundaries to prevent you from becoming emotionally attached.

There was no worrying about doing something too freaky too soon because it would fuck up his ego to think you weren't a virginal demure lady that he got to turn out and make a bad girl just for him. Nah. I could do every filthy, slutty, whorish thing I conjured up to make him clutch the sheets, clench his teeth, curl his toes, and convulse with multiple orgasms. Then I'd send him back to his wife with drained raisin nuts.

And lastly, though initially it was the hardest part, eventually I desensitized myself to the pain of the wife. No one cared when it was me. Not the men I committed myself to and supported, not the women who knew about me, not his boys who met these other women and kept their silence as part of some "bro code," not their mamas and sisters who swapped recipes with me and let me watch their kids and smiled in my face while protecting their loved one. No one.

Fuck all those books and life coach quotes. There was no self-healing like fucking another bitch's husband. For all my sincerest efforts, they were the most honest unions I had. And if you think it's hot fucking someplace you might get caught, it pales vastly compared to fucking where your lover's wife might catch you.

Now, before you bail on my tales for being a horrible person, please understand that I didn't just select any old married men. Nope. With the assistance of social media, I found the girls who had been the other woman in *my* relationships. If you're a turn the other cheek, two wrongs don't make a right type of person, *now's* the time to bail on my tales of vindication.

If you've ever been hurt, pull up a chair.

I made an account with a fake photo, added plenty of random people so the account looked real, and whenever I was in predator mode, I'd find the girl's "love of her life" and add him to my page. If he accepted, I'd do a quick scan on his page, read all the things he liked, etc. Then I would share similar things on my page and chat him up with what would appear to be harmless conversation. Eventually, I'd dip into their inbox with a joke or a meme about something they liked or I felt would appeal to their humor with a simple, "Thought you would enjoy this." Once they responded, the door to private communication was opened.

Next, I'd mention my boyfriend so he wouldn't feel like I'm a threat, but also toss around how incompatible my boyfriend and I were. I'd mention how it must be an "opposites attract" thing. Confide in him how he doesn't like sports, or beer. How my family teased I was the man in the relationship. Men love feeling superior to other men, especially in a classic alpha male way. I'd ask how compatible he is with his girlfriend, and that is where they began to spill every shortcoming she had. Like a boxing match, you begin to repeatedly attack the weakness.

A few messages later, I admit the photo in my profile isn't me and concoct a story like I had some stalker exes or left an abusive relationship. Empathy and their natural urge to protect is unlocked. Slide in how you didn't want him to feel lied to in case you two ever want to meet up. Gauge his response to see how close you are to that point.

If he's open to it, go in for the kill with a photo. It has to be one that highlights your physical assets but doesn't seem too obvious. A beach photo will always do the trick. There's an excuse for showing so much skin and why the photo was taken. Everyone snaps pictures on vacation! I choose one where I'm smiling, add a caption like, sunshine makes me happy! If he doesn't mention my body, I have to put a bit more work in, but if he does... he's as good as mine. I request a beach picture of him in return to be fair since he's seen me "basically naked" and let that idea warm up to him. After he sends, I soak and stroke his ego in compliments, the perfect bait to the neglected. I wait to see what events his girl has RSVP'd to and ask if he's free that night. Of course he is. Add alcohol and a dress that looks painted on my hourglass frame and he'll be between my legs in an hour, usually less than.

If he's a good fuck, I add him to my roster. If not, the first time will have to do. Between those inbox conversations, and a brief liquored up chat, I know everything his girl doesn't do, and the freaky shit he's been too scared to ask for. If she's a spitter,

306

I'm a swallower. If she's anti-backdoor, I'm an anal queen. If she lies there like a dead fish, I'm a wild rider. If she always has to be in control, I submit. I'm a fantasy fulfiller focused on making my prey a spousal amnesiac. Their vanilla sex life at home no longer satisfies them now that they are aware of what they'd been missing. It's hard to go backwards sexually for men.

Once I had him hooked harder than a dope fiend, I would push the limits of what he would do to keep me around and make her insane. Oh, she had a fit when you stayed out late last time? Now you have to spend the night with me. She doesn't buy that you fell asleep at your friend's house? Good. Let's take a quick vacation. Let's see how she feels about a string of nights away. But the key was to not let them split up before she knew why.

These two were on the verge. He stopped making excuses to be with me and would simply disappear on ole "Babygirl" as he called her. He picked stupid fights to justify leaving often. But that wasn't enough. I wanted her furious, confused, and vulnerable. I wanted her to feel all that I felt years ago when the tables were turned. I wanted her to know I was aware of her existence and that I blatantly disregarded it. I wanted revenge.

Over the phone? Page 308
In person? Page 311

Wi-Fired Up

On such a vacation, we checked into a room under my name, Amy Gdala. When we settled into our room, he got comfortable and stripped down to his boxers and a t-shirt and sat propped up against the headboard watching the Eagles lose.

Before complete decompression, he decided to call Autumn and let her know he'd arrived safely.

I decided it was a great time to go down on him.

She could tell something was off. I was sucking the thoughts out of his head. He couldn't hold a conversation if his life depended on it. She was suspicious. I could tell in his responses.

"I'm... I'm... I'm just watching the game. What do you mean? I am listening to you. No. Babe, stop."

I popped my head up like I believed he might be talking to me. I mouthed, "Stop?"

He pulled the phone away and shook his head vigorously. "Hell nah," he whispered.

He placed the phone back on his ear "Nah, I heard you. I just accidentally hit mute. Video chat? What? Why? I don't even know if my service is strong enough to..."

I heard the familiar ring of a video call on his phone. He had to answer. She knew he was available with his phone in his hand.

He tried to get me to stop but I vacuum sucked him in.

He needed to take this call.

"Hey! See. I'm right here. Watching the game." He switched to the rear camera so she could see the TV, then back to himself. "Told you."

I took him balls deep, and stuck my tongue out to lick them too. It always drove him crazy.

"Hawke! What the fuck are you doing? Are you jerking off?" she asked in a seething accusatory tone. Her gut insisted, but she needed proof. She was about to get it.

"Yeah!" he responded excitedly, grateful for an out that made sense.

Now.

This was it.

I popped my head up into frame. "Yeah, he's jerking off using my mouth. You're kinda interrupting us, Autumn."

I smiled at her recognition of my face then I hit the end button.

"What the fuck, Amy? Are you crazy? Why would you do that?" His eyes were wide and wild, bewildered I would even do such a thing.

"You two are over. You spend more time with me than her. You lie to her all the time. Her voice was annoying me, and blocking your orgasm. I just... sped up the inevitable." I shrugged. "Now let me finish."

"Are you fucking crazy?! You are. You're fucking crazy!" he shouted in disbelief.

His phone was vibrating repeatedly in his hand. Autumn, of course.

"Listen," I said calmly, "she knows. She's known. Women have intuition. You may as well take all your frustrations out on me. If you answer that phone for her, she's just going to ask you a bunch of bullshit that doesn't matter and stress you out. Fuck that. Matter of fact..." I swiped the phone from his hand and put it on my pussy. "Mmmmm. This shit is better than a bullet. I hope she doesn't stop calling before I cum."

He was having a hard time trying to comprehend everything that happened. He stood

309

over me, stiff as a statue. Except for the part of him I usually put to use.

"Let me make you cum. Shoot it down my throat like you like, Daddy." I made puppy eyes at him, gyrating against his vibrating phone.

He knew I had a point. The damage was done. I was there and willing to suck and fuck him exactly how he liked. And he couldn't rectify the damage no matter what he said.

He heaved a sigh of frustration.

"Fuck me."

He shook his head. "You're crazy."

"Fuck. Me."

He shook his head again. "Fuck it."

He straddled my chest and humped my mouth while the incessant vibrating of his girlfriend calling got me off.

Meet Moana

He was too into it. He started falling. It was about to get messy. I suggested he ask her about a threesome since she was already suspicious he wanted to experience something else, and she claimed to be bisexual. I know at this point Autumn was grasping at straws. She was desperate to keep her man. I coached him on how to get her to agree to it without her flipping out. The hardest part was usually convincing a woman that she should let her man choose the woman. Finally, after a few weeks of hints, she agreed to a threesome.

I rented the room next door to where the action would take place and had a bottle of champagne on ice. That night would be worth toasting to. My hair looked like angels descended from the heavens to lay it down proper. My body was snatched. My lingerie was the sexiest—and priciest—I owned, but well worth the price tag. With all due humility, I would have pounced on me.

Once he sent me the text that they arrived, I walked next door to their room. I had a masquerade mask on to hide my identity. I told Hawke that I'd rather she didn't know who I was. Part of what convinced her to agree was me coaching him to tell her that I was a little insecure, and after I saw what she looked like, I was intimidated by her beauty. He fed her my sweet lies because in the end, he was going to get double the pussy. He didn't care about her feelings, and I was down for it. It sold itself.

We started out with a soft embrace. I introduced myself as Mona, like I told Hawke I would. She introduced herself as her real name. He asked how we should start. I suggested that, "Maybe you could do the beautiful Autumn from behind, and if she wants, she can go down on me at the same time?" She looked nervous, but then quickly agreed before she lost her nerve.

"Okay."

Hawke looked shocked that was all it took. I lay down and spread my legs, she knelt between them, and he glided himself into her from behind. She had a nice set of chocolate perky titties, her ass was a full round bubble, but not sloppy. Under normal circumstances, I would probably be into this for real. But no body was bad enough to make me lose sight of my vision. She sprung headfirst inside my pum pum, two fingers and tongue deep. I reveled in it. I let her eat me for a good ten minutes before I made my move.

I slid my fingers down to open my pussy up, letting her get deeper. She started to get pretty good and even though it wasn't part of my plan, I came. I gushed in her mouth, opened my lips and let her suck up all my juices. Then I closed my fingers around my entire pussy, cupping it. She looked up concerned. I removed my mask and smiled at her.

Her mouth agape, she recognized me instantly.

"Hey, Autumn," I giggled happily. "Hawke, what do you say we teach her what you really like? I've learned a lot in these seven months. Or is it eight?"

Hawke stared at me, frozen with panic that I'd admitted we'd been seeing each other that long.

"Amy? Amy!" Autumn repeated in a panic.

"Wait… you two…?" Hawke's eyes darted between us, trying to piece things together.

"Yeah, I met Autumn when she was fucking my boyfriend John some time ago. Isn't that right, sweetie?"

"So you... you bitch!" she cried.

She jumped to lunge at me, but Hawke caught her mid-flight. He wrapped his arms under hers and stood straight up with both their legs pressed into the foot of the bed.

"I can understand why you want to fight. Look at your face. You don't have as much to lose," I teased. "And you're not clever enough to mastermind something like this. Of course you want to resort to violence."

She struggled and screamed with Hawke to let her go.

"But it won't help. Punching me won't change that Hawke has been cumming inside me, moaning my name, telling me how much better I am than you at... well, everything, for nearly a year."

"Get out! Get out before I let her go, Amy! Get the fuck out," Hawke threatened.

"You could let her go. I'm not scared of that bitch. I feel rather relaxed. She did make me cum pretty hard." I smirked antagonistically. "I taste good, baby? Hawke thinks so. He tells me all the time."

Autumn was fuming, with her piercing eyes and screwed up face, she was nearly frothing at the mouth still screaming to be let go.

Hawke, desperate to not have this unfold as a bloody mess asked me to please leave.

I climbed off the bed, and started for the door. "You did ask nicely. For old time's sake, why not just call me your 'Babygirl,' Hawke?"

"Amy!"

"Alright, alright. I'll go. Call me when this blows over. You and I both know how tired you are of her."

"Amy," he growled. He was growing impatient with me, and exhausted with her.

"Bye, Autumn." I waved happily like we were best friends.

She spit in my direction.

"That's part of why he's been fucking me for damn near a year. Spitters are quitters, 'Babygirl,'" I said, mocking Hawke, "And... you missed."

I stepped into the hallway, and waited a few minutes to see if he let her go and if she would come out ready to rumble.

She didn't. I guess he didn't let go until he thought I'd be far enough away.

But do you think I'd leave before I missed the show? Never.

I stepped into my room, poured myself a glass of champagne, listening to my favorite tune, the cries of a chick who'd felt the wrath of my vengeance.

TEASE

Tease is an acronym for
Titillating/Erotic/Anecdotes/Symbolism/Etymology

Essentially, it's the story, behind the story. I share why I selected a particular character's name, location, my inspiration, etc. I personally love inside information and literary "Easter eggs." It makes me appreciate the original content more. I hope this does the same for you.

Hoelistic Healing

Well, the title of the story is a spin on holistic healing because in today's society, a group of women finding healing in anything sex-related would be considered hoeish or whoreish behavior. I believe with the right partner, or setting, or whatever makes it right for you, it can absolutely be healing. Seeing as singer Marvin Gaye was known for singing "Sexual Healing," I gave the main character his middle name, Pentz.

Amrita means sweet nectar of the Gods or divine nectar for the yoni. Yoni is the Sanskrit term for vagina so what better name for a fantasy universe in which it's all about worshiping the yoni than yoniverse.

Haven - safe haven because she was the "scary one."

Mustache

I named it Mustache because she enjoys doing it right under his nose.

The name Tahir means innocent. Her husband was an innocent bystander in all of this. Surname Trotter just because "Break You Off" by the Roots is one of my favorite songs about infidelity and frontman Black Thought's last name is Trotter.

His name is Justin Cider because when they are caught and he introduces himself, he's literally saying I was "just inside her."

The app name JFT is also a foreshadowing that Justin Fucks Tymber.

Tymber, I liked the name and I selected it for this story because she had something that was deeply rooted, like a tree, and then it came falling down.

Company

I named the characters versions of the names of either the cast or characters of *Three's Company*. Jaxon for the character Jack Tripper played by John Ritter, Joyce for the actress who played Janet Wood, and Sioux for Suzanne Somers who played Chrissy Snow.

The name of the swinger club is called Company in Italian. I really wanted to drive the point home that three can be company and not a crowd. I think there are a lot of misconceptions about swinger clubs. Any time I've gone to one, they were very accepting and respectful. I've found men in swinger clubs respect boundaries better than your average club. I also wanted to note that even in a group setting, the sex can be loving in all its moving parts. My objective was to widen the scope on what people who've never indulged believe is transpiring behind those doors.
Additionally, anyone who's followed me on social media is aware that I love and identify heavily with Harley Quinn, so my characters going with those aliases is my way of injecting myself into the book.

Trixxx are for Adults

Character named Taylor because that's the legal surname for music artist Tony Matterhorn, creator of the dutty wine anthem. Grapes make wine, and I thought because it was a dirty version of feeding him grapes, I'd do a different spin on the infamous dutty wine.

Family Affair

Neme - because it's her sister, makes her her nemesis.

August – hot-tempered, vindictive. (Decides to pursue affair with sis-in-law after watching her get badgered for not choosing his boring life.)

Viri - Short for viridescent (she was jealous of her sister's freedom and bravery to live her life freely and not on their mother's terms).

Leña - firewood (mom adds fuel to fire), essentially being the catalyst for their illicit affair.

First option named Held in High Ahh-Steam because she learns he's an ally in the family and also because they have sex in front of the steamy bathroom mirror.

Second option is "Mom's Maple" because everyone else assumes his ending remark is about the syrup their mother Leña made, and not about Neme.

Hostel Situation

Iris and Siri's names are anagrams because the names, like the characters, are similar but switch order.

Neven and Otto are palindromes because to the girls, it's the same to them either way, front to back.

I didn't have any real reason for selecting Morocco other than I like some of the "high end" hostels there.

Fonder

Callie is thought to be a Greek variant of Kallista meaning fairest or most beautiful. I felt like since they were in front of the mirror, her name should answer that age-old fairy tale question.

The.rapist

I watch the show *Jeopardy*™ every day. *Saturday Night Live* had a skit where they'd mock the show and "Sean Connery" would mispronounce things as a contestant. He pronounced therapist as the rapist and that always stuck with me. Rape fantasies are very common so I thought it would set the stage to discuss it openly in a therapy session.

Named Atlas because he opened up her world, but in a semi-superficial way.

Mentioning Nonna to reveal she's at least half Italian so I thought it would suit her to have her name be temptress in Italian

Ultimately, she forced him to do something he didn't really want to. She overpowered him with seduction. In a sense she becomes "the rapist."

The abduction element was an added fantasy because our culture can be so repressed sexually due to fear of being judged. In this scenario in addition to being free from having to be in control, psychologically you're also absolved from the responsibility that society would inflict upon you if they knew.

The peonies and jellyfish are my faves. Another opportunity for author insertion.

Her partner is named Maxon because he's giving her the max amount he can and it still isn't enough.

It's named CUNT for the slang way of calling someone a cunt by using the abbreviated acronym for "see you next Tuesday." Which Atlas says to her, but she's finished with therapy.

Jackson surname for the legendary Janet Jackson, Miss Jackson if you're nasty.

With all the nods to artists both of the musical and painting variety, I felt I would be remiss if I didn't include my absolute favorite since age 16: Shawn Corey Carter. I made the "Cock worship day" his birthday in case it caught on. I know there's already steak and BJ day as the male Valentine's Day but I wanted to create my own day. I'd be lying if I said I wasn't also part of the Hive so it seemed fair to include her in the story as well. Obviously I selected her middle name. I was going to name him Corey but I prefer the sound of phrases like "Jay's juice" instead of "Corey cum." I don't know. I guess it could have worked. Fans of the couple who've read this probably sussed this one out. It was more overt than the nod to others in the book.

I named the other titles Hard On, because the sauce dries on hard, on his hard on. Also, Cat and Mouse because they did it at his computer desk in his home office and her pussycat was on top of the mouse.

Bridal Blues

I thought of all the ways that people want to enact revenge on someone who has cheated on them. In this instance, the betrayal came from a close source. She was just as hurt by whom he chose to cheat with as she was by her best friend ruining her relationship.

Each section was named for what a bride is supposed to have on her wedding day. Something Old: her father. Bringing up old feelings from her past. Something New: using technology to expose her in front of everyone. Something Borrowed: her man and her dress. The title is referring to the obvious blues the bride is experiencing as a result of what transpires.

Her "bestie's" name is Tre Dawr, which spoken phonetically is "traitor" which her friend turns out to be. I felt like Dawr as the surname worked for her father as well since he opened the "door" for chaos with his behavior. I named her fiance Cheyn as the phonetic spelling on chain, because he's part of the chain/cycle of how history usually repeats itself. In the foreword, I mention Natalie Portman being one of my favorite actresses and how her lines in Closer played a part in my naming of this book, so it makes sense that I'd name a character whose retaliation really crosses that line be named Natalie. Natalie's boyfriend is named Dub because that's what he is, a dub. Depending on the context and your geographical location, dub is basically slang for whack, lame, etc.

Th-eat-er

Gala Dali's birth name was Elena. She too was drawn to, and by artists, namely her second husband Salvador Dali.

Gala and Dali were openly into candaulism and cuckolding. She continued a well-known extramarital affair with her first husband Paul. Which is why I named their involved friend Paula. I remember reading somewhere that it was rumored Salvador had an aversion to genitalia and that fear was the catalyst for their swinger-ish lifestyle.

Gala died on my birthday a year before I was born. I've always been drawn to artists. My father, among many things, is an artist. (I know Freud would have a field day with that.) My favorite artist for years has been Brian Kirhagis better known as "BK the Artist." I had the opportunity to meet him at a showing in NYC. He was a very nice man who took the time to give anecdotes on his paintings that made me love his work even more. He has a series putting his spin on Dali's oeuvre. It's really incredible. I found inspiration in so many pieces it'd be hard for me to narrow down a favorite. I named the character Brian in lieu of Salvador because I thought that would be too obvious.

Tribbing + Stimulation = Tribulation. I thought it would be fun to create a portmanteau for a different kind of trouble.

Since this story was inspired by artists, I felt one of the stories options should incorporate paint in some way.

Kinky Crank

Kinky Crank because crank is another name for the street drug speed, and since the speed dating was focused on their kinks I named it Kinky Crank instead of Kinky Speed, which I didn't believe had as much of a ring to it. Also one option includes an actual crank.

Solana for SZA. A few times fans have asked her how to get over relationships and she says some variation of self-care. Exfoliate, wash your hair, toke a lil something. I just feel like she's my "friend in my head" and would be the kind of friend who, if you came to her complaining about a lame dating pool, would offer an excellent alternative.

There is an actual BDSM test. I used a portion of my own results in the story.

Initially I was going to swap their scenes because they were numbered 6 and 9 during the speed dating, but I wanted to switch it up and not make it so predictable by having that duo perform 69. I also didn't want the test to "win" the best connection. Algorithms can help, but they cannot replace human interaction, they can't calculate energy, or create a spark. So while 6 scored lower than 11, they were better suited for each other in the end and they experienced that connection during the speed-dating event.

Sabaism is loosely defined as the "worship of stars/heavenly bodies as deities" so I named the character Sabian. Her name is Celeste because he views her freckles as celestial.

Drilled

Tahliah is FKA Twig's first name. The Papi Pacify video is in my top three sexiest. As someone with a hand fetish and affection for fish hooking, I gave her more than one nod in this book. I really dig her.

The restaurant Ji's Pot = G-Spot

Zahn - tooth in German

The pressure point was something I learned about some years ago. I began asking people I knew if they'd heard about it. Most of them were unaware so I decided to include it in the book. I aspire to enlighten as well as inspire.

Babydoll

In the dollification community, there are many people who like different dolls for different reasons. I wanted to represent a few of them so instead of having both characters like a specific kind of doll and doing different things with it, I had them both be open to versatility to shine a light on various types and expound on the ones my personal curiosity gravitated to the most. Babydoll is a fairly common pet name, so it seemed fitting to name the story something that sounds simple and familiar and then dive into a kink not so familiar. I aspire to surprise my readers sometimes. I had the female character named Latoya, with her nickname being "Toy" for obvious reasons.

Barnett, surname of FKA Twigs. "I'm Your Doll." Aside from making some of (in my opinion) the sexiest fucking music ever, I also love her visuals. What I envisioned for the character Marion is a mash up of her Pendulum video and how she looked when she was just a dancer, in singer Jesse J's "Price Tag" video. While trying to jog my memory to ensure I was referencing the correct video, I decided to do a quick search for FKA Twigs as a doll when she was just a dancer, and stumbled upon her song called "I'm Your Doll." I knew then that I had to incorporate her on this particular story. For the Papi Pacify video alone, her inspiration was going to make its way into this book. I'm grateful it unfolded so perfectly.

Marion is named for dressing like a marionette. Heirian is named as such because that's when she's emulating a doll full of air. The name was originally Airian, to make it more obvious. I decided I liked the spelling and look of Heirian better and went with it. The other names were inspired by their doll type as well. Anne, like Raggedy Ann, China as a porcelain doll.

Hell of a Dilemma

Kanye's "Hell of a Life" from *My Beautiful Dark Twisted Fantasy* was the inspiration behind this. Not just in content, but making a song that had lines like, "make a nun cum, make her cream-ate" was some bold shit. I loved it. I knew that I wanted to have the character named after him, but Kanye was too obvious. So I went for his middle name which coincidentally means "God the highest" in Swahili. It was perfect for this story. I originally wanted to name the female character Trinity. I like it as a name, and thought of naming this story "Holy Trinity" but seeing as how temptation is referred to as the devil's work, I thought it best to change her name to "Lucy Furr" (Lucifer). Since her friend became the good conscience on her shoulder that attempted to dissuade her thrice from tempting Omari, I thought maybe she could be the holy trinity as the voice of reason.

Lent because she had a hand in him giving up the priesthood. Some of the Christian faith give up certain things for about six weeks during this time. But also a play a words on how she had a hand in his life-altering decision.

It's Written All Over You

Not sure how the universe saw fit to bless us with Robyn Rihanna Fenty but I'm grateful. As a Navy member, it was imperative I included something that paid homage to her. Her videos have consistently been my favorite visuals of any artist. My best friend, or as we refer to each other "Life Wife" called me the day the "We Found Love" video was released and said, "It was made for you." I hurriedly pulled it up online and it instantly became my favorite. I called my Life Wife back excitedly squealing, "She even puked ribbons. It's like she knew I have a weak ass stomach and couldn't handle real vomit so she replaced them with ribbons! She's for sure my spirit animal." The colors, that wardrobe, the fine ass man she cast as her love interest, the representation of a wild tumultuous relationship, it really spoke to me. The scene where he tattoos "MINE" on her ass was hotter than most porn I'd watched. I loved it. I hadn't been that excited by a video since Madonna's "Cherish" where she had mermen. The youngest merman, who at the time I believed to be a girl, looked Black. I was convinced I could be a mermaid. Disney exacerbated this mermaid obsession with Ariel three months later. Both Rihanna and Madonna's videos are still two of my favorites to date. When I decided to write a story based on graphoerotica (sexual arousal from being written on or writing on your lover's body), I knew I wanted to have it escalate to something permanent and that I would name the character Robyn.

I named the second version menial matrimony because menial also means domestic servant or a servile person. Being his submissive slave was a more fitting matrimony for the couple than going to the altar.

Cumming To

"Cumming to" as one comes to your senses, but in this instance she came to a state of euphoric consciousness after being knocked out.

His name is Joe because some folks refer to their coffee as a cup of Joe.

In stories where the content is risky, I usually situate the characters as novices so their dialogue can hopefully answer some of the questions the reader might have. People have frowned upon somnophilia, likening it to rape as the sleeping person cannot consent. It's been said it's a sign that a person wants to be a rapist or they're into necrophilia. While there are some similarities between somnophilia and necrophilia, they are quite different. The most important distinction between fantasy and the real thing is consent. Somnophilia hasn't been studied very much and there isn't an official term for someone who likes to be on the receiving end of it. In the kink community some refer to it as inverse somnophilia. I felt it was an underserved kink and wanted to act out a bit of it in my writing. I struggled with whether this one would be understood so I created a lot of dialogue between the characters and made sure to establish that they had a loving relationship where her consent was absolutely given, and he took measures to ensure her health wasn't in danger. Of course, there was still some risk, but he felt confident that in their relationship, it was worth the reward.

Kahlo bar, Frida Kahlo the painter captured the vibrant colors of Mexico where the story took place.

I was nervous about writing this because no matter how much you try to dissuade people and say, "Don't try this at home," some fool who believes they're impervious to consequence or somehow immortal will attempt to do what you have warned against.

In the Brothers Grimm version of Sleeping Beauty, she was named Briar Rose. Somnophilia is also referred to as Sleeping Beauty Syndrome, so I named the character Briar.

Tea With A Twist

I placed this story in Philly because during my early twenties, I was in my first lesbian relationship and my very best friend at the time was a gay man. I spent some of the best nights of my life in the gayborhood. I liked the idea of having this high class restaurant that on the surface appeared to be about having proper etiquette and an alternative to what the night clubs offered, but really being something super kinky.

Newdah Tea said phonetically is nudity.

Boba tea also known as bubble tea is named that way because it's the Cantonese word for big-breasted woman. So a tea restaurant that could literally serve you a busty woman, I had to name that version of the story Boba Tea. Which I really enjoy by the way. It's another personal author insertion.

Fucking Falconry

Her name Amy Gdala (the amygdala is in both hemispheres of the brain and is responsible for our emotions). Her emotions overrode her logic and fueled her adulterous escapades.

His girlfriend Autumn was named such because she was part of the cycle like a season. Additionally, in this season, it was her turn to fall and their relationship was dying the way leaves do in that season.

Hawke because hawks are used in falconry, which is a way of hunting birds in their natural habitat by using a trained bird to lure out the prey you're actually after. Amy used him as a bird of prey to catch—or in this case play— - a wild game.

Mona - fake name because she was going to force Autumn to moan, "ahh" for the threesome. It was an inside joke to herself about her vengeful plan.

Bonus Stories!

Edict

For a number of months, my lover and I had been focusing on cumming on command. Many people believe it to be a myth. Women especially say men who believe this legend are just oblivious to how good women are at faking. Not to discredit the performance level of women on the whole, I've done it too, very well in fact. But I wised up. Pretending I was satisfied only got in the way of actually becoming satisfied. We both showed up for the same reasons, and I wasn't going to be accountable for short-changing myself. So, I spent time masturbating and learning my body. I made sure to communicate gently, articulately and concisely. When necessary, I'd move a hand to the right place, alter the pressure, give demonstrations. I wouldn't go, until I came. Fair was fair.

Having a lover who was totally connected, in tune, and invested in your pleasure made it that much easier to submit to them. Somehow it had become a common misconception that the expectation of a Dom is to be hard and demanding always. The truth is, your Dom has to be empathetic, humble, and understanding. You have to understand your partner on a deeper level to allow them to feel safe with you. They have to *want* to submit to you. The work you put in to earn such a responsibility surpasses the normal relationship standards. A true Dom, a good Dom, understands this well.

Dexter was no exception. Not only was he exceptionally attentive and intuitive but he was a great listener. He could read between lines and pull from my experiences that weren't sexually related in the slightest, and somehow use them to understand how and when to push me and when to hold back. My favorite thing about him was how he completely avoided giving me "baby blues." Baby blues, sub-drop—however you chose to refer to it—is when you are in a really vulnerable space post-play time and some Doms disconnect. The rush one experiences while sharing and connecting so intimately is a high that is not without a crash. Dexter was the only Dom to evade this issue with me. His generosity and attention to my needs not just during play, but before and after, encouraged me into full submission. I could trust him with myself. I was safe.

When he brought up this new concept, I had questions, but he was more than willing to answer. He was delighted that my reflex was to be inquisitive as to how we could do this and not an automatic dismissal. I wanted to know if he had accomplished it with a previous sub. He said he had many years ago. I wanted to know what I could do to help the process. He said the biggest step was believing it was plausible, so I was halfway there. Naturally I let out a subbie girl squeal excited by the prospect.

The next thing he explained, was understanding it was not permission, it was a command. We were already deep into edging practices, which he said would be incorporated into my training. Regularly, Dexter would have me masturbate in front of him. He'd coach me, asking, "Who does your orgasm belong to?" and watch my body: my eyes, my thighs, my toes, for signs I was close. Any sight or sound of indicators I was on the verge of climax and he'd pull my hands away. He explained that he'd begin to implement those same practices with sex. I was not allowed to cum unless he said so. I was submitting all my orgasms to him, not some, all. *This* was of the utmost importance.

Initially, when we had sex he'd see me getting closer to orgasm, and just as he did with my masturbation, he'd remind me to ask for permission: "Who does your orgasm belong to?" and I'd affirm, "You Sir." He stroked my face and said, "That's right. Good girl." As my impending orgasm grew closer, I was trained to ask, "May I?" and at first he'd allow it right away.

"Cum now, Ana." As I erupted, he said, "I feel your walls squeezing me. Those juices flowing for me. It's perfect. Just perfect. Good girl." He showered me with reinforcements. If you've ever been a sub, you want nothing more than to please your Dom. At the very height of my pleasure, to hear those words from him intensified my orgasm three-fold.

Then slowly he began to delay the time between my asking and when he would allow it to happen. This is the tricky part because as any sexually active person knows, the female orgasm can be quite elusive even when you're both trying your best. But I knew it was essential to the training process to learn to associate my orgasm exclusively upon his command.

Soon, I began to fear not being able to cum for Dexter more than I feared not cumming at all. There were a few times I couldn't hold off the way I intended to. He'd still shower me with positive reinforcements as though he'd said, "Cum now, Ana." He never made me feel like I disappointed him.

His patience was limitless; my determination would match it. I didn't pressure myself, I just committed to serving my loving Dex. I asked him if there was anything else we could do. He mentioned that maybe an added sensory aid might help. As natural music lovers, the obvious choice was a song.

Our very next masturbatory session, he had an mp3 player connected via Bluetooth and told me he'd begin playing it when I was into it but still had a ways to go to give it time to build. I was thrilled. I had no idea what kind of music he'd selected. As I was lost in pleasure, I heard instruments fading in softly. I couldn't identify which and I didn't want to get too distracted from the task to figure out what this piece was. I simply made a mental note to ask who was responsible for this composition later.

Everyone should make love to something this majestic. Making love, even with yourself, is such a grand gesture, its soundtrack should be no different.

Throughout the composition, there were many times I almost came, of course Dexter could tell. He asked, "Who does your orgasm belong to?"

Whimpering, I replied, "You, Sir," and averted. As I neared closer to climax once more, the horns began to descend into silence. Internally, I pleaded, "May I?" The rumbling of percussion goaded ,*Not without permission.*

"Cum now, Ana." A triumphant explosion of juices, exclamations, and trumpets filled the room in an orgasmic symphony. Dexter was so excited he was dripping precum without even laying a finger on me!

For the first time, I wanted to cum and held back multiple times until given the order. I was elated and proud of myself. Though no one could be more proud than my love. Finally, he owned the power of my pleasure and full submission. For me, there was nothing better than submitting that power to him. He charged me passionately, savagely. He consumed me, devoured me. It was as if my orgasm gave him the command to release a beast within himself.

"Good girl," he growled repeatedly as he thrust into me. Seeing him this primal revved me up all over again.

He was just a few strokes in when again I cried, "May I?" and he nodded excitedly, unable to get the words out as he gave himself permission to do the same. Mission accomplished, with a joint climax to boot!

The time came where during masturbation and sex, as he played what I learned was a Tchaikovsky piece, he removed all physical stimulation. Cemented in our memories the precise moment it happened on command, he selected that section to repeat magic.

When the room fell silent, just before percussion, eyes closed I felt him hovering over me. He took my hands away, and leaned in. "Cum now, Ana," and involuntarily, miraculously, on command, I came. Eventually, no physical stimulation of any sort was required. He could put on the song as I was doing something as mundane as washing the dishes, and at the specific section he'd come behind me and command, "Cum now, Ana" and I would.

One afternoon, Dexter phoned me and said he'd have a dress waiting for me that night to go out. I was thrilled. It wasn't our anniversary or either of our birthdays. All of those milestones were in the spring and summer. It was February. I couldn't think of where he'd want to go that required a dress. My mind was spinning with possibilities! Work can drag any day, but none more than when you have a surprise waiting for you. Each torturous minute ticked by tediously. I hurried out of there precisely at 4:00.

I rushed home full of questions I was eager to ask Dexter. The moment I stepped in the door and tossed my keys on the stand, I opened my mouth to call out to him, but I was engulfed by the scent of the most beautifully aromatic boxed arrangement from my favorite florist in the foyer. The note read to be ready by 6:30. It was just 4:15. Where was Dex?

I hurried to the bedroom to see the dress I knew was waiting for me. I saw an exquisite black lace gown. I held it up to me, spinning whimsically. I felt like I was in a fairy tale. I needed to take a shower so I could try this thing on. I stepped into the bathroom and froze. I'd know that web logo anywhere.

"Charlotte Olympia!" I shrieked. Perched atop the small cabinet where we kept our towels was a box of shoes from my favorite designer. Inside the box sitting on top of the shoes was an envelope that I admittedly read after gazing at, holding, and squeezing the pumps.

The card read, "You didn't think I'd forget shoes did you?" They were a marvelous work of art, a suede black pump with hollow gold details in the heel and platform. I would have selected them myself; he did an excellent job. I couldn't resist trying them on.

"Oh." I exhaled the moan only a good shoe can bring. I felt sexier immediately. I had to shower quickly so I could see the whole look. Operation exfoliate, lubricate, and dash off to slip into my dress was in full effect!

Once I was in it, I noticed just how deep the V-neck plunge was. Minimal breast coverage meant double-sided tape would be a necessity. It was also backless and the mermaid fit hugged my curvy hips and long thick thighs before it trumpeted out just below my knees. I still had no idea where we were going. I decided on a fiery red-stained lip and some mascara, and figured a pinned up-do was suitable for the type of formal affair I presumed we were attending.

I slipped on my new shoes, stepped back and upon seeing the full ensemble in my full-length mahogany framed mirror, I was turned on by my damn self! It was 6:00 and belly butterflies were aflutter. I selected earrings and a clutch and went to the closet to decide on the last finishing touch, a coat. My black hooded floor-length faux fur seemed appropriate.

At promptly 6:30, a car arrived and my love was inside.

"Baby!"

"There's my good girl."

I squeezed him tightly before I slid into my seat, "Where?"

"Tut, tut, tut," he warned before redirecting. "Do you like your selections?"

"Like? I love them! You know me so well. Thank you!" I gushed.

Somehow, he looked happier than me. "Perfect."

I rested my head upon his shoulder until the vehicle slowed, and before me was the magnificently regal Opera House.

When we stepped in and checked our coats, Dexter got his first look at me in the dress.

He stared without blinking before telling me I was the most beautiful woman in the world. Right now, it truly felt like it. My eyes began to search for clues to what performance was taking place that night.

"Swan Lake!" I squealed.

He squeezed my hand in the affirmative. Dex knew I'd always wanted to go to the ballet.

We made our way to the Champagne Bar where all eyes, were, in fact on me. Men who couldn't get their fill, and their spouses disapproving glares were no match for the only eyes that mattered. I ordered a "Black Swan Bellini" that was served in a champagne flute garnished with a fresh blackberry. I sipped as though unawares of the gawking committee.

An announcement informed us it was ten minutes to curtain up. I quickly finished my second Bellini to head to our section in the auditorium. We headed up to our seats, center mezzanine where Dex said we'd have the best view. My head swimming on a Bellini and love high, I immersed myself in the art in motion playing out before me. The dancers were phenomenal, the story was enchanting, and the music... the music was very familiar.

Throughout the ballet, there were several moments I thought I heard our song, but it was just a variation. My heart began to race, my heaving chest causing my breasts to tug at the tape that stood between discretion and exposure. I could feel other eyes on me. Opera glasses intended for viewing the stage were transfixed in my direction. Salivating, licking their lips, and nearly panting like dogs in heat, they watched me.

As the version of "Swan Lake" played that was no longer a variation, but in fact the version I'd been trained to, began, it dawned on me that if my lover allowed, they might just see a show worth watching through those glasses. I felt my face flush a deep crimson. I squeezed Dexter's hand but he stared calmly ahead, as though this song had no relevance in our lives whatsoever. The piccolo and harp guided graceful dancers on pointe about the stage, encircling Odette & Prince Siegfried as he tried to make amends for his mistake. Von Rothbart arrived, his moves grander than the other dancers. Frantic strings symbolizing his movements also mirrored the thoughts in my mind. Cymbals crashed together with each pounding of my heart. The menacing Von Rothbart was making demands. My heart was racing at the prospect that Dex might just make me cum. I wanted him to... I hoped he would.

Desperate, Odette and I were on the edge. Tension built in the momentary ritenuto. This was when he does it. Will he? Squirming in my seat, I begged internally. *Say it. Say it please.* Just as when we're at home, my body was buzzing with the desire to orgasm, but magnified, perhaps by the public setting, perhaps by the rumbling vibration of percussion coming directly from the orchestra, but definitely, most definitely by the prospective command of my lover.

Trembling with zeal, I was hoping that when the trumpets came, I could too. He leaned in. "Cum now, Ana." On cue, I exploded as she leapt. It was the last thing I saw before my head fell back in ecstasy. My double-sided tape snapped and I heard a collective gasp of the diverted, hungry eyes who probably willed that tape to give out, showcasing a sliver of areola. The moan I belted out could not be completely drowned out by the triumphant horn section. In fact, the acoustics carried it throughout the theatre. For the first time, the principal dancer was upstaged by someone who'd never taken a ballet class in her life. As I descended from my climactic high, I fixed my near nip slip as best I could. The remaining swans were grateful for Odette's sacrifice dance, a dance of liberation. My heart danced with them. At curtain close, my lover was beaming with pride. He stood, applauding his star for a job well done. The ovation was mine alone.

Nip Quick

Sometimes more sensitive than others
Always a pleasure
Encircled by tongue...
or a quick flick of it.
Soft nibble that nearly makes you wince
Only to quickly give way to the pleasure of relief,
and the memory of your mouth.

Acknowledgments

To my Stink,
I have no idea how this would have been possible without you. Thankfully, I didn't have to find out.

To my own "the.rapist" Dr. J., thank you for your encouragement and reminding me how to be a star and effectively outshine my understudy. That is a lesson I will carry for a lifetime.

Thank you to every person on social media who asked for new "Slurred Word" videos or my new book. You all reminded me some people were actually interested in what I do.

Lastly, my family for always being supportive.
Xo -

Lo

Do you or someone you love wish to be a Cum Clinic attendee? Got Chloroform Coochie? Enjoy Tea With A Twist? Have A Golden throat that can gargle peanut butter?
Shop for FLICK merch at
TheLoyalist.com/FLICKThis

Other Titles by Lola LePaon:
Playlist of my Australian Lips
Available on Amazon & Barnes & Noble